THE GIFT COUNSELOR

THE GIFT COUNSELOR

SHEILA M. CRONIN

To: Susan,
Merry Christmas
& Happy reading!
Shue

Chicago, Illinois

First printing, 2014

Cover design by Katherine Kuszmaul

Library of Congress Control Number: 2014909528
Publisher: Sheila M. Cronin, Chicago, Illinois

ISBN-10: 0996046003
ISBN-13: 978-0-9960460-0-8

Printed in the United States of America

To the people of
South Shore,
the neighborhood in Chicago,
where I grew up,
with love.

"The gift you have received, give as a gift."

St. Matthew 10:8

THE GIFT COUNSELOR

CHAPTER ONE

Monday, December 1st

Potlatch (pot-latch). Ceremonial distribution by a
man of gifts to his own and neighboring tribesmen,
often, formerly, to his own impoverishment.

Webster's Revised Unabridged Dictionary

J onquil had just sat down to her desk at Children's
Home when she heard a faint tap on her door. Two
things occurred to her at once: the Coles kid was
standing outside her door and he was being discharged
that morning.

"It's open!" she called out brightly.

The Coles kid negotiated the entire visit in under nine
seconds, barely making eye contact and stuttering in that
adolescent twang of his. "M-Ms. Bloom, th-thanks f-for
helping m-me. I m-m-made this f-for you."

He dropped something into her lap. Then, before she

could react, he bolted out the door, the squishy sounds of his sneakers echoing down the linoleum corridor.

Left to make the discovery in private, she held the object up to the light. It was one of his woodcarvings made in art therapy, she surmised. Roughly four inches long, it appeared to be a crude rendering of a reclining Irish Setter. Pet dog? She couldn't recall him ever mentioning one, so she examined the piece more closely as her analytical skills kicked into gear. Why a setter? Why the literal pose? Could this be a good omen, another sign of his passivity or—

"Oh, God," she gasped. The carving slipped from her fingers. Her eyes darted up to the bulletin board on the wall above her desk.

There, beneath layers of memos and schedules, hung a faded snapshot of her husband, Gerry, and at his feet, all doggy adoration, Baron, taken days before a house fire had killed them both. She'd tacked up the photo when her internship began, but then had covered it over, so conflicted were her feelings. Uncanny, how the Coles kid had selected the most hidden, painful image in her office to serve as his model.

Was it still there? Jonquil jumped up and furiously ripped down the papers. The photo was gone. The Coles kid must have removed it in order to make the gift and surprise her.

She turned pale. What if her son Billy, on one of his rare visits to her office, had ever seen that photo?

She sank back down in her chair, her heart pounding as though she, not Stanley Coles, had just sprinted down the hall.

Moments passed. Gradually, her pulse slowed. Fingers shaking, she again picked up the carving. The Coles kid had even stained the wood to make it more life-like. *Baron!* A gush of dark memories, like smoke, engulfed her. She was afraid she might pass out. Just then the hall buzzer sounded, shattering the moment.

Jonquil jammed the carving into the pocket of her corduroy jumper, stood up, and after giving her face a quick scan and lipstick touch up, she locked her office and nipped over to the nurses' station.

Up and down the long corridor, Thanksgiving decorations drooped from the walls, while doors swung open on both sides, lending some light to the dingy hallway. Children's Home, where UCLA's graduate school of psychology had placed her, was a residential treatment facility and school for emotionally disturbed, and in rare cases, abandoned minors. Rumor had it some movie mogul in the thirties had hidden his pregnant girlfriend here. Whether true or false, the rambling edifice now housed a hodgepodge of children whom Jonquil knew well.

The children, ages four through sixteen, appeared normal during routine moments such as changing classes. Even so, there were those who would not let Jonquil pass without needing a hug, while others seemed to stare through her, more aware of their "voices" than the commotion in their direct path.

Jonquil knew that her frizzy auburn hair and freckles often sparked snickers among the older residents but she took their reactions in stride. What she would never get used to was the sight of a schizophrenic boy her son's age, hallucinating on his way to his next class.

When she entered the nurses' station, her two favorite staff members were busy charting: Nurse Betsy, a bleached-blonde, nurturing type, indispensable in this setting, and Phil, a nursing student from Manila and a natural at dealing with the adolescents.

They both looked up and greeted her as she poured herself a cup of coffee. Then Betsy asked, "How was your Thanksgiving weekend, Jonquil?"

"Long." Jonquil was glad that the weekend had ended and another full work week lay ahead. "How was yours?" She leaned against the counter and let the coffee soothe her.

"I was here 'cause I usually work on holidays. It's quieter since most of the patients have weekend passes. I like to take my vacation when all hell is breaking loose

6

around here," Betsy replied with a giggle.

Jonquil chuckled. "Smart. Good thing the weather changed this morning or else Billy and I might still be down at the beach."

"You don't sunburn with that Irish skin?" asked Betsy.

"I'm really lucky because I love having a tan. It makes my eyes greener and makes me feel younger. Maybe my mother's Swedish genes made the difference."

Betsy asked if Jonquil had seen the Coles kid before he left that morning. Nodding her head, she withdrew the carving and watched their reactions. After initial oohs and aahs, Betsy commented, "But that boy couldn't so much as share a lunch table when he came here. Now look at him, doling out hand-made gifts. Jonquil, you're a wonder with these kids."

She waved off the compliment like a jinx, tossed her cup in the wastebasket and turned to go.

Phil snapped his fingers rapidly to claim her attention. "It's a gift, right? Will you use it as an example in your research project?"

Jonquil glanced at him, startled. "Maybe."

"What's it about again?" asked Betsy, her back toward Jonquil as she handed a chart to Phil and selected and opened another one.

"The title is: 'The Psychodynamics of Gift-giving'," Jonquil replied.

7

Betsy faced Jonquil and rolled her eyes. "What does that mean in plain English?" she asked.

"Oh, sorry." Jonquil colored slightly, remembering that she wasn't in front of her psychology class at UCLA but with co-workers. "I'm doing a study of gift-giving, using the children here as my subjects. Gifts fascinate me, like, when they are sincere and when they're not. The psyche literature has little to say about gift-giving, which is great, because maybe if I do a bang up job, I can turn my project into my career."

In the back of her mind, Jonquil realized that Phil's question about the carving and her project made sense. Surprisingly, she hadn't made the connection herself. Rather, the carving posed a most unwelcome reminder of the manner in which her young husband and that animal had both died. She'd never forgiven her husband for destroying his, hers, and Billy's happiness so needlessly nor had she ever gotten over her shame about what had happened. Except for the authorities she hadn't told anyone, not even Billy, the exact circumstances of Gerry's death. Soon after the funeral, she'd moved down from the Seattle area to Southern California. Billy was born seven months later.

Betsy remembered that Dr. Shore had been looking for her earlier. Relieved to have an excuse to cut the discussion short, Jonquil re-pocketed the carving and hastened to the administrative offices in the south wing.

The largest office at the end of the hall belonged to Dr. Mitchell Shore, the Medical Director of the home's treatment facilities. Jonquil looked around for his secretary who had stepped away and was startled to see two painters in white overalls unloading their gear in the reception area. No word of any paint job had been announced in last week's staff meeting that she could recall.

She knocked twice on the door and waited. Muffled voices from within invited her to enter. Only then did she realize that Miss Ida Hamilton, the home's live-in Head of Social Services, was already seated in one of Dr. Shore's slippery leather chairs. Jonquil thought to herself, *this day is* not *going well.*

Why was Miss Hamilton always interfering? Whenever she saw them together, Jonquil felt like the betrayed child who discovers too late that secrets are never confided to just one parent. Dr. Shore stood about eye level with Jonquil, while Miss Hamilton towered over both of them though she was no mental giant. *Well, well,* mused Jonquil, *what have we here?*

"Please sit down, Ms. Bloom," Dr. Shore said, clearing his throat while avoiding her eyes. She felt a prickle of alarm.

"You've done a marvelous job here," he continued,

"and I hate to have to do this, but, as we must paint the offices in order to pass state inspection, I am afraid we need your stipend to cover the expense—effective immediately." The room became so still Jonquil had no trouble hearing her hopes and dreams come crashing down inside her with all the fury of the glaciers in Alaska's Inside Passage.

"But—but—" she sputtered, feeling totally bushwhacked.

"Come now, Ms. Bloom, it's for the good of Children's Home. We mustn't exceed our budget, dear," said Miss Hamilton. "You see, don't you?"

The muscles around her mouth twitched, a sure sign that Miss Hamilton was determined to get her way.

"But the children count on me being here, Miss Hamilton. I can't even tell them good bye? That's not fair either to them or to me."

Jonquil paused to catch her breath. The faces of the children she was scheduled to see that day sprang to mind. "Couldn't this wait until after Christmas?"

"You don't need to remind us of our responsibility, Ms. Bloom. We see graduate students come and go all year long as part of our teaching mission. We know best how to handle the situation, I assure you."

"How am I supposed to complete my research?"

"You're a talented clinician. UCLA will find you

another placement. You'll have no trouble finding work. This *is* Southern California, after all," said Miss Hamilton. Dr. Shore nodded his headed vigorously.

Jonquil could think of no appropriate response to the cliché, so she addressed him. "How can I finish my research anywhere else? The project is based on these children, Dr. Shore." *Ergo, be a man and overrule this shrew posing as a housemother.*

"Ida, it does seem a shame. Perhaps we can make some other arrangement?" Unfortunately, his tone had too much whine in it to dissuade Miss Hamilton.

"Mitchell, we went over our options very carefully. The painters are already here." Jonquil detected evasion in the woman's voice and pressed her.

"Why me, Miss Hamilton? You've said I work well with the children." She saw a look pass between the two administrators. "What? Tell me." She bit her lip with frustration.

Miss Hamilton twisted around in her chair and faced Jonquil squarely.

"We have no complaints about your work with the children. They like you and trust you. We'd keep you on here if we could.

"But since you've asked, there is one thing that concerns me about you personally, Ms. Bloom. Much of the time, you seem preoccupied when you aren't seeing

11

patients. Closed off from the rest of us, aloof, unhappy. At meetings, too. You're a million miles away and not fully engaged in our program. I wonder if you are truly suited to doing psychotherapy."

Jonquil was taken aback. Hadn't the staff just showered her with compliments? Now, the administrators were telling her a different story. She wanted to defend herself but didn't know where to begin, so she said nothing.

"I'm sorry, dear, but I felt duty-bound to mention it. And now, I'm afraid we're out of time. Dr. Shore, we have an intake interview to attend." Without another word, Miss Hamilton rose, turned away from Jonquil and crossed the carpet to the door. Dr. Shore also stood. Jonquil's mouth felt dry; all the moisture in her body had gone to the palms of her hands.

"You mean I'm out of a job just like that?" she blurted.

"I'm afraid that's reality." His words were cut short by another feeble cough. "Coming, Miss Hamilton," he called and followed his colleague out of the door.

"Oh, yeah? Well, reality stinks!" Jonquil shouted after him. But they had both vanished down the hall.

The secretary eyed her with concern. "I am so sorry, Jonquil," she said. Ordinarily, the empathy in her voice would have reduced Jonquil to tears, except that she was angry. She knew this anger. It was old and seductive.

Once it resurfaced, fueled by every frustration in her present and past life, it would annihilate all other points of view but one: that she could not and would not ever succeed. It galled her—that's how angry she was.

"What will you do? Are you going to fight their decision?"

"I can't fight this. I don't have time." Without thinking, Jonquil lifted a brush out of a paint bucket near her. "I have a son to raise, bills to pay. I've got to put my energy into finding a job where I can feel secure and not have to worry about getting thrown out the next time the walls need painting."

With that, she flung the brush back into the bucket, causing a few drops of paint to spatter one of the kneeling workmen. Beneath a dripping bill cap, a pair of bemused eyes the color of black gemstones stared up at her.

"Oh, I'm so sorry!" She covered her mouth with her hand, embarrassed.

The painter calmly brushed away the paint drops and beamed back at her in such a mesmerizing way, that it felt as though they were the only two people in the room.

"No problem," he murmured.

Momentarily, she couldn't move. Her cheeks flamed, her knees froze, while an exhilarating jolt circuited her body, launching her spirits skyward, higher and higher, until the faraway sound of the secretary clearing her throat brought Jonquil back to earth.

What had just happened? Clearly, she was out of control; time to get out of sight.

"Good-bye," said the secretary. "We'll miss you."

Sure you will, for about an hour, she thought bitterly, the painter nearly forgotten. *Whatever was I thinking? How could I delude myself again? No one cares about you, no one except yourself. And, if you're lucky, a boy named Billy.* She was furiously beating a retreat back to her (former) office when a dark-skinned nine-year-old named Tommy Cregier approached her with his incandescent smile.

"Hey, Ms. Bloom. I got you today."

Afraid she might lose her composure altogether, Jonquil simply placed her hand on his shoulder and said, "Not today, Tommy. I'm not feeling well. I have to go now." She managed to keep her tone light. "Be a good boy and go to study hall. Good bye." Her words ended in a whisper.

"Hope you feel better soon. Bye." He flashed her another of his dazzling smiles before scampering away.

She took a deep breath, unlocked the door to the office, slammed it shut, and finally let the tears flow.

CHAPTER TWO

Monday Evening

E very Monday was the same for Billy Bloom. He got home from school and walked directly over to the farthest window in the main room. On the way, he tossed his bookbag, jacket, and a copy of the *Venice Independent* onto the couch. At the window, he tapped the pane, pretending to attract the hummingbird's attention but he never could. The bird was plastic, a toy from his mother.

Next he called out, "Hi, Mom. I'm home," expecting silence as usual. But today, to his astonishment, she answered him. Moreover, she emerged from the kitchen with a tray of freshly baked cookies and milk.

"How'd you know I was here?" she asked, amused.

"I didn't," he grinned. "I always say, 'Hi, Mom, I'm home.' You'd have to be a latchkey kid to understand."

15

She set the tray down on the coffee table. "C'mon now, we usually get home at the same time, don't we?" She touched his cheek. "Well, Billy, you're not a latchkey kid anymore. I lost my job today." She picked up the *Venice Independent* and settled into her favorite overstuffed chair.

"No way, Mom."

"It's true, Billy."

"What happened?"

"Seems they needed to paint some offices, and the budget is so tight, they had to use my salary to pay for it."

Billy pondered this information while he selected a cookie. But he couldn't make sense of it. For the past year, he'd hung on his mother's every word about her experiences at Children's Home. It was obvious to him that she liked her work.

Billy was a good listener, even though he couldn't understand all the strange words his mother used, like "id" and "ego," but that part didn't matter. As she said, it was like learning a new language called jargon and she had to practice the terms so she could pass tests.

Being the man of the house (actually a two-bedroom, corner, garden apartment), ten-year-old Billy was used to his mother telling him things he didn't fully comprehend.

But this? Impossible.

"Can't we cop a plea or something? How can they do

this to you?" He propped himself on the arm of her chair.

"I called UCLA and they can't place me again till after the holidays. I'll get a new assignment in January. Meanwhile, I just have to find something to tide us over till then."

She glanced briefly at the front page headline about Y2K and commented more to herself than to him, "2000 is still three years away and already we're millennium crazy," before quickly turning to the classified section.

"If only you'd let me get a paper route like Ramon."

"Oh, Billy, not before high school. Look, here's an idea."

He leaned over her shoulder and read the boxed ad she was pointing to:

SPEND YOUR HOLIDAYS

AT

CLYDE'S OF SANTA MONICA

F-T AND P-T POSITIONS

AVAILABLE

VISIT PERSONNEL

9-6, 5th FLOOR

"See? The large department stores always need extra help during the Christmas season. They offer discounts, too. And Clyde's isn't part of a chain. It's one of a kind, much nicer. Maybe I can even get you in to see Santa Claus."

At the mention of this childish ploy, Billy leapt to his feet and said plaintively, "Mo-om!"

She gazed back at him in that special way that told him he was loved and said, "Okay, brush your teeth and grab a sweater. We're going out to dinner and a movie."

"On a school night? Oh, wow."

He managed to run as far as the hallway before he spun on one foot and turned back to her.

"Mom, are we broke?"

She answered lightly. "Not yet. Remember? Rule number one: celebrate the good times and rule number two?"

He chimed in, "*Really* celebrate the bad times." He darted off in the direction of his room.

She sank deeper into the chair, glad to have broken the news to him without sounding too hurt. Yet, now that Billy had left the room, her emotions got the best of her.

She needed a shoulder to cry on, but no way would she put that burden on her son. Worse luck, it was one of those times when her support network was unavailable. Ann, her closest friend, was on a cruise to the South Pacific and wouldn't be back in Los Angeles until after New Year's. Wendy, in Seattle, whose friendship dated back to their grammar school days, had her hands full with a colicky new baby.

And Margo, her dear grandmother in Ireland, was nearly deaf and rarely used the telephone. It left Jonquil no choice. She would have to face the uncertain days ahead of her alone.

She stared across the room at the photo of her husband in the redwood frame on her desk. "Now, look at me," she muttered, tears threatening. "This is all your fault. If you only knew." It had been quite a while since she'd spoken aloud to his photo with any feeling at all.

Later that evening as she tucked Billy into bed after listening to his prayers, he asked, "Mom? How will the kids get along without you?" She tried to assure him that the staff at Children's Home would take good care of the residents, but he persisted.

"Yeah, but they aren't like you. You have the gift."

"What gift?"

"You know, your teacher told you the night of our Halloween party when we were all in the kitchen. He said you have the gift. What did he mean?" Jonquil sat down on the side of his bed, stroked his soft, sandy-colored buzz cut and saw her reflection in his grayish-blue eyes.

"Well, Billy, it's an expression adults use when someone is naturally good at something, like playing piano or doing their job. It's something God gives each of us to share with others. Sometimes if we're lucky, it becomes our work.

"Maybe Dr. Paxton meant that I seem to know how to help kids with problems. Not everyone does." She never felt quite as self-conscious talking about her skills as with this precious and precocious child.

Billy sat up in bed all excited. "He was right, Mom! Remember that skinny girl who wouldn't eat?"

Jonquil thought back on her caseload of the past summer and recalled a shy, black adolescent in the early stages of anorexia. "You mean Luella?"

"That's the one. Luella's back in school 'cause of you. And Tommy didn't even talk till you helped him to." Tommy Cregier. With a pang, she remembered telling him good bye.

"Why, Billy Bloom, when I started this work, I thought you were jealous of these other kids in my life."

"Aw, I got over that. Besides, we're a team, right?"

"Right."

"So, since every team needs a mascot, can we get a dog? Please, Mom?"

She was annoyed, partly because, even though he'd had dinner at his favorite restaurant and a trip to the movies on a school night, he wanted more, like all kids do.

He also knew the subject of dogs was taboo with her.

Yet, sometimes such as on that night, he brought it up anyway, hoping in a good mood, she'd relent. Mrs. Crandon down the block raised dogs, and he had his eye on a black cocker spaniel, just three months old.

"Billy, you know how I feel about dogs," she said, her voice a warning.

"Yeah, I know. You're allergic." Foiled again.

"And that's not going to change. Now, sweetie, it's late. You have to get up early tomorrow to do your homework, and I have to get a new job."

Without thinking, she slipped her hand into her jumper pocket and discovered the carving there. She extracted it and presented it to Billy.

"Here. One of the children made this for me. You keep it."

"Oh man, a setter! I never had one of these before. Thanks, Mom." He put it on his nightstand near his other miniature animal models, and then kissed her goodnight.

"Remember, Billy, no dogs." She turned out the light and softly closed the door on her way out.

Billy rolled over toward the wooden setter, now silhouetted by the moonlight pouring in from the window, and whispered, "No dogs—yet."

CHAPTER THREE

Tuesday, December 2nd

T he day dawned foggy and cool. Driving over to Clyde's after dropping Billy off at school, Jonquil realized she'd forgotten to bring along a copy of her résumé. Her limited retail experience dated back to college, when she'd cashiered two summers at a coffee house. After her husband's untimely death, she'd worked at home as a private tutor and banked the insurance money, intending one day to continue her education. When the time was right, she knew she wanted to study psychology and chose the graduate school at UCLA.

Billy had never wanted for anything or so Jonquil thought. There were times when the rent was overdue or the car was in the shop an extra week. Yet, she managed to keep him in parochial school—thank God for uniforms!—and keep them both in good health. Had she not had a son to raise, perhaps her life would have taken a different turn. There was the remote possibility she might marry again. But Jonquil hadn't dated anyone in years. Grief had fashioned her into an intensely private person and her sexual drive had been reduced, like some archaic reference in her research, to a footnote. She mistakenly blamed Gerry for that, too. There was a wound deep inside her that no man could touch much less heal. Gerry hadn't caused it. His mistake had been to get her to trust love again, only to abandon her just as abruptly as her beloved father had years earlier. Even in her therapy sessions, required as part of the program's curriculum, she never faced the full impact that these two traumas had had on her life. Her therapist, noting Jonquil's reluctance to talk freely about her childhood, invited her to return when she felt willing, a choice Jonquil had put off indefinitely.

Suffice it to say that after her husband's death, Jonquil vowed she would make something of herself, so she would never again be dependent on anyone.

It was with that same determination that she reached her destination. Clyde's was Santa Monica's oldest department store. Five stories high, a tan-colored brick building, it stood somewhat faded in the California sun.

She parked, used the Fourth Street entrance, and took

the elevator straight up to the Personnel Department on the fifth floor. After filling out an application, she was shown into the office of the manager, Mr. Bramson. He was a tall, spare man, who occupied a long, narrow space. One large window dominated his office, featuring a spectacular view of Santa Monica Pier, but Jonquil doubted he ever took time to smell the hot dogs.

It looked to her like he was having too much fun maneuvering himself from his oversized roll-top desk at one end of the room to the metal file cabinets, positioned like bumpers on the opposite wall. To cover the ground between them in the shortest time, he had the aid of a chair with wheels and a vinyl floor mat. Using his foot to push off, he almost seemed to cry, "Wheee!" as he flew by her, processing her application in a blur of motions.

When he finally handed her a Clyde's nametag, she got a welcoming handshake and a dose of static shock. She was told to report immediately to Ms. Rita Oglesby, in the Scentsations Department, first floor north, for training.

Jonquil returned to the main floor with mixed emotions. She was relieved to be employed again so soon. Yet, when she glanced up at the ornate Strobel clock hanging opposite the front entrance, she couldn't help but recall that eleven o'clock was the time of the community meeting at Children's Home, a daily gathering of staff and residents to talk over the problems of living together.

What was she doing here, walking through the handbag section into ladies' shoes, onto hosiery, past hair accessories? How could she go from helping needy children to selling cologne to well-off matrons?

It was then that she became aware of the holiday Muzak in the air, the festive Christmas decorations popping up everywhere, the complimentary coffee and cookie tables, the store gongs, the upbeat hum on all sides.

Wait, store gongs? Jonquil was surprised she recognized them until she remembered that each Christmas, Clyde's decked its halls in nostalgia—from the gongs, old clerk uniforms and liveried doormen, to hairnets on the restaurant staff, even a few cash registers that rang.

At the kick-off party on the day after Thanksgiving, Mr. Merrill, Clyde's owner and president, literally turned back the hands of time on the fabled Strobel clock.

Though Jonquil couldn't relate to the memories this theme evoked in the store's older customers, the nostalgic sounds and decorations created a welcoming mood her first morning in the store. She was beginning to relish the charged atmosphere.

As she approached the Scentsations Department, she saw a woman C.G. Jung would have instantly appended to his list of archetypes. What would the Swiss analyst have called her—the tall, plumpish, middle-aged cornball with the dyed red hair, overdone make-up, false eyelashes, coquettish smile, and loud, sunny voice? Had he lived longer, he might have dubbed her the "Lucy" anima.

Like other novice therapists, Jonquil had the habit of labeling people. She had yet to learn how inadequate a label or diagnosis is when it comes to describing the unique qualities of a person's smile. For when she stepped up to the center perfume counter and introduced herself, the woman behind it flung out both arms in greeting and said, "So! You've come to your scents(es)," then giggled at her pun.

She had to be fifty, yet she laughed with abandon, like a girl. "Don't mind me, that's just my little joke. I'm Ms. Oglesby, but you may call me Rita," she added with a soft Southern drawl. She glanced at Jonquil's name tag.

"Do you go by Jonquil? Pretty name, sounds like one of my fragrances. Personnel called down and said you were on your way. Got any sales experience? Ever work in a department store during the Christmas season?" she asked, taking Jonquil's purse and jacket and stashing them in a drawer. Jonquil shook her head no, but Rita was already handing her a gaudy pink smock, as if it were made of pure silk. The one-size-fits-all cotton cover-up hung down nearly to her knees. She felt absurd in it, until Rita adjusted the matching belt, puffed out the sleeves, and affixed her nametag. Then, she stood back to appraise her handiwork.

"Got any allergies?" After Jonquil shook her head no again, Rita explained. "Last week they sent me a part-time college student, big sun-of-a-gun, six feet two. On his first day of work, he keeled right over the Chanel display and caused quite a stink. Case of a slight hangover and no breakfast. They transferred him to mattresses." *Is she pulling my leg?* thought Jonquil.

"Since it's your first day, I recommend Destiny—it might bring you luck," said Rita, reaching for a perfume applicator. She prepared to perform a baptism on the spot.

"Oh, but I never wear perfume," Jonquil objected. Nothing could have stunned Rita more. She froze, perfume atomizer in mid-air, mouth ajar, eyes glassy, a textbook example of shock.

"Maybe it's my destiny to start," said Jonquil with a quick smile, hoping as much to assuage Rita's feelings as to avoid a transfer to mattresses or a more remote outpost.

Jonquil was to learn that choosing the scent for the day was Rita's morning ritual, every bit as important as arranging the counter. It was her introit, weather vane, and form of journaling.

After dousing her new protégé with the fragrance, Rita

lovingly contemplated the array of glass samplers before her, remarking how she loved Christmas at Clyde's because the trendy scent cards were put away in lieu of the real thing. She selected her Tuesday favorite—Red. She explained in her chatty, just-us-gals voice that Tuesdays could always stand some brightening up. Jonquil had to agree. If nothing else, Rita's antics were making her first Tuesday on the job pass quickly.

Once Rita had amply applied Red both to herself and the surrounding area, pointing it in all directions like room freshener, she began Jonquil's training while another pink-smocked employee assisted shoppers.

"If your customer is a woman, you spray a sample on her wrist, but not too much. I always say: be frugal with the fragrances." Rita took Jonquil's left wrist and applied the scent with the dexterity of a pro.

"Now, when it's a man, you spray it on your wrist and then slowly wave it under his nose. Don't let him take your hand, sugar, 'taint necessary, and 'taint easy to get it back! We've had a few broken bottles on that account."

Again, Jonquil suspected Rita was exaggerating, yet her passion for perfume was genuine.

Rita firmly believed that every woman should have a wardrobe of fragrances. She also advocated the use of scented candles, soaps, and powders in the bath to create what she called a "scent"-ual cocoon.

While she gushed on, Jonquil realized she hadn't given any of these feminine indulgences the slightest thought in years.

They were going over the cash register procedures when Rita's head shot up like a radarscope. Quickly scanning the floor, she homed in on the object of her search. Then, she nodded her head in that direction.

"There's Al Yates, store manager. Twice divorced, bit of a starched shirt. Nice eyes. He's headed our way. Listen, sugar, I'll do the talking."

Her conspiratorial tone, along with a quick touch-up to her hair, alerted Jonquil that Rita's attention was riveted on the impeccably dressed, broad-shouldered, gray-haired gentleman approaching the counter.

As he came closer, Jonquil noted his commanding stride, balanced evenly by a pockmarked face and toothy grin.

"Good morning, Ms. Oglesby, how's it goin'?" His booming voice suggested a mixture of Marine drill sergeant, seasoned salesman, and high blood pressure.

"Why, Al, I was just showing my new assistant how to enter a sale. This is Ms. Bloom."

"Excellent! Welcome to Clyde's, Ms. Bloom. Is Rita treating you okay?"

"Fine," she said agreeably to his startling blue eyes, after a nudge from Rita.

"That's what I like to hear. Now, Rita, where is that new product from Frankio's?"

"You mean, Stony Island?" she asked with misgivings.

"Stony Island, that's the one. Makes me think of a love nest far, far away," he said dreamily, which struck Jonquil as peculiar until she remembered that Al was at heart a salesman.

Rita, minus her usual aplomb, reached into the bottom drawer of the counter cabinet and removed a bottle shaped like a rock. Then she pulled out the stopper, took a whiff, grimaced, and reported, "If you ask me, it smells more like a street I knew in Chicago."

"Say, your right," said Al. "Stony Island Avenue. I grew up in the Windy City on the south side."

"I sold my first bottle of perfume at Walgreens on the corner of 71st and Jeffery," Rita proudly retorted.

"And I passed there every day on the Illinois Central going back and forth to high school," said Al.

Next thing Jonquil knew, their eyes locked onto each other's like two pairs of oncoming headlights in a desert night. *Aha,* she thought, *he's interested too.*

The sound of store gongs brought Al back to his surroundings. "How many gongs was that? Was that for me? Ahem, well, we'll have to talk about Chicago some other time." He turned to Jonquil. "Ms. Bloom, have you sold perfume before?"

"Actually, no. You see, in real life I'm working on my Ph.D. in psychology." Al blinked while Rita regarded her with frank surprise. Perhaps she thought anyone who didn't like perfume couldn't be all that bright. However, what she said was, "P-H-D? Whoa, Nellie! Why, I shouldn't be training you, you should be training me."

"But, Rita, I need this job."

"You're in the right place," Al assured her. "When it comes to perfume, Rita's the best. Now, get out the Stony Island and move the merchandise. That's how we celebrate the Christmas season at Clyde's." With a wink at Rita, he hurried away.

"Now how in the world does he expect me to sell this stuff?" she grumbled more to herself than to Jonquil.

"Rita, I think Al likes you." Jonquil hoped she hadn't gotten too personal.

"You do?" Rita perked up right away. Her attention reverted back to her fragrances.

"Too bad Stony Island isn't a Red Door product," she chortled. "Otherwise, we could park it right next to Fifth Avenue."

After lunch, Rita walked Jonquil through several routine sales and then took her afternoon break. She gave Jonquil a layout of the store and a list of the Scentsations Department inventory to memorize. It was a daunting forty-page document.

Jonquil felt dismayed as she skimmed down the computerized printout, again asking herself what this detour from her meaning-filled work at Children's Home had to do with anything. It reminded her of having to take algebra in high school. She saw no point to that mental exercise either, and now as then, she balked.

Fortunately, at that precise moment, a handsome black man stepped up to the counter. He wore a flattering camel's hair blazer and red scarf, but his youthful face looked drawn, as though he hadn't slept all night.

"May I help you?" she asked.

"I need a gift to fix a problem," he said. Instantly, she was intrigued. Seeing no wedding band, she asked, "Is it for your girlfriend or your wife?"

"Girl—friend," he stammered. "At least I think she's still my girl. We had a little misunderstanding."

Something about his tone sounded familiar. Up until then, her dealings with customers had been supervised and the transactions had each been straightforward sales. Just yesterday she'd been totally immersed in nomenclature. Today's situation called for maximum dexterity with plastic credit cards. The change was more jarring than she had anticipated. This man and his dilemma were welcome indeed.

"Then, she's someone special?" asked Jonquil.

"Oh, very special," he said, anxiously fingering one

bottle after another. The urgency he displayed tapped her compassion. The gift was manipulative, sure. On the other hand, wouldn't the wrong gift do further damage to his relationship? He was about to pull the stopper out of the Stony Island sampler when she interrupted him with a nervy suggestion.

"Wait! I know what you should do, sir. If this was my problem, I'd forget perfume and buy her jewelry— diamonds—something so beautiful it will make her cry. Then, she'll be your girl again." He stared back at her speechless.

"Hey, you're right. I'll do it." All the worry in his face gave way to patent relief.

Above the din of Muzak and store gongs, she called out freshly memorized store directions at his retreating figure.

"Thank you, ma'am, thank you." He backed away, unaware of two people behind him, briefly collided with them, begged their pardon, and trotted off to the jewelry department.

Watching him go, she let her mind wander and found herself imagining it was the handsome painter at Children's Home running off to buy her sparkly diamonds. The painter had been coming up more and more in her thoughts lately, much to her surprise.

"Say, what's the big idea?" Rita's tone ended her

reverie. Jonquil hadn't noticed that Rita, back from her break, had witnessed the entire episode. "You sent him to another department. That's not going to help us reach our sales quota or earn us commissions." Rita sounded quite perturbed.

"I don't know what came over me, Rita," Jonquil said with dismay. "I wanted to help him solve his problem and it's not like I sent him to another store."

"Humph," was her concise retort.

"I'm sorry. It won't happen again."

Both of them became aware of a loud tapping sound. About three feet from them, a feisty old woman dressed to her teeth in winter clothing, stood impatiently rapping her cane against the counter. "Jabber on your coffee break, I need some cologne." she croaked.

Rita moaned and whispered loud enough for only Jonquil to hear, "It's the old battle ax, Mrs. Rose. If sour-grapes were a fragrance, she'd be wearing it."

"I'll help her," Jonquil volunteered. Rita gave her a grateful look and turned to assist another customer.

"May I help you?" Jonquil asked, business-like, determined to stick to the task at hand.

"I want eight ounces of Country Club Cologne," the lady stated.

"Certainly," said Jonquil, opening a cabinet drawer behind her. "Will that be cash or charge, Mrs. Rose?"

34

"Cash. Say, how do you know my name?" There was an edge to her voice.

"Rita—er—Ms. Oglesby, my supervisor, told me," Jonquil explained while tapping in the sale into the register.

"The redhead? Yes, I saw you two goofing off."

"Can I get anything else for you?" inquired Jonquil, slipping the cologne into a bag.

"I doubt it. What I need, no one can give me."

Jonquil heard the challenge in the woman's voice and found herself responding to it.

"Why not give me a try?" offered Jonquil, putting on her sweetest smile.

Mrs. Rose eyed her with disdain then let her have it with both barrels. "Can you make my husband healthy again? Can you make him remember we've been married fifty-one years today? He used to buy me my favorite cologne for our anniversary. Now, like everything else, I have to do it myself."

How sad and lonely she sounded in contrast to the activities going on around them. Jonquil suppressed a sigh. She had often felt a similar sadness on her own wedding anniversary. "That must be difficult for you. How do you manage?"

"None of your business. Here's what I owe you." The woman laid two twenty-dollar bills and some change on the counter. After depositing the money in the register drawer, Jonquil stapled the receipt to the bag, but she couldn't ignore the woman's distress.

"You sound upset. Have you been under this stress very long?" Jonquil persisted.

"What do you mean? Say, what right have you to pry into my personal life? You're just a sales clerk." But though she looked displeased, she waited for Jonquil's reply.

"May I make a suggestion? Buy the cologne for yourself, like you would buy a gift for your best friend. Have it gift-wrapped, include a card too and see if you don't feel better. And cherish all the loving things your husband did for you in the past. You know if he still could, he would."

Mrs. Rose glared at her but didn't budge. Then, tears began to roll down her lined cheeks. Jonquil offered her tissues, but she fished a beautiful lace handkerchief out of her purse and blew her nose.

"It's been so long since anyone cared how I felt. Thank you for listening, Miss—?"

"Bloom, Jonquil Bloom. Happy anniversary, Mrs. Rose."

With a cathartic sigh, she picked up her purchase and slowly ambled away. Rita watched her go and immediately dashed over.

"What did you *do* to her, Jonquil?" she demanded.

"I told her to have it gift wrapped, Rita. She did buy some cologne." Jonquil was talking as if she had to protect patient-therapist confidentiality. Odd, very odd.

Rita continued to stare after the woman. "She's been coming here for at least six years, and I don't ever remember her saying a kind word. She's always ordered the same old thing in the same rude way. Today, she actually looked human."

Jonquil hoped Rita regarded the change in Mrs. Rose as an improvement and not further evidence that she didn't belong in the Scentsations Department, for Jonquil was beginning to like what she was doing—whatever it was she was doing.

Rita showed her how to close out the cash register. Then, it was time to leave. Jonquil felt better than she had at the start of the day. The young man's words haunted her: "I need a gift to fix a problem." They seemed to be telling her something, but she couldn't yet discern their full import. She collected her jacket and purse and headed for the parking garage.

* * *

Billy Bloom usually took the bus partway home from school and walked the rest of the way with his best friend, Ramon DeWitt, whose coarse black hair always needed combing, shirttail tucking in, and shoelaces tying.

Grooming aside, you'd be hard pressed to find a more loyal friend. His family lived on the other side of the park in Venice Beach's poorer section. Ramon frequently dodged school and flunked third grade altogether but his paper route helped put food on the crowded DeWitt table.

"My mom is working at Clyde's now," announced Billy.

Ramon, a year older and three inches taller, sucked in his breath in surprise. "Why, dude?"

"She had to stop being a psychologist on account of they needed to paint some offices at her job. I think she'll go back there after Christmas."

"I sure hope so. My mom worked at Clyde's and it tired her out, all the noise, the people. She couldn't take it for long. You should get a job, buddy, and help your mom."

"She won't let me get a paper route until I'm older," Billy grumbled.

"Aw, look around, dude, there's something you can do." At the corner, they parted, and Ramon started to cross the street. "Bye, Billy," he cried and ran out of sight.

Billy continued down his own street toward the yellow apartment building with the purple bougainvillea vines. The area of Venice where the Blooms lived featured winding streets, each lined with a row of tightly arranged bungalows. In front of most, a patch of well-manicured lawn sloped from the front porch to the sidewalk. The two-story dwelling they occupied was the sole apartment building on the block.

As he continued along, he spied one of his elderly neighbors, Mr. Neri, attempting unsuccessfully to untangle the front yard hose. Billy stopped and called out to him, "Hi ya, Mr. Neri!"

The stooped, elderly man turned in all directions looking for the person who had called his name. "I'm over here," yelled Billy.

"Oh, hi, yourself," Mr. Neri grumbled. "Can't you see I'm busy?"

"Is your arthritis acting up?" shouted Billy to the hard-of-hearing Italian. Billy's mom had explained to him that Mr. Neri lived in a lot of pain, which made him cranky all the time.

"No, it's killing me, but the grass don't care—it just keeps a-growing."

Billy had a sudden inspiration. "Mr. Neri, how much would you pay me to water your lawn?"

The old man peered suspiciously at Billy through piercing eyes. "Pay you!" he sputtered, putting emphasis on the word pay.

"A dollar an hour is my final offer!" announced Billy.

"Twice a week? Front and back?"

Billy nodded affirmatively. The old man let go of the hose and started up his front steps. "My son cuts the grass on Saturdays," he said, "no touch-a the mower."

Billy dropped his bookbag and ran to pick up the hose.

"And if you feel like pulling a few weeds," Mr. Neri added, as he lowered himself gently into the porch rocker, "who's gonna stop ya?"

CHAPTER FOUR

Wednesday, December 3rd

On the way home, Jonquil reviewed her agenda for the evening: macaroni and cheese and broccoli with Billy, followed by the evening news on television, a look at Billy's homework, and finally, one quick load of laundry. But after dinner, she tuned in Tom Brokaw, parked her sore feet up on the couch, and promptly dozed off.

The next morning when she arrived at work, Rita greeted her with her usual effervescence, which, come to think of it, would make a fine name for a fragrance if you could design a large enough label. As they carefully dusted the counter, Rita voiced her perplexity with the human race. "What is wrong with people?" she asked.

Before Jonquil could reply, Rita continued, "This morning on the radio, there was another story about folks freaking out because the millennium is coming. All over the world, wars, bombings and suicides are up on account of a change in the calendar."

Jonquil guessed correctly that it was Calvin Klein day from the denim blouse and skirt that peeked out from under Rita's pink smock. While she treated them both to a veritable shower of the trendy scent, Jonquil resisted waving off the cloying fumes and addressed the issue. "You know, there's a good deal of superstitious thinking about the approach of a millennium. Some people think the end of the world is coming, but how do you treat a worldwide case of the jitters? On the Internet?

"Me? I'd rather deal with anxiety on a one-to-one basis. Like that fellow yesterday who needed a gift to fix his problem with his girlfriend. Know what I mean, Rita?"

Rita's face relaxed into a wistful expression as she observed the security guard unlocking the front doors. "You sure do pick up on things, Jonquil. I never finished high school but sometimes I think I would like to do more than this." She made a gesture encompassing the perfume counter. "Maybe even open my own boutique one day except I'm always too darned scared to try. Surprised? Well, other times I tell myself the trick in life is to find out where you belong, get there, and make the most of it."

They watched the first shoppers of the day file into the

store when all of a sudden an idea hit Jonquil with less warning than an aftershock.

She clapped her hands and exclaimed, "Rita, I've got it!"

"Got what, sugar?" Rita asked, startled.

"I'm going to turn this job around," she said. "I'm going to counsel gift givers. And you're going to help."

"Oh, my," Rita breathed and waited expectantly.

"See, I've just got to finish my research project. It's on the psychodynamics of gift-giving—what motivates people to give gifts. The children I used to work with were my sample population, but since I'm no longer at that facility, all the data I collected there would normally go to waste. Except that here I am, in a department store at the start of the holiday season, surrounded by all kinds of gift givers. I can collect new data here and maybe come up with a theory. Halleluiah!" At that point, they were each approached by customers who then drifted away.

Rita said, "I don't quite understand. Don't people usually give gifts because they want to?"

"Not always," Jonquil replied mischievously. "Consider the goddess Medea. She was so ticked off about not being invited to a royal baby shower, she had a gift basket of snakes delivered to the hostess. The snakes devoured everyone at the party."

Rita shuddered.

"Look, you'll be in charge of the control group," Jonquil continued, improvising a research design that would have made her faculty advisor howl with pain. "That way, you can keep up with your commissions." Rita liked the sound of that, though she hadn't a glimmer of what Jonquil was babbling about.

"I'll offer counseling to the shoppers who need special help like Mrs. Rose or that man I sent to jewelry." Jonquil felt her cheeks burning hot with self-consciousness. It was not an altogether unpleasant sensation.

"But what about Al?" Rita queried, as Jonquil maneuvered her toward the opposite end of the counter. "Won't he find out?"

"I won't tell if you won't tell." Jonquil was banking on Rita's ability to find fun in almost anything.

That is how, in under an hour, they had transformed the perfume counter into a makeshift laboratory. Rita, at one end, handled the customers who were there to make routine purchases. Anyone who showed the slightest hesitation or had questions, she referred to Jonquil. One woman, for example, was the mother of twin daughters—should she continue to buy them identical Christmas presents? (They were aged forty.) A silver-haired, dapper gentleman wearing expensive cashmere and khaki could not decide if a bottle of "Beautiful" were the appropriate birthday gift for his brand new twenty-two-year-old secretary. Jonquil sent him to stationery.

The morning passed so quickly, Jonquil hadn't found time to jot down her observations for her project. Nor had she any idea that a certain clerk in Men's Neckwear had tipped off Al Yates that something strange was going on in Scents.

Meanwhile, Rita proved to be the ideal decoy because of her penchant for matching the store's visitors with the appropriate scents. Jonquil had observed Rita the previous day, mumbling under her breath as customers walked by, "She's so White Diamonds" or "She's a walking Picasso if ever I saw one," much as Jonquil might label the clerk in purses—who rearranged her counter five times in an hour—compulsive.

It was a win-win situation.

Rita was chanting, "Express line, no waiting," while Jonquil was about to greet her next customer, when Al Yates arrived on the scene. He realized he was witnessing a situation not covered in Clyde's Training Manual.

"What the heck is going on?" he asked Rita. It was Jonquil's customer who answered.

"This lady's counseling me on which perfume to get my sister for Christmas."

Another voice behind her chimed in, "That's not all. This morning, she sent a neighbor of mine to the sweater department for a gift that shows warmth. Isn't that adorable?"

Though the people in line nodded in agreement, apparently "adorable" was not the word that occurred to Al, for he said with a stunned tone, "Rita, are you part of this?"

Rita's chin trembled slightly, but to her credit, she stood tall and replied, "In a way, I am, Al." Their eyes met for an instant and then both looked abruptly away, one abashed, the other furious. Jonquil hadn't anticipated such personal consequences to Rita's involvement.

"Please, Mr. Yates, this is entirely my fault. I asked Rita to help me with an experiment," said Jonquil.

"Young lady, who gave you permission to conduct experiments on clodhoppers—er—Clyde's shoppers?" he sputtered.

Jonquil sidestepped his question and launched into a spontaneous lecture on the psychodynamics of gift-giving. She failed to consider how the harried manager of an upscale department store might receive her remarks, but when she implied that some people give gifts for the wrong reason, while others spend too much money due to guilt feelings, Al's right hand shot up in the air like a traffic signal. "Stop! Those are the most traitorous words I have ever heard from a Clyde's employee, and lady, I've heard 'em all."

"Al!" Rita exclaimed, chagrined.

Al ignored her. He motioned to the clerk at the next counter to take over their registers. Next, he addressed the people who, up until then, had been patiently waiting in line. "Miss Steinway will be glad to assist you. Ms. Oglesby, Ms. Bloom, come with me."

Scowling, Al led them both over to the first floor elevators. While he banged the call button, he gloated. "Just wait until Mr. Merrill gets a load of you two. He knows the bottom line when it comes to retail."

* * *

Mr. Merrill, the founder's son-in-law and Clyde's current sixty-one-year-old president, was at that moment in his office behind closed doors immersed in his favorite fire truck toy. Of all the departments in the store, the toy section on the fourth floor won his most enthusiastic support. He made it a point to test every new toy, doll, or game, fresh from the manufacturers before they were stocked on Clyde's shelves.

For this reason, Miss Egnar, his bemused secretary, kept his door closed whenever he was in the office. If it became necessary to interrupt her boss, such as when an indignant Al Yates appeared that day with two contrite employees, she gave him a warning beep on his phone.

"Mr. Yates is here to see you, Mr. Merrill, along with

47

two clerks from Scents. He says it's urgent."

"Give me a minute, please. Then, send them in," shouted the executive, above the fire truck's ear-splitting siren. He cleared his desk, flipped his computer screen to a dummy spread sheet, straightened his tie, put on his presidential bifocals and clasped his hands firmly on the spotless blotter in front of him just as Miss Egnar opened the door.

Al strode into the president's office with Jonquil and Rita trailing behind. At the sight of Rita, Mr. Merrill rose and smiled. "Hello, Rita, it's good to see you."

Al wasted no time on chitchat. "Mr. Merrill, these ladies have been conducting experiments on our valued customers without permission."

"Is that so?" asked Mr. Merrill in a mild tone known in the past to diffuse agitated store managers. Deftly sliding the newest Hot Wheels under his desk and out of sight, he suggested they all sit down and talk it over. It had been years since he'd shown any real interest in the store because the large chains had made it virtually impossible to remain independent and profitable. Just that week he'd entertained another offer from a competitor to buy out Clyde's. He'd been able to keep the doors open and his staff, who were like family, employed. But he'd been unable to offer raises or bonuses in two years. Rita reminded him of better times. It was unthinkable that she could be mixed up in any real trouble.

However, twenty minutes later, after he grasped the gist of the situation, he reluctantly had to agree with Al Yates that store policy prohibited experiments of any kind. The infraction was serious enough to warrant suspension for Rita and termination for Jonquil. In over seventeen years of faithful service, Rita had never been in a similar predicament and her tearful regret was obvious to everyone. Even Al squirmed in his seat, his flashy blue eyes concealed behind lowered lids.

They were about to conclude the meeting, when Miss Egnar beeped on the inter-office line. Mr. Merrill picked up the receiver and listened briefly. "A riot in Scents?" he echoed for all to hear. "Demanding what? See here, we do not negotiate with terrorists!" Yet, after Miss Egnar furnished a few more pertinent details, his tone changed dramatically and his eyes focused. "That's a different matter. We'll be right down." He cradled the phone receiver and announced, "The customers are demanding gift counseling." His reaction resembled a rooky fireman answering his first call to action. He jumped up and gestured for them to accompany him downstairs.

When they arrived on the first floor, they couldn't believe their eyes. Ever since Al had whisked the two clerks off the floor, the patrons who had been standing in line to speak to Jonquil in the Scents Department hadn't moved an inch. The eight women and two men insisted they weren't leaving without gift counseling. With growing fascination, Mr. Merrill recognized two platinum-card customers among them. Moreover, a dozen or so curious shoppers had gathered to observe the impromptu protest in progress. To top things off, a student-intern from the radio station at nearby Santa Monica College lingered on the sidelines. He was at Clyde's to tape another "nostalgic moment" for a mid-afternoon program.

Al rushed over to apoplectic Miss Steinway to obtain an explanation, while Mr. Merrill hung back to observe. The reporter approached him, notebook in hand.

"Mr. Merrill, these people are demanding gift counseling. They claim no other store offers it. But Clyde's suddenly withdrew the service—some of these people believe—'cause it was a free-bee. Care to comment?"

Mr. Merrill massaged the back of his neck while he mulled things over. He was fond of saying to those he mentored: when opportunity knocks, you'd better be pressed, dressed, and ready to go. Leigh Usher agreed wholeheartedly. Leigh Usher was Clyde's smart, sophisticated Head Buyer and Mr. Merrill's closest advisor.

Both he and Leigh had the store's best interest in mind.

Of that, he was sure. Yet, they had their differences, too. She called him a dinosaur because he still believed good customer service was the hallmark of a successful business while Leigh pushed for more modern stock and procedures and heavily relied on technology.

How would she handle this minor contretemps? Since Leigh was traveling and not easily accessible, the decision rested with him.

Maybe it was time he did some experimenting of his own, he thought, brought Clyde's up to date, offered the holiday market something new. People sought counseling for many reasons—especially in California—so why not *gift* counseling? After all, the young woman in question— Bloom—was no dummy. Even if he couldn't understand her experiment, wasn't the customer always right? He could hear Leigh jeering at him: *that old saw?*

Yet, if these folks truly thought they needed gift counseling, perhaps they did. Supposing there were radio spots and television commercials and inducements in newspaper ads, would business pick up?

Mr. Merrill saw opportunity and risk written all over the tableau before him, and he decided to jump in with both feet. Speaking to the reporter, he said, "Stick around, young man, till we see which way the wind blows in Scents."

Before Al could report back with his appraisal of the

situation, Mr. Merrill took Jonquil aside. "Ms. Bloom, would you consider heading your own Gift Counseling Department here at Clyde's? For the entire Christmas season? Would you like that? We'll adjust your pay accordingly."

Jonquil reacted immediately. "On one condition: that Rita works with me, as my assistant, and that she gets a raise to make up for her commissions." Jonquil glanced at Rita and held her breath.

"Agreed," said Mr. Merrill.

"Agreed!" echoed Rita.

Mr. Merrill turned to the waiting patrons and announced the exclusive opening of the Gift Counseling Department, which would take place the following afternoon. As the radio reporter and the others began to crowd around him and Jonquil, Rita swiftly removed her pink smock and tossed it into a handy wastebasket.

Al caught sight of her and was about to react to the wanton disposal of company property, until he saw Rita cheerfully wave "bye bye" to the garish cover-up. Then she called out to the people milling around, "I'm setting up gift counseling appointments!" It dawned on him that there was more to Rita than perfume. There always had been—it just hadn't been plain to him until that moment.

* * *

On his way home from school that afternoon, Billy encountered Mrs. Crandon, the Neris' honey-coifed next door neighbor, out walking her dogs. Mrs. Crandon, who raised show dogs, also kept cocker spaniels as pets. Over Labor Day, they'd become parents. Today, she clutched three straining leashes, which made her clunky gold bracelets jingle-jangle like miniature sleigh bells.

Billy immediately spotted his favorite, a three-month-old puppy that he called Blackie because of his licorice-colored coat. "Hi ya, Mrs. Crandon," Billy said.

"Well, hello, Billy Bloom, how was school today?"

Billy knelt on the grass to pet Blackie who leapt high in the air with joyous barks signaling to his siblings, paws off—this is my friend.

"Okay, I guess," Billy said and laughed, but he couldn't say more until Blackie finished licking his face. They'd become acquainted recently the night Billy slept over at Mrs. Crandon's as a special treat when Jonquil had to attend a weekend seminar on campus.

"I'm feeling kinda punk myself," confessed Mrs. Crandon. "These puppies are getting to be a handful. They're the last of the litter. I'm giving them to my grandchildren as Hanukkah presents, but in the meantime, I have to walk them, and I'm at a critical stage with the poodles."

Billy knew what that meant. When Mrs. Crandon was

at a critical stage in the training of her charges, she would disappear into her home for days and devote herself wholeheartedly to preparing the show dogs for their next competition.

"I'll walk them for you," Billy volunteered.

"Billy, dear, could you? Twice up and down the block—oh, you know the routine. Listen, could you come back tomorrow, too, about this time?"

"Sure," said Billy.

"If you can also come Friday, I'll pay you five dollars in advance." She transferred the leashes over to Billy, and dug into the pockets of her pantsuit for her shiny coin purse.

"Mrs. Crandon, you don't have to pay me." The puppies were doing their very best to knock him off his high-tops, but after he ordered them "Down!" twice in a firm tone, the way Mrs. Crandon had taught him to, they contented themselves with sniffing the cracks in the pavement.

"Yes, I do, Billy. You'll earn it. Besides, it's not everyone I'd trust with my babies. I know you'll do a good job," she said as she slipped the five-dollar bill into the back pocket of his uniform pants. "I'm pressed for time and puppies know how to make a ten-minute walk last until suppertime. You, on the other hand, love every dragged out minute, don't you?"

54

"Sure I do. Thanks, Mrs. Crandon."

* * *

When he heard Jonquil's car turning into the garage, Billy ran to meet her. "Mom, Mom, guess what. I got two new jobs!" he yelled as he held the screen door open for her.

"Golly, I got only one new job today," she replied in her kidding tone. She walked out to the kitchen with a bag of groceries. While she and Billy emptied its contents, he told her about the watering job. She only half-listened to him because her mind was busy selecting an outfit for tomorrow's opening at Clyde's. Yet, when he told her he would be walking Mrs. Crandon's pups, she firmly cautioned him not to become too attached to them. Billy told her not to worry—the puppies were going to be Hanukkah gifts for Mrs. Crandon's grandchildren. She let it go.

She told him about the new Gift Counseling Department she would be managing at Clyde's and described it as an experiment.

Billy had a hard time understanding this change in her job at the store, but he was happy to see her smiling again. It gave him a terrific idea.

"Mom, can we go out for dinner tonight? Remember? Rule number one: celebrate the good times? I've got money, I can treat." With that, he extracted the bill Mrs. Crandon had given him.

"Oh, sweetie, that's very generous of you, but I have a zillion things to do to get ready for tomorrow. Why not use your money to buy Ramon a Christmas present?"

Billy frowned and started to trudge away. Jonquil thought quickly.

"Tell you what, we'll have a special dinner tonight. Now, what culinary delight will put a smile on that long face?"

"Sloppy joes?" he asked hopefully. "With pickles and shoestrings and chocolate milk?"

She arched an eyebrow, nodded, and laughed.

He rewarded her with roars and a split-second hug.

"Start your homework."

"Okay, Mom."

As she began to prepare dinner, her mind moved on to the next problem—what to say at tomorrow's opening.

CHAPTER FIVE

Thursday, December 4th

D imly, Jonquil heard clanging, then banging, followed by the whir of some kind of drill. She rolled over and snuggled under the covers. The last thing she needed was a bad dream.

Bam! There it was again, no mistaking it. Someone nearby was hammering the daylights out of something. She threw back the covers, fully alert now. The digital clock on her nightstand read 6:23 a.m.

"What the—?" she asked the furniture.

She peered out the window nearest her bed into darkness. Then she groped her way over to the opposite window, automatically recalling the Northridge quake, which had lurched the beach communities to consciousness in the winter of 1994. Gingerly, she stepped out on the balcony. Dark as it was, she perceived movement on the building across the street. Her worst suspicions were confirmed when she also detected a half dozen pickup trucks and the undeniable wail of country western music. Construction workers!

"Damn!" she said, mindful of the short night behind her and the new challenge facing her in a matter of hours. Overnight, it had become warm—the Santa Anas were blowing. Rapidly, she threw on a T-shirt, jogging shorts and sandals, then stomped off in the direction of the noise.

Dawn broke just as she positioned herself in front of the dwelling across from her apartment, which had been vacant for nearly two years. Her anger so energized her that she swayed from one foot to the other, fists at her waist, her face puckered in a mask of rage.

"Who's in charge here?" she yelled toward the men overhead. "WHO-IS-IN-CHARGE?" she repeated with more gusto. Her inquiry met with catcalls and derision.

"Look-y what we got here," one voice taunted.

"Ooo-ee, we got legs," another weighed in.

"Oh, Claudie, you got company," sang out a third.

Then, from out of the uppermost window, a man emerged dressed more business-like than the other workers, in a beige suit, tie and white hardhat. He took a few steps toward the edge of the roof overhanging a second floor porch.

She stood her ground.

"How dare you!" She flung the words up at him. "Ruining the sleep of this entire neighborhood. Who do you think you are?"

He removed his hard hat and knelt down on one knee to get a better look at her. She could see that he had dark hair and a muscular build, but with his back to the sun, the rest of his features were in shadow.

"Claude Chappel," he said, putting emphasis on "pel." *Sha-pell,* her mind echoed. *Sha-pell, sha-pell, sha-pell.*

"And you are?" His voice sounded melodious with something extra mixed in—possibly French. His pleasant greeting caught her off guard.

"My name is Jon—" she began, then, coming to her senses, she exploded, "*Mrs.* Bloom. And, thanks to you, I lost a precious half-hour's sleep. My, uh, family, too. Now, there must be ordinances or laws against this mayhem, and I will look into it, and I will have you stopped. Are you even listening? Today I start a new job, and it's important that I'm awake while I'm doing it." Her tirade met with a deafening silence.

"Well? Say something!" she shouted up at him in exasperation.

Claude Chappel, meanwhile, studied the agitated figure below him and wondered to the high heavens how such coincidences were possible in a place as spread out as Southern California. Hadn't she spattered his face with wall paint just four days ago? Hadn't the secretary in that broken down excuse for a home told him how much his moonlighting paint gig had cost this woman? Twice in one week their paths had crossed. Both times she'd been furious about something he was doing. Thank God she did not recognize him.

"I apologize, madam," he said. "The ordinance says work can begin at 7 a.m. We jumped the gun. It won't happen again."

"It had better not," Jonquil muttered before she jerkily marched back to her apartment, maddeningly conscious of tingles running up and down her body, which she blamed on the tilt of his head and the intoxicating tones in his voice.

* * *

When Jonquil entered the store that morning, she was amazed by the speed with which the Gift Counseling Department™, complete with presumptive trademark, had materialized. She had to keep reminding herself that Clyde's had once been a thriving emporium, not the crumbling state-funded facility where she had previously interned.

Even if the store was now perched precariously on the bubble as rumors implied, its buoyant spirit could still rise to the occasion when necessary.

Mr. Merrill, relishing the challenge, had called into play the store's resources, including maintenance; housekeeping; marketing; public relations; legal, and personnel. Overnight a sunny suite of offices on the first floor—site of Clyde's defunct travel bureau—had been aired, scrubbed, and tastefully refurnished. New blinds hung on the floor-to-ceiling windows facing Fourth Street. Poinsettia plants offered holiday color.

It was Al's idea that decorative wall posters should feature Clyde's hot products, including a blow-up of noxious Stony Island perfume. Before Jonquil could lodge a diplomatic protest, Rita took herself up to Gallery on Three and selected several charming prints, framed and ready for display. They were hung in the reception area, office, and powder room. In deference to Al, Mr. Merrill had a hard copy of the store's inventory, all twenty binders' worth, delivered to the suite, and then made sure Jonquil got the hint: push Clyde's merchandise! She got the message loud and clear.

The net result was a little island of serenity separated from the main floor by a short hallway that offered respite to the undecided (conflicted from Jonquil's point of view) shopper. Tea, coffee, and Perrier invited sipping in the reception area where Rita would hold forth, making appointments and greeting visitors. The unit was not connected to the store's repetitive Muzak either. Here, one could find peace and quiet. Taking it all in, Jonquil hoped she could meet and exceed Mr. Merrill's quicksilver expectations.

Between the back-to-back meetings with staff to acquaint them with the concept of gift counseling, and reviewing the opening ceremony agenda for the press and media, she managed a pit stop at the ladies' restroom. Jonquil stood stock still in front of a full-length mirror and privately thanked God for this new adventure. She noticed that, while her make-up needed touching up, her green eyes sparkled. While her hair needed adjustment, her energy level had never been higher.

After making sure no one else was in the room, she took the opportunity to shake her fist at her reflection and declared, "This is for me. This is mine. I'll show 'em all!" Then, she high-fived the mirror.

She hurried to the opening ceremony, her heart pounding louder than her heels hitting the floor. Excitement permeated the air like one of Rita's fragrances. She could see it on the faces of the employees, feel it in the way they waved her good luck. They had a stake in the outcome of this venture, too.

Strangely, the words Jonquil had written to a childhood friend after her husband's death broke into her thoughts.

I've not only lost Gerry but also everything that made me tick—marriage, home, family—so, it's no wonder I've lost time as well. Time doesn't weigh heavily or stand still or pass slowly. Time has no relevance whatsoever.

She batted the air as if tearing away cobwebs. She was ticking now—tick, tick, tick! Cooking on all four burners and damn the mixed metaphors! She didn't need a man in her life—*hear that, Mr. Chappel?* she wanted to yell. She had Billy and this fantastic opportunity. Love and work, wasn't that Dr. Freud's pithy prescription for fulfillment? Well, at last she had both. So, why were these painful memories about Gerry surfacing after so many years?

Moments before noon, they assembled outside the suite—Mr. Merrill, Al Yates, PR manager Inez Escanaba, Mr. Bramson, Rita, Jonquil, and two dozen invited guests. Beaming, Mr. Merrill cut in half the wide scarlet ribbon garnished with a king-sized gift bow that had been taped across the entrance. Cameras flashed to the accompaniment of spontaneous applause, even cheers. Then, Mr. Merrill spoke a few words.

"In keeping with its long tradition of serving this community, Clyde's is proud to offer a new and exclusive service to its loyal customers. We call it gift counseling. And now, I call upon Ms. Jonquil Bloom, our resident gift

SHEILA M. CRONIN

counselor, to tell us more about this exciting and free benefit available to all."

Jonquil stepped forward to shake his hand, then made some remarks that later she couldn't recall—too many perhaps, because she became aware of Al, off to one side, vigorously pantomiming self-decapitation. She nodded, smiled, and concluded by welcoming everyone to the Gift Counseling Department.

Al smirked as he handed her a jumbo box of facial tissues, his version of a kick-off gift. Rita, who had uncharacteristically stayed in the background, now came forward. She whisked out an atomizer and showed Jonquil the label. It read "Champagne." Touched, Jonquil watched as she marched through the suite, spraying it right and left, like an acolyte in church dispensing incense. With that, they were launched.

That first afternoon was in many ways chaotic. None of them could estimate how many people would sign up for the new service or how long a typical session would take. They had plunged into this endeavor on little more than a whim and had to feel their way through the early stages.

Rita took on the role of gatekeeper. Through a brief intake interview, she determined whether gift counseling was indicated or if one of Clyde's personal shoppers could handle the situation. This cadre of store employees

64

performed the legwork for customers who knew what they wanted but didn't have time to shop.

Those who wanted counseling were asked by Rita to furnish specific information, including the relationship between the "giver" and the "receiver," the gift occasion, and the budget parameters.

Rita was not computer literate, and both she and Jonquil preferred an atmosphere free of technological gadgetry, so she jotted down these facts on an index card, which she then handed to Jonquil, while ushering each person into her office.

On more than one of these cards, Rita scribbled her own cryptic appraisal. When Jonquil saw "Opium" written on the back of one card, she wondered if this was Rita's signal to her that the sophisticated, tailored lady seated across from her was an addict. She should have known better.

The day unfolded in unexpected ways. There was a young man, for example, in his early twenties, who couldn't sit still. Though he wore a smart suit, his bleached blond hair and sunburned face suggested weekend surfer.

He'd come to discuss the purchase of a Christmas present for his office's Secret Santa grab bag. He had drawn the name of an older colleague whom he did not like.

When Jonquil asked him for further details, he threw his hands up in the air and said, "It's a personality conflict, that's what. She bugs me. She's rude, she's nosy, she's always late for work, and she never gets docked. And don't tell me to get her a watch—we're only supposed to spend ten dollars."

"If you don't mind my saying so, you sound upset," Jonquil observed.

"I am. Why do we have stupid grab bags anyway? Why all these fake office parties at Christmastime? If I didn't work there, I wouldn't even know the witch." He glanced at her and mumbled, "Sorry."

"Please sit down," said Jonquil. Sighing, he did.

"Perhaps your co-worker reminds you of someone?" she asked.

"No way," he said with a snort.

"Way," Jonquil was tempted to retort, like Billy often did when he contradicted her. But if she was going to make a success of this position, she could not overstep the boundaries of supportive, reality-based counseling. *I'm not here to analyze him,* she thought, *only to help him give this woman a present.* "What would you like your gift to say or do?" she asked patiently.

"I guess," he answered, studying the floor, "I want something safe. Nothing too personal or nothing that says how I really feel about her."

"The store is full of such items," she remarked dismissively, much as she might have said, "Quit wasting my time." That mustn't have sounded supportive, she realized too late.

He looked at her sharply. "I get it. In other words, do it right or don't do it at all." She hadn't meant that at all but he had interpreted her words in his own way. "Okay," he continued in a different tone, "I have a week before this office shindig to find out what she likes. I'll study her desk before she gets to work in the morning—maybe find a clue." He got up and walked out, charting aloud his plan of action.

The minute he reached the threshold of Jonquil's office, Rita would hand him a Clyde's gift certificate. There was no obligation to shop at Clyde's but the certificate provided a smart inducement. It also allowed Marketing to track the tangible benefits of the store's newest department, plus keep Mr. Merrill and Al Yates informed.

Meanwhile, Jonquil scratched fast notes on the back of his filing card. At night, after Billy went to bed, she intended to transcribe these notes onto her laptop. By the end of that afternoon, she had accumulated twenty cards to input.

She stopped at the bank after work and then got gas before picking up Billy at Ramon's house. There was no sign of activity on the jobsite by the time they reached home. The vivid image from that morning of Claude Chappel dropping to one knee to give her his full attention kept recurring to her. She was so distracted that while preparing dinner she burned the pork chops.

CHAPTER SIX

Friday, December 5th

B illy woke her from a deep slumber, quite upset. "Mom, Mom! We're late!" he cried.

Immediately she sat up and checked the digital clock on her bed stand. It was flashing 12:00, a sure sign that there had been a power outage during the night.

"What time is it, Billy?" she asked.

"Almost eight o'clock. Hurry up, Mom."

Pulling on her terrycloth robe, Jonquil flew to the kitchen and prepared him a quick breakfast, all the while thinking how odd it was that they had both overslept. When they heard his carpool driver honk, she ran out to beg a few extra minutes so Billy could brush his teeth. She had completely forgotten about the construction job across the street, but as she scurried down the driveway to where a minivan waited for Billy, she became aware of a curious phenomenon. Approximately thirty men, scattered all over the jobsite, appeared to be hard at work, yet she couldn't hear a single hammer hitting a single nail.

She recognized Claude Chappel standing on the top level. When he spotted her, he yelled to his crew, "All right, men, let 'em rip!" Immediately, the men pulled what looked from a distance like rags off their hammers and tools. The morning erupted with noise, scattering birds out of the trees. Claude turned back in her direction, bowed deeply, and called out, "Morning, Mrs. Bloom. I trust you slept well."

She blushed to the roots of her tangled hair. The carpool driver, Georgina Phillips, leaned out of her window to get a better look at Claude while Billy came bounding up behind her, demanding to know who that man was.

"Nobody," lied Jonquil, handing him his lunch bag.

After they drove away, Claude continued to gaze down at her serenely. Against her will, her right hand rose above her head and waved him a speechless thanks. When she discovered that even her own hand seemed to be drawn to this annoying man, she stomped back to the apartment in turmoil.

Jonquil was trembling by the time she got inside and slammed the door. "No!" she bellowed at the walls. "No, no, no!" She ran to the picture window, lowered one of the mini blind slats, and peered over at the jobsite. If she so much as caught him laughing, or glad handing the foreman, or mimicking her in any way, she'd, she'd—but Claude was nowhere in sight.

"Fine, Mr. Claude Chappel," she grunted, letting the blind snap back into place. "We're one on one. But don't get any more cute ideas, see? Because you don't stand a chance with Jonquil Bloom." So saying, she dressed quickly and decided to stop for coffee on the way to work. A calming cup of java, along with an exhilarating view of the Pacific would surely settle her nerves.

However, she had not counted on traffic being a problem. Road construction—what else?—at the entrance of the Number Ten Freeway reduced all motor activity to a crawl. She turned on the radio in time to catch the lead-in to a ballad Tony Bennett had recently debuted at a splashy Hollywood Bowl benefit for children with AIDS.

> *"When there's nothing left to give,*
> *Give love..."* he began with halting tones.
> *"When there's no more you can do,*
> *Give love..."* he continued, his voice building momentum.
> *"While you struggle with living,*
> *Let your heart do the giving.*

For best of all gifts
Is your love ..."

Just then, an Essex convertible with an attitude and no turn signal cut her off and made her miss the light. Jonquil switched off the radio and fumed.

* * *

By the time she reached Clyde's, she was seething. She stormed into the office and literally bumped into Rita.

"Hey, sugar, what's up?" asked Rita, surveying her pumped-up demeanor.

"Men, that's what."

"Coffee's on. There's bagels in the lunchroom."

"Rita, I'd *kill* for a bagel," Jonquil said between clenched teeth.

"That won't be necessary," Rita deadpanned. "I'll go get us each one and then you must tell Rita all about the nasty man or men who upset you this morning. You may not leave out any details, or else ..." She rolled her eyes and had Jonquil chuckling before she dashed off to the lunchroom.

Rita, as it turned out, approved of Claude Chappel sight unseen. She admired his style. She claimed he was a romantic. She pronounced him probably unattached, definitely interested and undeniably sexy. From the way she took over the conversation, Jonquil assumed that, next to perfume, romance was Rita's favorite topic, but then, the two went hand in hand, so to speak. She proceeded to tell Jonquil about the love of her life, one Edwin Oglesby, a traveling salesman whom she met at a square dance in her native Arkansas when she was just shy of eighteen. Tall, stout, though fleet of foot, he had a zest for life that wouldn't quit. After a few "dosey-does," he rakishly proposed. After a couple more "allemande lefts," she impulsively accepted. They eloped and set out for Chicago. "The city," he said, "where you can dance till dawn."

He was twenty years her senior, the most fun loving man she'd ever known, and so crazy about her that he quit the road and found work closer to home. He also urged her to sell perfume if that was her yen. They raised two boys while she grew up and he grew older and, if it weren't pure joy, it was more happiness than she could ever have imagined, given the hard rural life she'd known before he came along.

"My favorite sound in the whole world was the little knock his car made when he pulled into the driveway each evening before supper."

They were married nineteen years until a month after his long retirement began, when he suffered a fatal heart attack while stringing bulbs for the annual block party.

Her eyes glistened brightly and she smiled.

"We always dreamed of moving to California, so, after Ed passed over and the boys started college, that's what I did. And here I am, sugar, talking off your ear when we should be plotting your next move with Claude what's-his-name."

"You were lucky, Rita," said Jonquil. The envy in her voice eluded Rita.

"Lord, don't I know," Rita sighed in agreement.

It was time for the store to open, the phones to be answered, and the workday to begin. As they gathered up the cups and crumbs, a thought occurred to Rita. "Why, Jonquil Bloom, here I am yakking my head off and you haven't said 'boo' about your son or your—"

"My husband died before Billy was born," Jonquil interrupted. "I don't remember the sound his car made."

"Oh." She heard the mixed emotions in Jonquil's voice. "Did he make you happy?"

"Who, Gerry? At first, yes, but in the end he made me the saddest woman on earth." Letting go of that admission for the first time in the presence of another person was akin to hearing the hinges creak on a corroded door. Jonquil dreaded everything behind that door and had kept it sealed, but some force beyond her control had succeeded at pushing it open from the other side. Even so, she could have kicked herself for saying anything so self-pitiful after Rita had shared her happiest memories with

74

her. Rita may have sensed the awkwardness, too, for she deftly maneuvered them back to the present.

"Say, aren't you on television tonight?"

Talk about your non sequiturs. She invited herself over to Jonquil's apartment so that together they could watch the local six o'clock news which was to feature a snippet on gift counseling. She said she wanted to meet Billy but Jonquil suspected that what she really wanted was a peek at Claude. Nonetheless, the idea of sharing the television event with another adult appealed to her. And who better than Rita?

Claude and crew were nowhere in sight when Billy ran to open the door for them. Billy and Rita took to each other right away, especially after she seconded his motion for take-out pizza.

"Great, guys," said Jonquil. "I'll order dinner and make a salad while you crank up the TV."

A while later they were gathered around the tube when a reporter from KTLA, who had taped the interview with Jonquil earlier that day, introduced the feature story.

"Help for the beleaguered holiday shopper can be found at Clyde's of Santa Monica this season in the form of gift counseling. Here with me is psychologist Jonquil Bloom to tell us about Clyde's new and exclusive service." As the camera focused on Jonquil, Billy let out a whoop. She remembered how she'd avoided craning her neck to look up at the interviewer by training her eyes on the camera instead.

"Jonquil, what is gift counseling?"

"Gift counseling is the process by which a person receives help in overcoming problems associated with giving or receiving. Gift-giving is an ancient custom. Some say it originated with sacrifices to appease the gods. Today, we often find ourselves in situations where giving the appropriate gift can be the defining moment in a relationship."

"Can you give our viewers some examples?"

"Well, there's the proverbial what-do-you-get-the-person-who-has-everything. But no, I'm talking about ordinary situations. For example, if both parents work and feel guilty about the time they spend away from their children, do they compensate with expensive or exorbitant gifts? Does a divorced couple compete for their kids' love by their individual pile of presents? Or, say you are on strained terms with a member of your family but you pick that person's name out of the holiday grab bag."

"And what do you do for these folks?"

"I help them figure out what they want the gift to do."

There was a pause, while the interviewer waited for Jonquil to elaborate. When she didn't, he plunged on.

"I see. Well, good luck to you." The camera focused on him again and he reminded everyone watching that gift counseling was offered exclusively at Clyde's before turning the show back to the anchor team.

Rita jumped up and threw her arms around Jonquil. "You were tops, sugar."

The phone and doorbell rang simultaneously. "That will be the pizza—it's my treat," cried Rita, reaching for her purse.

"Thanks, Rita," Jonquil shouted as she grabbed the kitchen receiver. "Billy, set the table, please," she said before taking the call.

It was Nurse Betsy from Children's Home. They had all seen Jonquil on television. A born gusher, Betsy couldn't stop saying, "I'm so happy for you!" Jonquil hated to interrupt but her phone was beeping with another call.

"Bets, thanks so much for calling. Sorry, I have to go now," she said.

"Right. Say, you'll be glad to know the Coles kid hasn't come back."

"Wow, that's good news." The persistent beep broke up the rest of her words. Jonquil blurted, "Thanks again for calling," and took the next call.

The caller was Father Tim Moran. A retired parish priest, he lived in St. Monica's Church rectory over in Santa Monica. They had met at the hospital the night Billy was born. Father Tim was practically a member of their family. Now in his mid-seventies and frail, his voice still carried a musical lilt.

"Jonquil, me dear, you're a star!" he piped.

"Hi, Father Tim, how are you—did you see me on TV?"

"Sure and isn't that why I'm callin'? You were a smash, dearie, but what's all this claptrap about pay-gun rituals?"

"To tell the truth, Father, I was so nervous I didn't know what I was saying."

"You could have fooled me. Well, this will make the lads come knockin' down yer door."

The call-waiting signal beeped again. Jonquil apologized to him that she had to take another call.

"I'll be off, then," he said and kindly hung up. Billy was at her side, tugging her arm.

"Can I speak to Father Tim, Mom?"

"I'm sorry, Billy, he hung up already. We can call him back." She asked her caller to hang on a sec.

"That's okay," he muttered and his shoulders sagged.

Rita got him started on dinner while Jonquil spoke to one of her graduate school classmates. The phone rang on and off for the next two hours. Jonquil was glad Rita was there to keep Billy company. Nor did she mind one bit eating cold pizza.

Later that night, passing Billy's bedroom, Jonquil

heard the unmistakable sounds of an old Kenny Loggins cassette tape and paused. Billy, in a certain mood, would play and replay a tune called, "Return to Pooh Corner." It was his signal to her that he wanted to be left alone. One weekend years ago when they'd driven north to Santa Barbara to visit former neighbors, the whimsical song had played on the car radio.

"Your dad's voice sounded like that," Jonquil remarked half to herself. Billy, just four years old, diligently asked for and received the cassette on his next birthday.

Although she wanted to knock on his door, they had painstakingly forged a mutual understanding, gleaned from his periodic "time outs" and her occasional stormy retreats to her bedroom, that he was entitled to his privacy as much as she was to hers. Yet, tonight after they'd enjoyed such a splendid time with Rita, after all the excitement of the television interview, why had Billy retreated to his room to play that childish song?

She could barge in on the pretext of saying bedtime prayers with him. On the other hand, he might not be expecting her since it was so late. Prayers? Privacy? Which held sway? As always, she had no husband to consult with, no other children to contend with, only the dirty dishes and Billy's closed door. She tapped once, then pushed the door open a crack. Billy was in bed fast asleep. She tiptoed over to the cassette player, punched the "off" button, and then pulled the covers up over her son.

The enormity of being a mother—a single one at that—swept over her again. Tomorrow, no matter what, she must remember to ask him why he withdrew from the celebration.

CHAPTER SEVEN

Saturday, December 6th

J onquil caught herself peering over at the jobsite as she did the breakfast dishes. All was quiet. Inexplicably, she felt a stab of disappointment.

Claude Chappel had replaced the painter from Children's Home in her romantic fantasies which had increased noticeably since her chat with Rita about him. Her anger toward the sexy construction boss had morphed into curiosity since she knew nothing about him.

She dried her hands and turned her mind to practical matters. This was her first working Saturday in years. She reviewed her schedule and Billy's for the week, as well as grocery, laundry, and house-cleaning chores.

"Billy, take out the garbage before you leave, please," she yelled. "No more reminders."

"Sure Mom," he yelled back.

Georgina Phillips arrived minutes before nine. Annually, cool mom that she was, Georgina took her carpool kids to the Farmers Market in Los Angeles to do their Christmas shopping. Afterward, they would chow down on whatever food they craved since the famed outdoor tourist attraction offered every cuisine imaginable.

Before they drove away, Georgina confided to Jonquil that the handsome construction boss had worked on her neighbor's house addition, that he was single and owned his own company. Jonquil, though impatient to get to work, listened carefully to every word.

Both her hours and Rita's were 10 a.m. to 4 p.m. on weekends. The phone never let up. The television plug had generated many inquiries. A steady trickle of walk-ins kept Jonquil busy. Mrs. Rose, the woman who had purchased Country Club Cologne from her, stopped by with a long gift list. It had been years, she confessed to Jonquil, since she had written one out. Rather than going down each entry, she sat back and recounted an experience from childhood.

"You told me to make the cologne a gift to myself. It sparked a memory of something that happened when I was just a schoolgirl. Right before my twelfth birthday, my mother had to go nurse her maiden aunt in another state. It was left to my father to organize my birthday party. He did all right—ordered a cake, made a nice lunch and so forth. But when the day came, none of my friends showed up, not even my bosom buddy, Maribeth Hussey.

"Well, I was a proud little thing even then. I wouldn't cry or call any of them to find out why they had snubbed me. Instead, that afternoon I broke my piggy bank and spent all my savings at Woolworth's. I went on my first shopping spree. I bought myself a pretty hand mirror and a bag of sweets and oh, I don't recall now what all. It was during the Depression and such behavior was considered sinfully frivolous. I loved every minute.

"Days later, my poor father discovered the packet of invitations in one of his suit blazers. He'd never mailed them. But I learned a lesson—you must be good to yourself. It starts there. You reminded me of something important I'd forgotten, Miss Bloom, and for that I am grateful."

Jonquil marveled at the change in Mrs. Rose. An inconsequential bottle of cologne had opened up, not just memories, but her heart and generous nature. It excited Jonquil, for this is what she wanted to do: help individuals give to themselves and to others. She knew from personal experience, however, that people often lived in self-imposed prisons, hiding their needs, strangling their power to share.

CHAPTER EIGHT

Sunday, December 7th

Sunday morning, after early Mass at St. Monica's, Jonquil and Billy took Father Tim out for breakfast. It was too breezy for him to sit outdoors so they settled on Polly's Pie House on Wilshire.

Father Tim and Billy had an affinity for one another. Sometimes Billy would tell him things that Jonquil hadn't already heard.

That morning, Billy, between mouthfuls of dollar pancakes, announced that he was nervous about an upcoming test in fractions. Jonquil made a mental note to help him prepare for it.

Turning to matters that concerned her, Father Tim, as usual, mentioned that there were several additions to the parish men's group that he'd like her to meet. He was determined to find Jonquil a husband and Billy a dad and nothing Jonquil said ever discouraged him. As always, she listened politely.

The waitress appeared pot in hand to freshen up their coffee. Jonquil reached for her cup too quickly and some of the steaming liquid splashed onto her fingers. Her hand flew to her lips while a stark memory flashed through her mind.

She stood underneath the full-skirted fir tree at the edge of their property about fifty feet away from the house where Gerry had left her. Their house that was burning down before her singed eyes.

Gerry was running away from her, toward the house, calling the dog's name. The night was black with clouds and smoke and very cold. The noise of the windows shattering and the water heater exploding were barely heard above the wind's heartless gusts.

It was all beyond the valiant, futile efforts of the volunteer fire brigade.

Where was Gerry?

One of the neighbors threw a heavy shawl around Jonquil's shoulders which she clutched to her womb. Another friend handed her a mug of fresh coffee but she was shivering so violently that its contents splashed and scalded her hands.

Her hands were burning, everything was burning on that February night long ago.

She came to with a start.

"Jonquil, dearie, are you all right?" asked Father Tim with alarm.

"Yes, how clumsy of me." It hadn't been much of a spill. The pain was negligible and the memory quickly faded away.

"I worry about you, darlin'," said Father Tim.

"And I love you for it," she replied patting his arm.

She paid the bill and dropped him off at the rectory, reminding him that they'd be celebrating Christmas together. She then drove Billy to the sitter's and headed to work.

CHAPTER NINE

Monday, December 8th

M inutes after Jonquil arrived at work, Rita rushed into her office and announced, "Just got a call from Ms. Egnar. We're to clear the decks so you can attend an urgent meeting in the fifth floor conference room in ten minutes."

"Did she say why?" asked Jonquil as she shrugged off her coat.

"Nada. She told me to cancel and reset all your appointments for this morning."

"How many is that?" Rita consulted her appointments calendar.

"You're booked solid. I don't know what I'm going to do with those people." They stared at each other, not moving. Jonquil's phone rang. She lunged for it.

"Jonquil Bloom. How may I help you?"

"Jonquil, good morning. Dr. Paxton here." It took her a moment to match the clipped British accent with her UCLA faculty advisor's voice, possibly because he was on a speakerphone. "Busy?"

"Uh, actually I'm on my way to a meeting. May I call you back this afternoon?"

She could hear muffled sounds at the other end. Then, he picked up the receiver and said tersely, "My office hours are from three to five today. Be sure to call." He disconnected before she could reply.

Slowly replacing the receiver, she looked over at Rita. "That was my faculty advisor. What's going on?"

"Search me. What should I tell the folks I have to cancel?" she asked. The sight of Rita wringing her hands tried Jonquil's patience because it suddenly occurred to her that she could be facing the awful possibly of losing a second job in the same week!

"Oh, Rita, I don't know. Whatever you do, please don't let on that anything's wrong until we know for sure."

Rita looked chagrined but quickly rallied. "I've got it. I'll call the Beauty Salon on Two. They have to cancel appointments on short notice whenever a stylist calls in sick, so they may know what to say. Think that will work?"

"Great idea!" Jonquil enthused, relieved that the

problem was solved. She exited the suite without another word, knowing full well she owed Rita an apology for her abruptness, but later.

* * *

On the fifth floor, Jonquil met up with Mr. Bramson and accompanied him to the conference room on the floor's east end. There, already seated on both sides of a lacquered, wood-stained oval shaped table, were people Jonquil remembered from her orientation: Al Yates, Inez Escanaba from Public Relations, Rich Ridgeland, VP of Marketing and Advertising, the Burney Brothers— Clyde's twin accountants, a woman whom Jonquil recognized from a photo as the Head Buyer, and the store's legal counsel, Cyril Saginaw. She slid into an empty seat across from him. A side door opened and Mr. Merrill entered, taking the seat at the head of the table.

He opened the meeting by thanking Jonquil for coming to the weekly executive meeting on such short notice. "Do you know everyone here? Let's go around the table and introduce ourselves."

The Head Buyer's name was Leigh Usher, which she announced while casting a frosty glance in Jonquil's direction.

Jonquil's reaction was immediate. Here was a beautiful woman, conscious of her stunning, blonde looks and her effect on men. Leigh Usher accepted their

89

attentions as though it were her birthright, flashing a smile no orthodontist had ever touched. The mere sight of her, from the top of her precision cut bob to her manicured fingertips, made Jonquil feel awkward and drab. Leigh wore a clingy sweater dress the color of palest lavender, accented by a flowing scarf. Her pearl earrings seemed extensions of her perfect teeth. Jonquil couldn't help but notice that the young woman's lightly tanned, glowing skin and sapphire blue eyes were enhanced by just the right shade of blush and lip gloss. Though she couldn't guess why the woman seemed hostile toward her, her own feelings were no mystery. She was envious.

At that point, Jonquil looked down and spotted the toothpaste stain on the front of her navy suit. She sighed. It was ever thus.

"Ladies and gentlemen," continued Mr. Merrill, "there is good news and not so good news this morning. The good news is that thanks to Jonquil, Clyde's is back on the map. Sales are up, visits and calls to the store have increased significantly, and Al tells me that our wonderful employees, for the most part, are rising to the occasion.

"On the downside, we may have leaped into the fray too impetuously and for that I take full credit." He beamed at them like a man who had rediscovered his zest for hard work. "Al, what's your take on our situation?"

"Two points, sir. First, our most valuable patrons should get preferential treatment. We're getting some complaints that our biggest accounts can't get immediate appointments.

"Secondly, we should be charging a fee to discourage the merely curious and offset the cost of additional phone operators, clerks, and security guards. Frankly, sir, I don't think one gift counselor can handle the volume."

Mr. Merrill saw that Jonquil wanted to respond but he asked that discussion wait until after they had aired all the issues. Next he called on Sy for his comments.

Sy, a beefier version of Alec Baldwin, leaned forward in his chair. "Our insurance carrier has voiced concern over potential malpractice lawsuits. We are in the retail business, not the counseling business. We could be vulnerable to all sorts of half-baked claims. Rich might want to put a disclaimer in his ads. Ms. Bloom, do you currently have malpractice insurance?"

"I'm in the doctorate program at UCLA. I'm covered as a student there."

"Student?" repeated Leigh Usher, arching one brow.

"I have completed my Master's degree. I could start a private practice right now but I chose to go on for my doctorate. Most psychologists do." She delivered this information with equanimity but her guard was up.

Mr. Merrill intervened. "Then it's simple. Sy, get her

some malpractice insurance for her work here. Who else?"

Leigh Usher spoke up demurely. "May I?"

"Yes, Leigh?" asked Mr. Merrill, sending a warm smile in her direction.

"Sy has thoughtfully reminded us of what business we're in. Now, I don't know what gift counseling purports to be and I was in New York when all this was decided, but five of our biggest suppliers have requested—via fax, over the weekend—specific details, namely whether or not their products will be recommended to our customers by Ms. Bloom, or their competitors' brands."

"That's a hot one," said Mr. Merrill, enjoying every minute. "Any other issues?"

The twin Burney Brothers coughed in unison. How strange it was to see two grown men in their late fifties clad identically in glen plaid suits, bow ties, and suspenders. BB1 was slightly heavier than BB2. No one called them by their first names except Mr. Merrill.

"Barney?"

"As to the budget, we could add a few more seasonal employees with no difficulty. We are not yet at our full holiday headcount." BB1 addressed these immortal words to the contents of his coffee mug.

"Excellent." The other twin coughed again.

"Yes, Bernie?"

"No matter how many store employees we employ, we still have only the one, uh, counselor, Ms. Bloom." BB2 aimed his profound observation at a crack in the wall behind Mr. Merrill's right ear.

"Right. Anyone else? Inez? Rich?"

"We need to sort this out quickly. My department is working overtime on a media blitz. I don't have to remind anyone what day it is," said Rich.

They each nodded their heads in complete understanding. Quickly, Jonquil calculated—December 8th—two days before her thirty-fourth birthday. Surely, they couldn't be referring to that. "What day is it?" she asked, baffled.

As with one voice they replied, "It's sixteen shopping days until Christmas."

"Oh, of course," Jonquil mumbled and blushed. Leigh Usher threw her a drop dead look.

Mr. Merrill then opened the meeting up for discussion. The next forty minutes were spent hashing out the salient points mentioned earlier. How strongly their deliberations contrasted with staff meetings in mental health units. There, so much analysis and theory went into every decision that meetings typically went overtime and few problems were resolved. Here on the other hand, things were more direct. Nearly every issue boiled down to dollars and cents. Jonquil sat back, an observer, as they literally haggled over her job description.

At last Mr. Merrill rapped the table and said, "It's been more years than I care to remember since I've chaired a discussion about too much demand at Clyde's. It feels great. Now, I'd like to hear from Ms. Bloom."

"Thank you, Mr. Merrill." Jonquil gazed down the table and felt the urge to rise. She pressed down the front of her suit jacket, wet her lips, and prepared to take them on. This was it. If she could keep her voice steady, she might hang on to the tiny niche she had created.

"First of all, since there are only sixteen days till Christmas, I'll work as many hours as are necessary to meet with those seeking gift counseling. Tomorrow will be my last day off until December twenty-fifth.

"Secondly, to charge a fee would be detrimental. Perhaps we can return to this topic after the holidays. I come from a professional discipline where preferential treatment has no meaning. I urge that gift counseling remain on a first come, first served basis for now. Rita's doing a great job screening the calls. As for brands and competitors," she said, eyeing Leigh Usher, "I have no interest in what people buy. My job is to help them do it.

"Finally, I am a fully trained, licensed psychologist. I meet all the state requirements. I've been researching gift-giving for the past two years. You have in me the only expert in the world in what I hope will be a new field of study. It is too soon to train others. I'm not even quite sure myself how it works. But I can't divide the limited time I have between training others and serving Clyde's clientele. I'm asking you for the chance to make this work. Hire the extra phone people and counter people and I will do my part." She sat down.

"Well said," commented Mr. Merrill. "Glad to have you on board this season, Jonquil. You'll have our unstinting support." The others took their cue from Mr. Merrill and rewarded Jonquil with warm smiles and agreeable grunts. All but Leigh, who slouched back in her chair and looked suspiciously to Jonquil as though she might be coolly plotting the swift dismissal of Clyde's new gift counselor.

* * *

When she arrived back on the first floor, Jonquil spotted Rita chatting with a couple of Scents clerks. She wasn't going to interrupt them but they all saw her at the same time. Rita came over without hesitation.

"How'd it go, sugar?"

"Rita, I am so sorry for losing my temper." She felt she owed Rita an apology for her rude behavior that morning and wanted to clear the air as soon as possible.

"Big woo. We're both feeling the strain."

Jonquil smiled with relief at being forgiven so easily.

"What are you wearing today?" she asked as they strolled past busy counters.

"Escape," replied Rita with a mischievous glint in her eye.

"Ha! I'd like to try some of that!" Jonquil quipped.

They walked together back to the suite while Rita continued to press for details. No one was waiting, so they both took seats in the quiet reception area.

"Mr. Merrill is pleased, Rita."

"Sugar, if he's happy, there's nothing to worry about."

"On the other hand, Leigh Usher—"

"Uh-oh, is Lady Leigh back in town? She thinks she's God's gift to Clyde's." Rita removed a jar from her desk, smoothed cream on her hands and then offered it to Jonquil. The air became redolent with the fragrance of lilies.

"Is she?" Jonquil applied a dab to her hands and placed it back on the desk. "Mmm, smells delicious. Thanks, Rita." Vigorously, she rubbed in the cream and waited for Rita's answer.

"Well, she's got the glamour job, you know, travel, charity events, fashion shows, deciding next year's merchandise. But she has an attitude like she's better than the rest of us."

"No one is better than you, Rita," Jonquil assured her.

* * *

That afternoon, she telephoned Dr. Paxton and found him at his desk, chomping on a late lunch. "Ms. Bloom, what's this I hear? You've left the graduate program?"

"Not at all, Dr. Paxton. I've been meaning to call you—"

"Some of the faculty and students saw you on the news. I gather you're doing some kind of therapy in a department store?"

"Not therapy, I—"

"Ida Hamilton from Children's Home phoned me. She's rather put out. You never told me you were having difficulties there."

Jonquil yanked the phone receiver away from her ear and stared hard at it before answering. "They terminated me in order to use my paltry stipend to paint a few offices for an alleged state inspection, sir."

Her acid-toned remarks were met with his silence. She took a deep breath and continued. "I contacted the graduate school and was told I could not be reassigned until after the holidays. I took a temporary job at Clyde's and that's when—"

"They want you back now. Seems they'll lose their state funding without a psychologist on staff."

Now it was Jonquil's turn to fall silent.

"Jonquil, you were one of my most promising students."

"I still am, Dr. Paxton."

"How soon can you start back at the home?"

"Um, I'm really not sure." Jonquil felt her fingers tighten on the receiver. Did she even want to go back? She thought of the children there and how they needed her. But, was that where she wanted to be now?

"Exactly what is it you're doing at Clyde's?"

"Gift counseling."

"What in hell is that?" The tone in his voice warned Jonquil that she'd better explain in person.

"Dr. Paxton, I should make an appointment to see you."

"Indeed. The sooner, the better." They agreed to meet the following afternoon in front of the medical library at four. Deep in thought, she cradled the receiver.

It was happening all over again. The anger she'd felt only one week ago, that blinding fury at being pushed here, shoved there, like a puzzle piece, flared up inside her. A golden opportunity she'd created by sheer chutzpah was about to be snatched away almost before it had begun. By the very same people who had hurt her so deeply one week ago. Her advisor intended to sanction their stupidity. Incredible!

Should she do it? Return to Children's Home, to the two administrators who considered her no more than a name in a slot to be added or erased at whim? Jonquil trembled with indignation. No one knew better than Jonquil that life holds no guarantees. Admittance to graduate school didn't *ipso facto* mean that she was cut out to be a psychotherapist. Her own life had been riddled with losses and more than once in the past year Jonquil had found herself questioning how much she had to offer the needy residents of Children's Home.

Whereas at Clyde's, her eyes were opening up to new possibilities each day. She felt alive and in charge. She looked forward each morning to the challenges that lay ahead. She liked her colleagues in the store, such down-to-earth people. She felt more in tune with life in general.

Even though, on the surface, her new position in the store might appear less important than her work as a child psychologist, the comparison seemed unfair. Something in her was stirring for the first time in years. The new job reopened old wounds. Instinctively she knew that in order for them to finally heal, she mustn't interfere with the process. It both terrified and exhilarated her. And nobody—not Billy, not Gerry's memory, not Dr. Paxton, not Ida Hamilton—nobody was going to take this opportunity away from her. She phoned Dr. Paxton back and canceled their meeting.

Jonquil's four o'clock appointment turned out to be none other than Leigh Usher. Rita must have penciled her in because Jonquil didn't recall seeing her name on the schedule. It was ten minutes past four and Leigh hadn't yet shown up. Jonquil heard muffled sounds outside her office and cracked open her door. She discovered Leigh, her back to Jonquil, perched on Rita's desk, one foot dangling as though she owned the place. Jonquil frowned and left the door ajar. Their voices floated into her office.

"Happy, Rita?" asked Leigh.

"Well, er, I mean, yes, of course," replied Rita with her usual fluster.

"Quite a change from being out on the floor, isn't it? Remember when I got hired and you were my first supervisor? You believed that perfume was the most important product in the store." Jonquil pictured Leigh tossing her hair as she laughed, each strand falling right back into place.

"I still do," said Rita.

"Miss it much? Come on, you can tell me."

"In a way. But this work is important, too. It helps the customers and it helps the store." *That's telling her*, thought Jonquil and pictured Leigh bending her head closer to Rita's.

"Suppose I could get you back in Scentsations tomorrow—today—this minute. You know I can. Just say the word." There followed a disconcerting pause before Rita answered. *Does Rita want to jump ship so soon?* worried Jonquil.

"How would Jonquil—Ms. Bloom—manage without me?" asked Rita and blinked.

"Eh, any high school dropout can do what she's got you doing: answer the phone, make appointments, schmooze the customers, hand out the incentive cards." Leigh broke off the sing-song chant with a groan. "Oh, Rita, it *pains* me to see your own talents going to waste!"

"You're late for your appointment, Leigh," retorted Rita. "It's not polite to keep people waiting." With that, Rita picked up her telephone.

Seconds later, Leigh took a seat across from Jonquil and crossed her legs. *She ought to be in movies*, thought Jonquil. Then Leigh pulled out a pocket-sized cassette tape recorder from her purse and set it squarely on the desk between them. Puzzled, Jonquil began to speak.

"Welcome, Leigh. Usually I begin by asking each client to sign a release form so I can use their data for my research—"

"Skip the intro, Doc," Leigh interrupted, "I have some questions I want you to answer." She leaned forward and pushed a button. The machine activated.

"What's your position on gift certificates, pro or con? How do you feel about our baby and bridal registries? Does using either one constitute a copout in your opinion? What's your take on Clyde's generous exchange policy? Do people have the right to return gifts they don't want? Even a gift you 'counseled' someone to buy?" She smirked.

"Please. I have no opinion about any of those things. They each serve a purpose. Let me explain—"

"You've had your say. Now it's my turn to clue you in on a few things. I've been at Clyde's for ten years. I was hired straight out of Gardner School of Art, where I graduated at the top of my class. After floating in various departments for six weeks, I took a sales position in women's gowns. Worked hard, learned retail, nailed down Clyde's clientele, earned the top sales award every year. Brought in new patrons, Bel Air types, whose mothers stopped coming to Clyde's ages ago. I made manager in two years. I know what they say about me— that I have the glamour job, that I get the special perks. But you and I know better, don't we? I'm the Head Buyer 'cause: A) I wanted it; B) I went after it; and C) I'm good. Saks offered me twice as much money four months ago. Do you know why I stay? Because I care."

"You're implying that I don't?" Jonquil's temper flared.

"You're only temporary." Leigh exaggerated each syllable. "You'll get what you want, stir up the place, then vamoose.

"Be honest. You have no real stake in Clyde's. Why else would you stick our top Scents associate behind a desk, away from her best customers during the biggest sales season of the year?

"You've created problems for Rita, for Al, for Sy, for Rich, for Inez, for Mr. Merrill—for everybody!"

"Can we turn off that machine and talk?" Jonquil said.

"No. I want to know what you meant this morning when you said at the meeting that we could review certain issues after the holidays."

"Guilty," Jonquil admitted and sighed. Her head began to throb. "I was deliberately planting the idea that gift counseling could become a permanent, year-round service. I like what I'm doing here."

Leigh's eyes narrowed. "Over my dead body. You've fooled Mr. Merrill, got his hopes up, but this store is failing. Look at this suite of offices. Ridiculous! You don't bring in a dime. You're a user, Ms. Bloom. I see right through you." Jonquil stiffened at the accusation.

"I've got news for you, Doc. No one in admin—and that includes Mr. Merrill—intends to float this department beyond Christmas. You can kiss your career plans sayonara." She shut off the recorder, jammed it into her purse, and stood. "Keep this in mind: I'm going to be president and CEO of the store one day soon. Until that happens, I won't let anyone or anything hasten its closing. I will reinvent Clyde's and when I do this store will rival Rodeo Drive."

Jonquil speculated glumly as she watched the woman trot out the door whether Leigh Usher and Miss Hamilton were in cahoots. Both women seemed intent on demolishing Jonquil's hopes and dreams.

Rita knocked softly, poked her head inside and looked around. "Can I sound the 'all clear' signal, boss?"

"Come in Rita, take a load off," said Jonquil, leaning her forehead against her balled fists.

"You look lower than a worm in a wagon rut," observed Rita sympathetically. "Can I get you anything? A Coke, coffee, a sledgehammer, anything?"

Jonquil glanced up at her and said, "We'll be out of business after Christmas. Can you hang on that long?"

"Hang on? Honey, what did Lady Leigh say to you?"

"She told me how selfish I've been, how I took you away from Scents and your best customers, and how the employees are all worried because of me."

"Bah-loney. In the first place, it was my choice to become your assistant. I wanted to, remember? Still do. In the second place, we were much more worried before you came here. Haven't you felt the change in the store? Folks are keyed up about this department. You could be voted Employee of the Month on the spot."

Jonquil relaxed slightly and shook her head. "I don't know, Rita. Now she's got it on tape that I want a permanent job."

"On tape? Say, this is Clyde's, not the White House for crying out loud."

"I don't trust her."

"No one does, sugar. Rumor has it Mr. Merrill is going to retire in the spring. Lady Leigh has made no secret of the fact she wants his job. Well, can you imagine? She'll change everything. She'll concentrate exclusively on clothes and hand over all the other departments to outside vendors.

"She says department stores are passé. So, between Mr. Merrill leaving and her taking over, many of us long-timers will lose our jobs. Except that now Mr. Merrill seems to be taking an interest in the store again. Al thinks he may delay retiring."

Jonquil made up her mind. "I'm not going to worry about this, Rita, not yet. I'm going to focus on being the best gift counselor I can be. Besides, as you already know, I'll be off tomorrow. Billy's school is closed for the day. I don't want to be stewing about Leigh Usher on my last day off."

"That's the spirit," cried Rita. "I mean, the poor woman's so dumb, she doesn't even know she's a Knock Out!"

Jonquil nodded grudgingly. Then she hit her forehead with the palm of her hand. "By any chance are you talking about perfume, Rita?"

SHEILA M. CRONIN

Rita put her fists on her hips and shook her head from side to side. "What else would I be talking about? And to think I trained you."

106

CHAPTER TEN

Monday Afternoon

Claude Chappel, the construction company owner, had meetings with the building owner and architect which delayed his arrival at the jobsite across the street from the Blooms' apartment until Monday afternoon. Most of the workmen had already packed up and left. He settled down at the desk in the trailer to delve into a pile of paperwork.

This was the best time of the day to get caught up, when things quieted down and the constant interruptions by the trades and his crew ceased. This renovation of a single dwelling into a six unit apartment complex was the largest project his fledgling company had tackled so far and he knew that staying on top of the plans, the budget and the correspondence was integral to its success.

After a couple of concentrated hours, he decided to stretch his legs so he stepped outside.

He filled his lungs with the tangy ocean air and squinted at the bright sun which had begun its slow descent. He loved Southern California, especially in the winter when the sunsets were their most spectacular. Maybe it was the painter in him, but he never tired of the sky's brilliant colors reflected on the clouds, or the sight of the blazing orb as it turned flaming red before it vanished from sight. With this particular jobsite being mere blocks from the beach, he intended to work late each day and enjoy the sunset before heading to Orange County and home.

Just as he was about to return to his desk, however, something caught his attention. Across the street, outside the opened garage door of the building where the captivating Bloom woman lived, stood a line of children. They each held an animal by leash or in their arms.

He continued watching as a black youth, perhaps nine years of age, left the garage carrying a small fish bowl. The boy turned and waved to someone unseen. Next, a smaller blonde-haired girl with pigtails skipped into the garage carrying a turtle large enough for Claude to identify its shape. Was there an adult in that garage? He decided to stroll over and take a cursory glance inside, but at the garage entrance, he paused.

Inside, behind a bench comprised of stacked, empty orange crates covered by a piece of plywood and spread out newspaper, stood Jonquil's son. Claude remembered seeing her put the boy in the van on Friday. He wore an oversized gray sweatshirt—probably belonging to one of his parents—with the words "UCLA Medical School" emblazoned in large black letters down its front. At his feet sat a pail of water and assorted boxes of pet food. A large stethoscope dangled from around his neck and behind him, tacked to the wall, was a piece of poster board with a bold red cross painted not too neatly on it.

"And my turtle just sleeps all day long," whined the flaxen-haired girl.

"Hmm," said Billy. "Have you tried talking to him? What's his name?"

"Princess Leia," she replied.

"Oh! Sorry, Princess," Billy said, peering into the shell. "Well, I recommend you talk to her and make friends. She's probably shy. You only got her over the weekend." This last bit of wisdom was delivered with a fair amount of male impatience. Claude stifled a chuckle.

"Thanks, Billy," cried the little girl. She scooped up Her Majesty and skipped out the door past Claude.

"Next!" shouted Billy.

Claude put a warning hand on the shoulder of the boy about to enter, collie in tow.

"Mind if I go next?" The boy shrugged and stepped aside. Claude entered the garage.

"May I have a moment of your time, young man?" asked Claude.

"Sure, mister. Aren't you the guy that works on the building across the street?"

"That's right. My name is Claude Chappel. And yours?"

"Billy Bloom." They shook hands.

"I gather you're running a pet clinic?" asked Claude in a man-to-man tone.

"Yeah. So? Hey, you gotta get in line."

Claude admired the boy's spunk. He seemed bright and friendly, plus he possessed a solid handshake. All the while that they were talking, Billy was removing old newspaper and laying out fresh pages of the *Los Angeles Times*. Next, he dipped his hands in the water pail and dried them off on his shirt. His sandy brown buzz and dark eyes contrasted with his mother's coloring. Claude figured he'd inherited his looks from his dad and his personality from his mom.

"Son, do you have a license to practice veterinary medicine in the state of California?"

Billy stopped moving and stared innocently up at Claude. "Huh?"

"You could go to jail for setting up a pet clinic in your garage. Do your parents know you're doing this?"

"It's just me and my mom. Man, she'd have a fit! See,

I want to be a vet when I grow up and I need to practice. I got the idea from this book," and he pointed to a copy of *All Creatures Great and Small* on the bench. "Mrs. Crandon up the block gave it to me for walking her dogs. See, my mom works late now and I started this to keep busy after school till she gets home. I don't charge nothin' either."

Billy concluded his rapid fire explanation by reluctantly yanking the stethoscope from his neck. Claude registered the disappointment in his face, the way his shoulders slumped. He had the strong impression that the kid was lonely.

"Say, have you ever seen the inside of a construction site?"

Billy shook his head no without enthusiasm.

"Why don't you finish closing up shop and I'll walk you through. Your friends can come, too."

"I better not," said Billy becoming cautious. "I got homework." Mentally, Claude gave Jonquil high marks for teaching her child to beware of strangers.

"Fair enough. Some other time, Billy." Claude left it at that.

CHAPTER ELEVEN

Tuesday, December 9th

Shortly after noon the next day, Claude Chappel was at his desk when suddenly the power shut off. The fan stopped oscillating, the copier machine flicked off and the compact refrigerator quit humming. He bolted from his chair and angrily yelled out the window above his desk to one of the workman that someone had cut the power line again.

Then he saw Billy Bloom leaning against the doorway. "No school today?" he asked, still fuming.

"Half-day. Teachers' conference."

"I see. Is your mom home?"

"Yeah. She's sunning by the pool."

"Give me a sec. I have to call the electric company." Since an inspector was using the desk phone, Claude picked up the walkie-talkie on the file cabinet. "Fred, you got your phone with you? Mine's in the shop."

"No can do, Boss," bleated the walkie-talkie. "Mine was in the glove compartment when my pickup got stolen Saturday night."

"You can use our phone," said Billy.

"No, son, your mom—"

"She won't mind. Come on, I'll show you where it is."

"Fred, I'll be back in five." He tossed the walkie-talkie on the desk and followed Billy out the door and across the street. Jonquil was indeed reading and sunning herself in a chaise lounge by the oval-shaped swimming pool that formed the nucleus around which about sixteen apartment units were arranged. She wore a pretty green and white neon swimsuit that revealed an even prettier figure. Claude found it amusing that the amount of her apparel had progressively decreased with each sighting: from the blouse and jumper he'd first seen her in at Children's Home, to T-shirt and shorts, to a bathrobe, to this two-piece swimsuit. She put a halt to his tantalizing train of thought by sitting up and removing her sunglasses.

Billy blurted out, "Mom, Claude needs to call the 'lectric company."

"Our lines were cut just now," added Claude. "I'd be much obliged."

He reckoned that she felt on the spot with her son standing there eager to lend him the use of their phone, but she surprised him.

"All right," replied Jonquil. She was distracted by Claude's cement-encrusted boots. Following her gaze, he sat down at the pool's edge and removed them.

She stood up and pulled on her cover-up just as a neighbor called out to her. "Mrs. Bloom, are you doing laundry? If so, the washers are done and I need to use them." Jonquil gestured to Billy to take Claude inside.

"Follow me," said Billy. He threw open the screen door and led the way into the darkened apartment. It took a moment for Claude's eyes to adjust. He found himself standing in the main room.

Well under three hundred square feet, he judged, still, it was deceptively spacious. The bank of windows on the far wall were curtainless, opening up the room, while rattan furnishings—not his favorite—area rugs, and track lighting set an airy tone. Built-ins framed a dining area facing the street. He had no time to dally, but his brief impression was that some thought had gone into making the most of the area.

Comfortable as it seemed, it was Claude's opinion that growing boys needed a backyard with trees to climb and plenty of prickly green grass to daydream upon. He realized he'd lost sight of Billy. He started down a hallway and was about to turn back when an opened doorway set off alarm bells in his head.

"Claude!" called Billy from far away.

It was the boy's bedroom, judging by the baseball posters on the wall. They were hard to see, given the array of stuffed, plastic, childish or life-like animals that hung, sat or otherwise crammed the room. There was a giraffe that nearly touched the ceiling; a pile of Beanie Babies; every kind of teddy bear, dog and cat imaginable, frogs, horses, dinosaurs, lizards, birds, bats, elephants, even a smug looking kangaroo. They protruded off the shelves, covered the top of the bureau and peeked around the desk and chair.

Even the wallpaper was a page out of Dr. Doolittle. In fact, there didn't seem to be room for one more addition to the spooky menagerie.

"What's all this ...?" Claude wondered aloud with a frown.

"That's my room," said Billy behind him, defensively. "My mom won't let me have any live pets. She's allergic. Come on, the phone's in the kitchen," he added, tugging Claude away.

But though he let himself be led back to the main room, through the dining area and into the kitchen, his mind stayed stuck on the disturbing contents of Billy's room.

What did it mean? Was she nuts?

The boy had long ago outgrown nearly every item in that room. It reminded Claude of a taxidermist's lab or a

115

hunting lodge in Lake Tahoe, the walls of which were covered with trophy heads. It gave him the creeps.

Minutes later, they emerged from the apartment back into the sunlight. Claude inhaled deeply. It felt good to be outdoors again, away from that suffocating spectacle.

"Find everything all right?" called Jonquil.

Claude stooped to pull his boots back on, hoping to hide his immediate reaction to her question. "Yes, thanks," he mumbled.

"Mom, I'm going to ride my bike over to Ramon's," called Billy, and he darted out of sight. Jonquil watched him go which gave Claude the opportunity to briefly study her. He didn't believe she was crazy. After all, hadn't she worked at that home? Yet, there was something terribly awry between her and her son.

"Mrs. Bloom?"

"It's Jonquil. And thanks for the peace and quiet in the morning."

"You don't recognize me, Jonquil. But I was at Children's Home Monday. I was one of the painters."

"You're kidding! I was not myself that day," she admitted ruefully. "You're not the one I sprayed with paint?" She appeared to study his eyes more closely and blushed.

He was relieved that the discovery seemed to please her.

Claude grinned, jammed his hands in his pockets and said, "Eh, no problem, it washes off."

"I'm glad. And I apologize again. I had just been laid off from my job there and I was in shock. Now, I have a new job. Today is my last day off until Christmas."

"Billy told me. He's a good kid."

"I agree," she said, squinting up at his face.

"Did you know he runs some kind of animal hospital after school in your garage?"

"What did you say?" she asked, standing stock still.

"Yes, ma'am, I don't mean to interfere, but for a boy like Billy, if any of those creatures really were sick or even died—"

"No! No! That can't happen!" she cried. Swiftly, Jonquil bent down to gather up her things but not before Claude caught a stricken look that crossed her face like a speeding black cloud.

He bet that Jonquil's agitation and the boy's stuffed animal collection were related, but how? Claude tried not to stare at her which was next to impossible. Her hair was the color of wet autumn leaves, a tumble of rich brown, crimson and amber. Wide, curving eyebrows softened her frowns, broadened her smiles. The color of her eyes reminded him of a lily pond in Canada where he and his brothers often used to go fishing. He liked her freckles, too, though her face when relaxed held some residue of sorrow. Instinctively, he knew this was a woman to whom he could entrust his struggles, his hopes, and his dreams.

"When I worked at the home, Billy didn't need a regular sitter because we were both getting home about the same time each day." Her voice told him she had regained her composure. "This is 'mom' stuff," she said and grinned up at him while shading her eyes. "I shouldn't bore you with it."

"Look," Claude replied, folding his arms across his chest, "after school he's welcome to hang out in the trailer with me. It's clean and safe and the loudmouths are all gone by then. I stay and do paperwork till sundown. People drop by but he'd be no problem."

Her wariness was visible. "I'm not sure ..." she began but didn't complete her thought. What Claude didn't know was that a part of her wanted to be talked into his plan but for motives that had nothing to do with Billy.

"We could just try it. He'd be keeping me company. He could do his homework."

"He has a test coming up in math—"

"I'm good at math. Why don't we just try it for a couple of days?"

"I appreciate your interest. Billy's father is dead."

"Sorry to hear that."

"It happened a long time ago. This new job is temporary but my hours are longer. It's hard on him. He knows he can stay with the apartment manager until I get home and I'll remind him. That should work for the time being until I find a sitter. Besides, Mr. Chappel, you're a stranger."

"True. I'm also going to be working twelve-hour days across the street for the next year. I have a huge stake in that job. Hopefully, it will lead to others in this area and the odd paint job will no longer be necessary. My sister lives on Euclid Street in Santa Monica. Her boys are going to be working for me over Christmas vacation. Look, I only offered because I thought Billy—what?— might have fun wearing a hard hat while he does his homework."

She smiled up at him. "Let me think it over. I want to talk to Billy, too. What's your sister's name?"

"Katie. She's listed in the phone book under E.J. Ryan on Euclid. Give her a call if you like. She loves to sing my praises."

Her features softened into a spectacular smile.

"I may just do that …"

"Claude," he said and waited.

"Claude," she repeated. He definitely liked hearing her say his name.

* * *

Barney Miller. She'd seen the actor who played him— Hal Linden—on a PBS pledge night in August. That's who Claude reminded her of—a much younger-looking Hal Linden with thick, dark hair. To think that Claude and the painter were one and the same man! Up until their conversation, she hadn't noticed the similarities.

Now his features were clear in her mind: a deeply tanned, square face, a charming nose above a captivating smile, those intoxicating black eyes that barely held some secret merriment in check, and a relaxed stance which, despite his height and broad shoulders, put her immediately at ease. No use denying it: she was attracted to him.

She felt a chill. The warmest part of the day was over. For once, she wished that she could create one of Rita's "scent"-ual cocoons and bathe in fragrant splendor. But the larder was bare and she needed to stop at the dry cleaners. After chores, she must set up tables on her laptop for her project. With everything else on her mind, Jonquil did not expect to give Claude Chappel another thought. Her mind, however, was quite willing to multitask!

CHAPTER TWELVE

Wednesday, December 10th

Billy rolled over, realized what day it was, kicked off his covers and yawned. The sun wasn't even up yet. He glanced over at the Lion King clock above his desk. A full half hour would have to pass before he could wake his mom and give her birthday present to her. His stomach churned with excitement.

He got up and knelt down to retrieve the box from under his bed where it had stayed hidden since Saturday. He couldn't wait to see her face when she opened it. For the first time in his life he had picked out something he knew would please her. How many times had he heard her say, "Where are my pens?" Even Mrs. Phillips had complimented his thoughtfulness. He checked the clock again. The skinny hands hadn't moved at all.

Maybe if he used the toilet she would hear the sound of the flush. No such luck; her door was shut. On his way back to his room, he contemplated alternatives. He could go outside and bang the doorbell until she came running. Or, he could try to make a pot of coffee. That might do the trick. He stood in the hallway, undecided, when all of a sudden the Nike slogan popped into his head: *Just Do It.* He ran back to his room and retrieved the box and then barged straight into her room.

"Mom, wake up. It's your birthday," he cried. "Here's your present. Open it!"

Groggily, Jonquil stretched and sat up, glad for the warm glow from yesterday's sun that took the sting out of turning thirty-four. "It's so early, honey," she yawned.

"Open, open, open," Billy chanted, balling and splaying his fingers like the woman in the Mervyns television commercial. His urgency left her no choice. She tugged off the bows and gently pulled off the shiny wrapping paper, the sight of which sent Billy into paroxysms of indignation. "Sheesh, Mom, rip it already!"

"Honey, it's too nice to tear." Appeased, he plopped down beside her. When she finally reached the main event, Jonquil discovered a beautiful cloth-covered notebook and two chunky, multi colored ballpoint pens. "Oh, Billy," she murmured with surprise.

"They're for when you go back to Children's Home so you can write down what the kids tell you. Like 'em, Mom?"

"I love them!" she replied, fingering each item. He sprang up and pranced around like a victorious receiver in the end zone. "But what if I don't go back to Children's Home? Can I use them at the store?"

"But, Mom," he objected mid-prance, "those kids need you."

"Well, after Christmas we'll see." She drew him into her arms to hide the irritation she felt at the mention of her old job. Then it dawned on her: Billy's gift came with strings attached. Not like the decorative ribbons, no, these were more binding. He expected her to use the gifts in a certain way, at a certain place. Her thoughts gathered momentum. That seemed to be the exact opposite of giving. Or was it? Maybe it was the true dynamic of giving. Bargains were struck, deals were made, alliances were formed and sealed with a gift. It was the story of history. It was the subtext of the morning news. The right gift kept somebody quiet, kept somebody else dependent, kept somebody else in line. Deceptive, sneaky. *Let's not forget the Trojan Horse*, she thought. "That's it!" she cried, seeing the title on her dissertation. "Gifts and the Strings Attached!"

Billy squirmed in her arms.

"Oh, Billy, these are the very best presents I ever got!" She attempted to cover his face with kisses but he tore himself out of her arms, conscious that he himself was ten years old and no longer comfortable with lingering embraces. The look on her face, though, assured him that his gift had made her happy. Mission accomplished.

* * *

Apparently, birthdays were a big deal at Clyde's. When Jonquil arrived that morning, more preoccupied with the idea of "gifts and the strings attached" than with her natal celebration, Rita handed her a present. Also, in the middle of her desk sat a beautiful, blooming Christmas cactus from Personnel. Lunch for both Jonquil and Rita would be Mr. Merrill's treat at whatever eatery Jonquil desired.

"So, where do we eat?" Rita asked in her direct manner.

"My favorite spot is Rigby's on the Promenade," Jonquil replied, referring to a popular diner on the Third Street Mall nearby.

"Done. I'll make the reservation. We can scoot over there and be back here in plenty of time for your two o'clock. Guess who it is."

"Hal Linden?" Jonquil mused wistfully.

"Is he still around? No sugar, it's Constance!" Rita pronounced reverently and waited for Jonquil's response.

"Constance who?" asked Jonquil, tearing open her gift. Billy would have been proud.

"Who?! Why, *the* Constance. From Paris, France. For heaven's sake, Jonquil, you mean to tell me you actually

124

don't know who I'm talking about? Constance the model, Constance the designer, Constance fragrances, Constance boutiques."

Only then did Jonquil notice that Rita was decked out in a shimmering gown, nearly floor-length, with a loose jacket that swirled as she moved. She had arranged her henna colored curls with particular care. Even her heavy perfume was unfamiliar to Jonquil.

Jonquil removed the lid from the box and found a candle resting in a smoky blue cup. "Oh, Rita, I love it!" she cried.

"Tiffany's," Rita said offhandedly. Then, changing her voice to a distinctly conspiratorial tone, she said, "Now listen, sugar. Constance is the real thing. Big time. We have to get her in and out of here secretly."

"Why is that?" Jonquil inquired as she placed the cactus to one side of her desktop and the candle beside it.

"Haven't you been listening? She's mega, she's ultra, she's *People* mag and *Harper's Bazaar* rolled into one. Al's handling the details. It happened yesterday on your day off."

"Al?" asked Jonquil, more attentively.

"No problem. I'm cooking dinner for him Saturday night," Rita replied with a saucy wink as she twirled, like a ballroom dancer, back to the reception area.

As it turned out, they had to forego lunch because Constance's appointment required a strategic meeting with Al, Inez, Leigh and Mr. Merrill. Everyone seemed delighted.

Only Leigh Usher's nose appeared out of joint. First, she tried to inveigle her way into the Constance visit by offering her services as translator. Inez, however, assured them that Constance spoke English. Next, Leigh insisted she should be on hand to greet the celebrity because she had met her in Paris at the Fi Fi Awards. Nevertheless, it was agreed that the visit should be conducted with as little fanfare as possible. Finally, she brazenly suggested Clyde's would be the ideal location for a Constance Boutique. When a perplexed Mr. Merrill inquired how the store would accommodate it, Leigh set everyone's teeth on edge by replying, "The gift counseling suite, of course. Won't it be empty by the end of the month?"

Promptly before two o'clock that afternoon, Constance arrived via limousine at Clyde's receiving dock off the alley. Al whisked her away to the gift counseling suite where Rita fluttered painfully through the five seconds it took to usher her into Jonquil's office.

Constance was magnificent. She was clothed head to toe in peacock blue, including a calf-length skirt with matching jacket, chapeau and leather gloves. She had just come from a Beverly Hills luncheon where she'd met real estate agents about potential sites for her newest boutique. Divinely tall and slender, with a gorgeous head of brunette hair, she had piercing, black eyes and a milky-white complexion, both enhanced by a striking shade of coral on her flawlessly sculpted lips and long fingernails. Jonquil guesstimated her age to be about sixty, yet she moved with the grace of an haute couture model. Jonquil was dazzled until her visitor produced a package of slim cigars. Fortunately, Rita, who had attended a Constance product sales meeting two years earlier, had slipped an ashtray onto Jonquil's desk moments before her arrival.

The crux of Constance's dilemma, which she described in a thick, rapid-fire French accent, was her mama. Coming right to the point, Constance needed a suggestion for Mama's Christmas gift. Mama, she explained, had never lived anywhere but in the same tiny village in Normandy where she was born. In years past, Constance had given her a chalet, but Mama never took up residency. A yacht. But Mama returned it. A cruise around the world. But Mama conveniently suffered a sprained ankle and had to cancel. On the other hand, her younger sister, Jewel, which she pronounced "Zhooell," seemed to be right on target with her gifts: a scarf Mama wore till it was a rag, a bar of soap that Mama treasured like a relic, a trinket Mama wore on her left wrist night and day.

"Simple gifts," Jonquil murmured, wanting desperately to open a window as the smoke grew thick around them.

"Mais non, I want to geeve her zee world! I am, er, a zook-sess, n'est pas? I owe eet all to ma mere."

Yachts? Chalets? It was too much. "What do you want from your mother?" Jonquil asked her, more confident than ever that a gift had a deliberate purpose.

Her reply was immediate. "Er, I want to see her smile again like she deed when I was steel her leetl girl. Alors, je serai très contente."

It was time for Jonquil to speak. She was amazed at her own ingenuity. "You must select a gift not worth more than, say, five dollars American," she declared. "Can you do it?"

Constance gasped. "Quel dommage! Zhoan-keel! Five dolors, Rideeculooz!"

There goes the ballgame, Jonquil thought. Constance would make a "steenk" about the absurd gift advice she received and Jonquil would be fired. She was about to advance a second, more calculated suggestion, when the woman's tense, pampered face lit up.

"Seemple geefts!" Je comprends! I weel do eet! Merci, mon chérie, merci beaucoup!"

Jonquil picked up a gift counseling flyer containing her phone number that the store had produced and handed it to Constance. "Please feel free to call me at any time,

Constance, if you have more questions or wish to discuss your gift choice again." Constance accepted the flyer amid more merci beaucoups.

With that, she deposited grateful kisses on Jonquil's cheeks and swept out of the office leaving behind the odor of exotic cigars. After she left with Al to return to her limo, Rita struck a dramatic pose in the doorway.

"Belle Constance," she informed Jonquil. "Not in the states yet. And she knew I was wearing Belle Marie, her flagship fragrance."

"Named for her mother no doubt," said Jonquil, bending over her appointment calendar. At which point, Rita broke her silly pose to peer at her with profound respect. "Sugar, how *ever* did you know?"

CHAPTER THIRTEEN

Thursday, December 11th

J onquil and Billy had lived in the Venice Beach garden apartment off Main Street ever since he entered preschool. Jonquil chose the building for its location, affordability, garage parking, and because at the time, no pets were allowed.

Then, about a year ago, the management changed hands and the new owner welcomed tenants with pets. Several cats and at least one parakeet now resided in the building. Billy pointed out each new arrival to his mother with intense interest. Yet, he remained steadfast in his desire for a puppy.

Every time the subject came up, she scoured the toy stores for a substitute stuffed animal. She was afraid that Billy's love for pets would lead to disaster as it had for his father. In one of those utterly inconsistent decisions that moms make now and then, Jonquil hit upon using toys as safe substitutes. She was at her wit's end over the appearance of giga-pets which "died" if they weren't monitored every couple of hours. Fortunately, Billy scorned them more than the stuffed animals. For him, the only pet worth having was a real one.

She thought about Billy when her next client, an architect about her age, described his situation. The index card Rita handed her as he commandeered the seat across from her indicated that Dan Burnham was the Giver and his eight-year-old son, Danny, Jr., was the intended Receiver. Adoption was listed as the unusual gift occasion. Next to budget parameters was scribbled, "Whatever it takes!"

Jonquil looked up from the card and studied him in silence. There was nothing remarkable about either his face or his suit. Yet, he had an unmistakable vitality that she found attractive. She smiled and asked how she could assist him.

"Danny, my son, is autistic. Are you familiar with the term?" he asked while he settled back in his chair. She noted how calmly he delivered the information.

"Yes, I treated autistic children at my former job. You have quite a challenge on your hands. Does Danny live at home?"

"He does and he attends a special school in the valley.

He's making limited progress but Joan, my wife, and I have high hopes. The thing is, we put in for an overseas adoption about a year ago. Tricky, given our situation. Well, we just learned that our four-year-old daughter will be arriving from Korea at LAX on or about Christmas Eve!" Dan Burnham clapped his hands as though he'd just won the California lottery.

"Congratulations," she murmured while privately registering the enormity of his obligations.

"We're thrilled. Our only concern is about Danny's reaction. We don't want him to feel we love him any less. Joan miscarried twice after Danny's birth. We always wanted a larger family. I got this idea, and when Joan heard about you, she said I should talk it over with you. See, it's my idea to get Danny a puppy to help him through his new sister's arrival."

Jonquil blanched. He pretended to not notice and continued, "Even his teachers think it's a good idea—" He broke off mid-sentence. "Ms. Bloom, are you with me?"

She wasn't.

She was back at the breakfast table listening once again to Billy's pleas for a cocker spaniel named Blackie. She shook away the memory. "I apologize, Mr. Burnham. Please continue."

"What do you think about my idea?"

"My theory, Mr. Burnham, is that people give gifts that do something or get them something in return."

"I'm not interested in your theory. Is a dog a good idea or not?"

"Let's put the dog aside for a minute. What is it you want from your son?" Smiling ingratiatingly as she waited for him to reply, she was conscious of a self-important nuance that had come creeping into her voice during the session. What had prompted it?

"I don't want anything from Danny. I want to show him I love him."

"Then a dog would be totally inappropriate. It's work, it's responsibility, and it's trouble."

"We wouldn't expect him to take care of it. My God, do you think I'm stupid?"

"No, of course not. I didn't mean to suggest any such thing." But had she? It must have been that reminder of Billy that had momentarily distracted her, summoning the edge to her tone.

He made a face. "I don't get you. What's the big idea? Boys and dogs go together, right?"

"That's a charming cliché," she interrupted. "The fact is—"

He cut in. "Forgive me, Ms. Bloom, but bull! I've dealt with scores of doctors and therapists over the years and I can tell when one's not playing straight with me."

She didn't respond. He was right, of course. He had accidently hit upon her vulnerable spot and she had lost her objectivity.

It happens to every therapist or counselor now and then. Freud called it countertransference. To Jonquil, it felt uncomfortably more like being up the creek without a paddle.

Mr. Burnham stood up. "I don't know what I expected gift counseling to be but this certainly has been a waste of my time.

"Tell me, is it your job to coerce folks into buying Clyde's merchandise? Do you want to talk me out of the pet idea 'cause Clyde's doesn't carry them? Why, you're nothing but a shill."

"I'm sorry I can't help you," she stammered lamely.

He stormed out in disgust and waved away the gift certificate Rita tried to hand him. Rita practically fell off her chair craning her neck to catch Jonquil's eye. Jonquil, meanwhile, got up and softly closed the door between them. Her heart was hammering. She took deep breaths to calm herself down.

What had just happened?

The man was more intelligent and aggressive than her typical clients and she had not been prepared. No, that wasn't the case. The truth was she could be objective about most gift ideas but not about pets.

This was not good news because it could happen again.

She resisted the obvious solutions, either to call her former therapist for a session or at least contact Dr. Paxton about getting supervision on this new job. Either course would mean she'd have to finally confront the traumatic events of ten years ago, Gerry's death and all that led up to it. She couldn't avoid the truth much longer and her failed meeting with Dan Burnham had demonstrated the pressing need. But the risk of jeopardizing her relationship with Billy stopped her from taking action as it always did.

Instead, she attempted to force some good out of the fiasco. Hadn't Dan Burnham wanted to control and manipulate his son by giving him a gift to keep him from becoming jealous of his new sister? Didn't that prove that every gift, however noble, comes with strings attached? The pieces didn't fit. Dan Burnham's motives went far beyond the scope of her dissertation. Jonquil tore up his index card. Rita gently tapped on the door and she braced herself for the next session.

* * *

Billy liked the idea of heading straight for the jobsite after he got home from school so much that he relinquished his chores, both watering Mr. Neri's lawn, and walking Mrs. Crandon's dogs, to willing Ramon, his friend.

Claude greeted him with obvious pleasure, the way Billy sometimes imagined his own dad would have done. His mom refused to discuss getting a puppy, the subject uppermost on his mind. It helped to sit for a couple of hours each afternoon beside Claude, who seemed willing to talk about anything and who knew practically everything.

Billy's test in fractions was scheduled for Friday morning so during their first two afternoons together, Claude made up problems for Billy to solve and then patiently went over his answers with him. At one point when Billy saw his mistake before Claude did, and hastily corrected the problem amid much erasing and smoothing down of paper, Claude remarked, "Atta boy, son!" Billy's face lit up like a Christmas candle.

That afternoon, after an hour of problem solving, Claude suggested they go outside and toss a Frisbee. Two of the neighborhood children who had brought their pets over to Billy's defunct garage-clinic joined them.

The next hour passed quickly with countless squeals of laughter.

Finally it grew dark and they went their separate ways: Claude to the beach, the other children to their homes and Billy to the manager's apartment to await Jonquil's arrival.

She arrived home after six o'clock.

"Mom, Mom! Claude says I'm going to ace my test!" Billy proudly announced as he held open the door for her.

"That's nice, honey," she replied wearily, while glancing through a stack of bills and Christmas cards.

There was one from funny Jackson Parker, the UCLA film student she had met during her pregnancy. Back then he was frantically writing a thesis showing the high incidence of the word "Chicago" in old film scripts. They went to a retrospective of film noirs once and he recorded the amount of time that elapsed before the city was first mentioned in each film. Funny guy. There was also a postcard from her friend, Ann.

"He's one cool dude," Billy continued.

"I'm glad honey." She checked the phone messages.

"You like him too, don't you?" he persisted.

"Sweetie, let me listen to the phone messages, please?"

"Sure, Mom."

She seemed out of sorts more of the time. Each night she came home so tired they spoke less and less to each other. Sure, it used to be like this when she worked at Children's Home, but not every night. Maybe, Billy thought to himself, if Claude came over for dinner one night, he'd make her laugh the way he made Billy and the other kids laugh today. It gave him a terrific idea.

CHAPTER FOURTEEN

Friday, December 12th

J onquil drove to work still shaken by her session with Dan Burnham. She'd blown it, pure and simple. Up until then, she'd arrived at solutions to people's problems effortlessly. A remark on her part, whether intuitive or offhanded, led to a plan of action. She could live with that.

After all, the whole point of her research was to explore an area of human behavior not well documented in psychology. She had to appear like she knew what she was doing while learning on the job.

Her mistake with Dan Burnham was to mention her project. That came off as pretentious and defensive and he'd seen right through her.

Oh well, she now assured herself, *I'm back in control. That was dumb but it won't happen again.* Her vigilant inner voice responded, *Oh really?*

Well, sure, she reasoned further as she headed toward Clyde's. There was a vast difference between helping someone make a ten-dollar purchase for the company grab bag and helping a caring parent find the right way to assure his young, autistic son that he was loved.

Still, it boiled down to the indisputable truth that gifts came with strings attached. How many times had her own adored father, John Bloom, a traveling salesman who frequently missed her birthdays and school functions, brought her home a surprise—the size of which probably corresponded to his guilt—hoping she would forgive his absence? His presents, though, never took the place of his presence and she quickly tired of them.

On the other hand, her mother's gifts tended to be practical—new clothes, new hair ribbons, a winter coat, party shoes. Pauline Bloom was a nervous, stern woman, the oldest of the Ditmar girls. Born to wealth (her father owned the largest Swedish bakery in the Twin Cities), she married late, after her younger sisters. She was obsessed with appearances and she always wanted Jonquil to look her best. So, while her dad practiced bribery, her mother's form of giving was closer to behavioral modification.

Then there were the birthday parties she attended as a little girl. Looking back on them now, she speculated that in many instances, the gifts—selected not by her friends but by their mothers—were supposed to impress or top all the others. She'd recognized this same phenomenon at baby showers and weddings over the years. People sometimes gave gifts to show off or compete. Jonquil hadn't realized until that moment how jaded her own opinions about giving had become. She sat hunched over the steering wheel at a stoplight on Lincoln Boulevard and brooded.

Her thoughts took her back to the evening of her eighth birthday and her father's shocking betrayal. After promising, even swearing on an unseen stack of Bibles, that he would be home before she blew out her candles, Jonquil's father instead vanished into thin air, never to be seen or heard from again. Not only did he break his promise to her, he broke her heart and destroyed her mother's fragile spirit. Four months later, her mother was incarcerated in a private Minneapolis hospital where she soon died. Jonquil, an only child, was dispatched to live with her paternal grandmother, Margo Bloom, in faraway Washington State.

With car horns blaring all around her, Jonquil continued driving to work and continued to work out her feelings.

"Call me Margo, I'm too damned cute to be a grandmother," trumpeted the plump, mannish lady with the Irish gleam in her eyes who met her at the airport.

Margo Bloom. A smile crossed Jonquil's face while a slew of golden memories replaced her pensive thoughts.

Margo Bloom, a widow, lived a semi-rustic life on Puget Sound when they met. She was as generous with hugs and kisses as she was with feeding the squirrels outside her back door, each of whom she named. She wore her long, gray mane artlessly in a ponytail and pulled on a skirt only for the Easter Vigil; otherwise, she preferred sweats and ponchos. She eked out a living as an artist and crafts designer. When school recesses permitted, she took Jonquil with her to fairs and crafts shows up and down the West Coast from Laguna Beach to Alaska.

The first time she and Margo squared off occurred over the dinner table on the night of Jonquil's arrival. "Are there any other kids around here? Where will I go to school?" fretted Jonquil to her mashed potatoes.

"St. Bride's down the road," replied Margo matter-of-factly. The house was shadowy, eerie, because Margo preferred candles at the evening meal rather than electric lights. Jonquil had made up her mind on the flight out there that she would hate Washington. It turned out to be easier than she imagined.

"Why?" she asked Margo.

"Eat your dinner, child."

"Why do I have to change schools? Why do I have to

live here? I want to go home!" Her voice escalated and Margo put down her fork.

"This is your home now," she said evenly.

Jonquil felt angry and helpless and realized that good manners were inconsistent with her goal. Then, she recalled a game her younger cousins used to play. It was called the "Why" game. It was clever because it unnerved adults. She'd play it until she got put back on a plane to Minnesota.

After dinner, which neither of them finished, Margo led her to her new bedroom. It was much smaller than the one in the white stucco house on Minihaha Avenue back in the Twin Cities. This one had stained wood walls rather than pretty wallpaper and was sparsely furnished with a narrow bed, a nightstand and lamp, a desk and bookcase, and a hobbyhorse on rockers.

The sight of the hobbyhorse stung her eight-and-a-half-year-old pride. "I'm no baby. That's a baby toy. I hate this place. I hate you. I want my daddy!" She kicked it.

"That toy belonged to your father when he was a little boy. I put it in here on purpose."

"Why?" demanded Jonquil.

"I don't want you to be afraid to talk about him or your mother. I may not have answers, child, but I will always listen to you."

Jonquil distrusted her. Adults always said one thing and meant another. Her father had promised to be home for her eighth birthday, and then vanished. After he left, her mother broke every rule she'd ever taught Jonquil by staying in bed all day weeping, not eating, not washing, until they took her away. Her Minnesota relatives, every time she brought up either of her parents, got peculiar. They changed the subject or offered her a sweet, or exchanged looks above her head, shutting her out. Jonquil exploded in anger.

"Where's my daddy?"

"I don't know," Margo replied unflinchingly.

"You're his mommy! You're s'pose to know!" shouted Jonquil.

Margo appraised the girl's passion and directness, her ability to feel as well as to inflict pain. There was hope for her waif-like granddaughter.

Jonquil had endured so much and her bloodless Minnesota aunts wanted no part of her upbringing. Margo believed that if she could love Jonquil through this crisis, perhaps they could both survive the trauma that her only son's disappearance had caused.

It had been many years since she'd dealt with a youngster full-time. She sat down on the bed so that their confrontation could continue at eye level.

"He began running away from me before he was old

enough to go to school. John never could stay in one place for long."

Jonquil watched her through hooded eyes. Was she making fun?

"I am sorry your father went away, especially on your birthday. You see, Jonquil, no one can control another person. Not even mommies. We begin letting go of those we love from the day they are born. With luck or grace, they don't usually wander far. But sometimes—"

"No! Leave me alone!" Jonquil covered her ears with her hands and screamed.

The battle she had been raging to cope with the bewildering changes in her life had required utmost vigilance.

Worst of all was any suggestion that her father might never come back. She wailed long and hard, finally accepting the strong arms that pulled her close. Later, exhausted, after Margo tucked her in bed, Jonquil thought that perhaps she would stay there for a while.

A week later, she began to have dreams about her father and the dreams troubled her. She came home on many occasions and told Margo that she had seen him at the mall, at church, getting on the ferry, getting off the bus. He was always in a crowd, always a few steps ahead of her and out of reach. Young Jonquil trembled with frustration.

Margo listened to the details of each sighting and dried many tears. Then, she placed a lit candle in the window so that he might find his way home. Margo couldn't give her back her father but neither would she let his memory fade.

Typically, Margo celebrated everything to the max— Christmas, Easter, birthdays, even feast days. This last gave her pause as Jonquil wasn't named after a saint.

"Never you mind," she told Jonquil. "Flowers are God's gifts, like stars, like butterflies. We'll make your day the first day of spring and we'll have ourselves a treat."

Margo's gifts were special, too; there were none like them. Whether they were homemade from bits of gauze, feathers and glitter, or the doll or book in the local store window she'd seen her granddaughter coveting made no difference. Each came wrapped with Margo's joy in being alive, creative, in loving and being loved.

How strange, Jonquil suddenly thought. How very strange that her troubles with Dan Burnham led to her brightest memories of Margo. Pulling into Clyde's parking garage, she could not fathom any connection.

Her inner voice commented, *Gotcha!*

CHAPTER FIFTEEN

Saturday, December 13th

That morning, Jonquil arranged with Billy's weekend sitter to drop him at the store at four o'clock so they could pick up a Christmas tree on their way home. The Christmas season in Southern California always made Jonquil long for more wintry climes. She wished she could take Billy skiing at Lake Tahoe, or better yet, to her grandmother's house on Puget Sound where at night they could pretend to be the Magi and search the spangled heavens for the beam that led to Bethlehem.

Except that Margo didn't live there anymore. She'd married again and moved to Ireland.

When they reached the crowded lot behind Lucky's Supermarket where they purchased their tree every year, sounds of the season filled the air. Nearby, the clang of a Salvation Army bell mixed with the carols blaring from

146

loudspeakers overhead. Car doors slammed, followed by children's shouts. All the scene lacked was snow and a thirty degree temperature drop.

Business was brisk. Both Jonquil and Billy saw friends and went in opposite directions. Later, as she poked through a lackluster row of firs, she heard Billy calling her name. "Mom, I found the best one!" he shouted. Impatiently, he tugged her over to the center of the lot. A man stood with his back to them, blocking their path.

"There it is!" cried Billy, pointing straight ahead. As if by signal, the man turned and faced them. It was Claude Chappel. A ripple of pleasure raced through Jonquil.

"Well, isn't this a pleasant coincidence?" Claude remarked with mock surprise. His cream-colored turtleneck, coffee-brown leather jacket, and chinos looked to her like dating attire.

"Coincidence? I rather doubt that," she said with a chuckle. One glance at Billy confirmed her suspicions.

"The truth is, Billy did tell me you were buying your tree here this afternoon. Well, from the way he described the selection, I thought I should check it out. Maybe find myself a tree." *Ri-ight,* she thought, *and we just happened to get here at the same time. If only the temperature would drop and put some color in her cheeks.*

"Do you live in the neighborhood?" she inquired.

"No," he said, "but I had to stop by the job, so—"

"Coming through!" shouted someone behind her. At the same time, Claude put his hand on her back and moved her aside so two men dragging a trussed tree could pass. His brief, firm touch sent tingles up her spine and warmth to her cheeks. *This guy is smooth*, she thought. *He doesn't seem to be aware that he touched me. Could it be possible he didn't engineer it?*

"Mom, this tree rocks!" cried Billy, grabbing the branch of a spiffy looking evergreen behind Claude. "Hmm," she said, walking around it. "You don't think it's too tall, do you?"

"Do you think so, Claude?" asked Billy.

Jonquil said quickly before Claude could reply, "We'll get it cut down a few inches, sweetie." Realizing she had cut in, she blushed.

Claude looked at Jonquil and commented to Billy, "Your mother's right." She couldn't help but notice the warm rapport between Claude and her son and decided she was glad for many reasons that the meet-up had occurred.

A young man in a scarlet stocking cap approached and asked if he could assist them. Soon the tree, minus four inches, lay strapped to the hood of Jonquil's VW.

"Well," said Jonquil demurely, "I hope you have as good luck finding your own tree, Claude."

"But Mom, can't Claude come home and help us set it

up?" pleaded Billy. He looked from one adult to the other. Jonquil felt cornered—no—she wanted Claude to take the initiative and not have Billy act as go-between.

"I wish I'd had advanced warning, Billy. I don't know what shape the apartment is in. You know how Mom likes things neat and tidy for guests. You do understand, don't you Claude?" She grinned up at him.

"Yes, Jonquil, I do." They regarded each other with amusement, both aware that Billy's plan had worked out better than he could have anticipated.

* * *

After dinner, while Jonquil untangled the tree lights and Billy unpacked the ornaments, he asked her to tell him the story of how she met his dad.

"Well, Billy, I was living in Washington with your great-grandmother," she began in the story-telling voice she invoked on these occasions.

"Yeah."

"And I was in college at the University of Washington in Seattle."

"Uh-huh. Look, Mom, here's the one I made in preschool. Remember?" He held up a paper wreathe plastered with stickers. She admired it all over again as she did every year. "Go on, Mom," Billy ordered as he reached for a box of ornament hooks.

"Now, where was I?"

"You were in college."

"Right. It was at the start of my junior year. Classes hadn't begun yet. I decided to take a walk. It's a beautiful campus. I used to love to stroll around it. So, there I was, minding my own business, not a care in the world, just bip-bopping along ..."

"Uh-huh."

"When from out of nowhere this blockhead comes charging right into me—practically knocks me to the ground! He and another guy were 'jogging.'" She rolled her eyes.

"Did you get mad at him?" he asked and giggled, anticipating the answer.

"You bet! I mean people like that slay me. Show-offs. They're so into health but they don't give a damn about who's in their way. 'Scuse my French!"

"What did he do?" Billy's giggles grew louder.

"Nothing! It was a hit and run accident. No, wait ... he yelled at me something like, 'Why don't you watch where you're going' and kept on jogging. Like it was my fault!"

"Then what happened?" Though Billy knew the story by heart, he never tired of it.

"Well, then the other fellow came over and asked if I was hurt."

"That was my dad," Billy stated proudly.

They had stopped working on the tree ornaments and

sat across from each other deep in discussion. The room grew quiet.

"Yes, that was your dad."

"Gerry."

"Yes."

"Gerry O'Keefe."

"Right."

"So, what happened next?"

"Well, Gerry asked me if I'd like a Coke or something and I said, 'Okay' and the rest, as they say, is history."

"I bet his friend was surprised," Billy chortled.

"He was a lot more surprised a year later when he was an usher at our wedding," countered Jonquil. Billy laughed, then his face puckered in concentration.

"Dad was an enviral—"

"Environmentalist. He helped write laws to protect the waterways, the forests and the parks."

Billy's gaze turned to the photo of his father resting on the desk. "And I look like him, don't I?"

"Yes, you do, Billy Bloom."

"Do I act like him? I mean, do I talk like him and stuff?"

She stood up and plugged in the last string of lights. "Every day you remind me of him more. You have his eyes and his dimples and a few of his expressions. He was smart and so are you." She omitted how Billy had also inherited his father's passion for animals or that his Irish Setter, Baron, had been with him on the day they met. A frisky pup, she took to him immediately, never suspecting how much he would take from her just three short years later. A long time ago she decided that Billy was better off not knowing about Baron.

"Mom, can you miss someone you never met before?" His question knocked her for a loop. Could he read her mind?

"Billy sweetheart, of course you can." She reached for him. "Come here. Let me give you a hug." She gathered him in her arms, amazed by how much he'd grown in recent weeks. "You can even love someone you never met," she whispered.

The one hundred eighty-degree shift in Billy's emotions caught them both off guard. "Why'd he have to d-die, Mom? W-Why?" he exploded in sobs nearly causing her to lose her balance. His body shuddered with wails and hiccups. She felt a catch in her throat and swallowed hard. "Billy, Billy," she whispered, rocking him gently while he cried out his pain. "Are you tired, honey? We can finish this tomorrow."

"Y-you have to w-work, don't you?" She could barely understand what he was saying, nor could she recall the last time Billy had cried so hard.

"Yes, but afterward—"

"No!" Immediately, he pulled away and struggled to gain control of himself. "I'm okay. I want to do it now." He sniffled with all his might.

"Sure?"

"Sure I'm sure." He wiped his eyes and nose with the front of his shirt. For once she let it pass.

"Say, you know what we could use? We could use a little music." She flipped on the radio. Choir voices filled the air.

"There 'mid the straw and gentle cows,
That precious baby smiled!"

Instinct told her that they needed something livelier than "Joseph's Song," even if it was the new American carol. She reached for the dial but stopped when she heard her son humming along, already absorbed in decorating the tree again. Watching him closely, Jonquil reminded herself that Billy was growing up. These questions were bound to arise more frequently. What would she say when he could no longer be distracted? How could she ever find the courage to tell him the truth?

"Hey, Mom," Billy exclaimed an hour later when the tree was finished and lights twinkled from every branch.

"Hey, what?" she asked from the stepladder.

"This! Tree! Rules! Yes, yes, yes," Billy pumped his

arm like Kirk Gibson rounding third base. Then he put his hands on her cheeks and gave her a boyish smooch before he took himself off to bed.

Thoughtfully, Jonquil gathered up the ornament boxes. The apartment grew quiet except for the Christmas music playing on the radio.

She shoved the empty boxes beneath the sofa, its floral apron concealing their whereabouts. Surveying the room, she caught sight of the manger scene sitting under the tree where Billy had set it up. She carefully lifted it and placed it on the coffee table. In past years, she and Billy had practiced the old custom, gleaned from her Minnesota relatives, of filling the bare, cheerless manger with pieces of fresh straw for each kind act they made during the four weeks of Advent leading up to Christmas, thereby ensuring a warm crib for the Babe. This year like so many other things, it had slipped her mind.

"O, on this holy night,
A new star shone so bright,
That when my wife and I stopped here,
The sky was filled with light."

"Joseph's Song" was playing once again, performed this time by a gifted tenor. Jonquil inhaled the spicy smell of pine and smiled. She knelt down on her haunches and fingered the painted, carved figures, trying to imagine the first Christmas.

"This holy night, dear God,
She said we'd have a Guest,
The town was full, we found a cave,
My wife paused there to rest."

Instead of Bethlehem, however, memories of her old apartment and Billy's birth came to mind.

* * *

Billy entered the world ten years ago during the first hour of the last day of August. Jonquil by that time had resided in Southern California several months.

Unemployed, she lived in a quiet apartment in West Los Angeles off Pico Boulevard. Her nearest friend was the cashier at the corner 7-Eleven. She had money and medical insurance to cover expenses and the obstetrician's fees, but she avoided all new social connections.

Her former Seattle neighbors urged her to make new friends. Tough order. Her former best friend, her husband, had abandoned her without warning, just like her father. She chose to concentrate on the new life in her womb while spending her days auditing classes at nearby UCLA.

It was her way of healing. She felt at home there. The campus was reminiscent of the University of Washington with more grass and fewer trees; the serenity it gave her was the same. An avid student since childhood, she felt protected as if she herself were in a womb. Everyone in the libraries, the cafeterias and bookstore was helpful, not prying. She sat in on a variety of lectures, from Frank McAdams' critique of "Casablanca" to Professor Joseph Mazziotti's lectures on psychodynamic theory. Best of all, she could read outdoors in the warm sunshine between classes on most afternoons.

Her water broke one sweltering evening while she was home doing laundry. She sagged against the sorting table, dismayed at how vulnerable and alone she was. By keeping to herself, she'd made a drastic mistake. Frantically pulling the still wet contents out of two dryers, she could think of no one to call for help. Then she discovered she couldn't even lift the clothesbasket.

At that moment, two young people, a neighbor and her boyfriend, barged into the laundry room arguing heatedly. The girl's name was Renata Pinz. She had two massive braids that hung down to her waist and an accent Jonquil guessed was Swiss or German. The chatty building manager had informed Jonquil that Renata spoke seven languages and worked in the movies translating foreign film dialogue into English subtitles. Her boyfriend,

Hector, a much tattooed and pierced dance club musician, began cursing at her in Spanish that bounced off the cinderblock walls.

"Shut up!" shouted Jonquil, topping their voices. "I'm having a baby. Tonight! Now!"

The combatants simultaneously dropped their laundry paraphernalia and rushed to her aid. Renata assisted Jonquil back to her apartment to call her doctor and grab her overnight bag while Hector followed with her wash, then pulled his '85 Olds convertible to the front of the building. They all crowded into the front seat and Hector sped off to UCLA's emergency room getting lost only twice. Upon arriving, Jonquil edged out of the car slightly winded but full of gratitude. They offered to stay with her—in several languages—but she turned them down. Perversely, she would go it alone.

Two hours into labor, a problem developed. Her contractions became erratic. The pain grew excruciating. One of the nurses leaned over and asked her with increasing urgency if there were anyone to notify should matters worsen.

"Priest," she grunted through clenched lips. She hadn't been inside a church since Gerry's funeral. "Catho-lic priest," she specified.

Chaplin Tim Moran was on duty at the hospital that night. Moments after her request, his hand locked onto hers in an arm wrestle like the grip between two varmints in a B-western movie scene. Appropriately, he was wearing a surgical face mask. *Fair enough*, she thought grimly, *I'll fight this out with God.*

Though his muscles were as strong as his brogue, his sixty-some-year-old life résumé contained no previous experience in the delivery room. The padre was flat-out ecstatic to be there. He prayed, he bullied, he coached her breathing, he bargained, he soothed. Four sweat-filled hours later, he hoarsely baptized William Timothy Bloom, all eight pounds and five ounces of him. Then he, the doctors and nurses, the technicians, the monitors and the overhead lights faded as Billy was placed in Jonquil's arms. She squinted down at his face in awe and peace. At last her isolation was over.

CHAPTER SIXTEEN

Sunday, December 14th

Billy's eyes looked puffy over breakfast; otherwise, he seemed in bright spirits. After Mass, Jonquil dropped him off at Georgina Phillips' house. She and Ted were taking a gang of kids to the Lakers' game. Jonquil gave Billy some money so he could treat them all to a snack at the Forum, explaining to him that that's how people thank other people for such a generous invitation. He suspected her comments would develop into a full-blown lecture about gift-giving as had happened so often in the past year. Billy, who had endured one sermon already that morning, nodded vigorously that he understood and tore out of the VW to join the other kids.

Jonquil's priority after she arrived at work that day was getting the play-by-play on Rita's dinner date with Al Yates. Rita obliged with soft spoken details and a secret smile about her lips that Jonquil had not seen before. He'd brought a bottle of sparkling wine to complement her Heavenly Hawaiian Chicken entrée. Left to himself in her living room while she went off to prepare drinks, he spied a shelf of well-worn record albums. To his immense delight, the collection was dominated by dance music: from ballroom classics, square dances, rock 'n roll to disco. By the time she re-entered the room with a tray of hors d'oeuvres, he'd pulled down a dozen albums and had begun opening the cupboards in search of a turntable.

"Do you dance?" he asked hopefully.

"Do I! Sugar, you are looking at the quintessential dancing fool." She pointed to where the stereo had gathered dust—only figuratively, she was a nut about house cleaning—and while the chicken overcooked and the sparkling wine lost its bubbles, Al and Rita found their rhythm. She could hardly put into words her intense pleasure at dancing and flirting away the hours again in the arms of a new partner. It was, she declared, the most romantic night she had enjoyed in years. She and Al planned to lunch together that afternoon. They both agreed there was no time to lose. If this were indeed another chance at happiness, they'd rather find out sooner than later.

Jonquil studied Rita's glow. Was there such a thing as a second chance for her, too? Would Claude call? Just remembering his touch set her pulse racing. That more than anything told her she was ready, that she wanted him to call, that if the truth be known, she was *aching* for him to call. But would he?

After work Jonquil decided to squeeze in a couple of hours shopping. She could take advantage of the employee discount as well as demonstrate her loyalty to the store. Maybe, she speculated grimly on her way up the escalator, word would get back to Lady Leigh.

From the moment she began her trek through the store though, Jonquil sensed something unusual in the air. People were watching her. The maintenance crew and cleaning staff waved to her. The harassed sales clerks, rather than counting down the minutes to closing time, kept alert eyes on her. Some of the customers pointed at her and whispered to each other. A security guard tipped his hat in her direction. Surmising that a VIP must be trailing her, twice she turned around to see who it could be. No one was behind her. *How strange*, she thought, checking for the third time to see if her slip was showing.

When she stalled in the book section to buy Father Tim a present, each of the clerks rushed over to meet her. A circle of employees and shoppers formed around her. One woman attempted to get Jonquil's opinion on two best sellers. "Actually, the meter is running on my babysitter, may I please shop in peace?" she nearly griped. Concealing her irritation, she suggested the woman make an appointment to see her.

As gracefully as possible, she disengaged herself from the group, made her selection, and hurried away. Unbeknownst to her, within minutes, five customers purchased the same book.

She was beginning to grasp the situation. She was no longer simply Jonquil Bloom, at least not under Clyde's roof. She was Jonquil Bloom, Gift Counselor, and all that the title entailed.

When had the metamorphosis occurred? Was it in response to the radio and television ads? The Constance visit? Word of mouth? Her mail was growing with invitations to charity events and speaker forums. Daily, requests to endorse this product or that brand of greeting card were trickling in by phone, fax and email. The *L.A. Times* article about her was set to appear in Sunday's edition. Where would that kind of publicity lead?

She was used to privacy at work. Her therapy sessions as Children's Home had been confidential and not open to scrutiny except by her colleagues and UCLA advisors. She could share few details with her friends, neighbors or even sympathetic Billy about her day to day work with the mentally ill.

She now knew that doing therapy was a profoundly lonely calling and she was not suited to it. Miss Hamilton had been right. She viewed her gift counseling sessions at Clyde's as confidential, too, but away from the actual sessions, the similarities ended. Why, the people in the store were reacting to her as if she were a VIP!

Before she dismissed the notion as laughable, she reconsidered. There was nothing inherently wrong with a little extra attention. She of all people could certainly handle it, being educated, level-headed and mature. If anything, she felt wary of it.

Moreover, the discovery of her new importance gave her a second wind. She straightened her spine, ran a hand through her hair, slowed down her pace and slapped a bright smile on her tired face.

Then she started acknowledging the looks and waves. Perhaps if she played the part of her role intelligently but didn't let it go to her head, it might help obtain for her what she now most wanted that Christmas—a full-time job at Clyde's. It might even be fun so long as it didn't interfere with her clients or her research.

Jonquil felt like Cinderella at the ball. The path through the Scentsations Department resembled a gauntlet. The sales reps squirted her with their samplers on all sides. She could almost hear her grandmother Margo whispering, "Bloom, Jonquil, bloom."

CHAPTER SEVENTEEN

Monday, December 15th

I t was one of those rarified days that just kept getting better. First Billy paged her from school with the happy bulletin that he had passed his fractions test. Jonquil could barely insert a word of congratulations, he was so keyed up. To celebrate, she promised him his favorite chicken tacos for dinner.

Then, about eleven o'clock, before her next appointment, Rita breezed in to her office to inform her, "You have a personal call on line four. A Mr. Claude Chappel." Jonquil clapped her hands with relief and anticipation. "Thanks, Rita." After Rita left, she snatched up the receiver.

"Claude?"

"Jonquil, how are you this morning?"

She swayed to the intoxicating music of his voice and

let it fill her head. "Oh, fine and you?"

"Eh, couldn't be better. Say, did you hear from Billy about his test yet?"

"I did. I talked to him a while ago. He got an A on the test. In fact, I wanted to call you today to thank you for helping him."

"Oh? Hmm. 'Fraid that's not good enough." She heard a creaking sound at his end as though he had leaned back in his chair.

"I beg your pardon?" What game was he playing now? The chair creaked louder as though he had snapped it back into place. His voice sounded closer, too.

"Ms. Bloom, will you do me the honor of having dinner with me Saturday night? Just you and me, Jonny. Nothing fancy. We're going on a picnic."

"Uh-huh …" *Did he just say Jonny? This guy does something intimate with each encounter*, she thought. Saturday, he had touched her back. Her heart thundered at the memory. Now he'd bestowed a nickname on her. Jonny.

"Are you thinking it over or checking your calendar?" he asked. She couldn't keep pace with the conversation. It had been quite a while since she'd last felt this giddy and feminine.

"Thinking it over," she admitted.

"That's as good as a 'yes' where I come from. I'll pick

you up at seven thirty sharp. And Jonquil, don't change your mind because these knuckleheads can cut my power line at any time. See you Saturday." The line went dead. Rita popped back into Jonquil's office.

"Ooo—was that the construction boss?" she asked.

"Yes, Rita, and he asked me out for a date!" Jonquil wailed. Rita ignored the panic in her voice.

"High time. Men these days. Stall City! Okay, when, where and what?"

"Saturday evening—dinner—a picnic!"

"Picnic? Not your typical December choice but then he's not your typical anything. Okay, sugar, here's the deal: we clear out of here as early as possible. I'll sit with Billy while you sneak in a beauty nap. Then I'll fix you one of my 'scent'-ual cocoons. Don't give me that look. It will be fun."

"But Rita, I haven't been on a date in eons. Yikes! What'll I wear?"

Rita chewed her lower lip in concentration. "Something alluring yet outdoorsy. I recommend Belle Fleur. Constance would agree."

The day's surprises were not over. When Jonquil returned to work after doing a little Christmas shopping at lunchtime, she found Rita bursting with news. While Jonquil was out, Rita had received a call from the Poppi Blair Show people from New York. Rita had been a fan ever since the hot jazz singer, turned television talk show host, had cut her first record album and joined the illustrious long line of entertainers who hailed from Arkansas. Excitedly, Rita had forwarded the call up to Inez Escanaba in Public Relations who had phoned back down minutes ago to confirm the rumor already circulating the store—that Jonquil had been invited to be the featured guest on the afternoon talk show on Christmas Eve. Live from Burbank!

"What?" exclaimed Jonquil as she lost her grip on the packages she was carrying.

"Glory be, Jonquil, I think I shall faint!" pronounced Rita.

"Don't do that, Rita. Talk! Why me of all people?"

"Because she's moving her talk show to the West Coast that week. Around Christmas time, Poppi puts a lot of young people on her show. I mean singers who want to be in showbiz but who need a break. She started out as a singer. It's her way of giving back. So this year, she's coming to Hollywood. Makes perfect sense."

"Rita," Jonquil said as she bent over to retrieve her purchases, "where do I fit in?"

"Have you ever seen the show?"

"I don't have much time for television. What night is it on?"

Rita groaned. "Sugar, it's a daytime daily, like Oprah

or Rosie. Here's where you come in: it's the Christmas Eve show, get it? Last minute gift ideas, that's what she'll be looking for from you. She likes to feature new fads and gift counseling is new."

"Hardly a fad," Jonquil commented. "So, if the show's on in the daytime, how come you know so much about it?"

"Simple, I tape it and watch it at night. She just cracks me up! Anyhow, Inez told me that Poppi's scouts have been casing the L.A. newspapers and media looking for local, seasonal stories. Inez said that when they heard about gift counseling, they pitched the idea to Poppi and she loved it because she's doing the one show on the afternoon of Christmas Eve live, with a call-in number."

"Call-in number? What do you mean?"

"I mean it's a Christmas Eve Special, sugar, and the viewers will be able to call you with their last minute gift questions."

Jonquil stared slack jawed at Rita.

"Christmas Eve—aren't we booked solid?" she stammered.

"We're wide open. Folks are leaving town by then. I managed to reschedule the two appointments you had for the twenty-third. The show airs next Wednesday at one o'clock at the NBC studios in Burbank. Inez has all the details."

That afternoon, Jonquil met for a half hour with Mr. Merrill and staff. First, she and the advertising department were congratulated for capturing Poppi Blair's attention. Already the show had faxed over a tentative agenda. Members of Poppi's staff were en route to the West Coast for a prescreening interview scheduled for Wednesday. On the day of the actual show, a limo would provide Jonquil with roundtrip service from her apartment in Venice. She would be on air during the first part of the show. After being introduced, she would be given one minute to summarize her occupation. Then Poppi would field questions from the studio audience and viewers about last minute gift problems.

In turn, the store would provide Jonquil with clothes, jewelry, accessories and hair styling by the store's own Pierre Andre. Also, during the next week, Ralph in the Teletronics Department would tape the show so she could view it at night and become familiar with Poppi's sassy style. Mr. Merrill made it clear that any and all store resources were available to her to make her television talk show debut a success. Leigh Usher never uttered a word.

Jonquil returned to her office in a daze. By then the store was all agog over another event—Amy Madigan and Ed Harris were spotted in the toy department. Rita rushed over to her friends in Scents to get the details, allowing Jonquil a few moments to assess her feelings. It was a bounty, pure and simple: Billy back in high gear after passing his test, Claude taking her cue and asking her on a date so soon, and now the fantastic opportunity to validate her new occupation in one minute on live network television in front of millions of viewers! Jonquil's heart skipped a beat.

What would she say? How could she phrase it without sounding like a cross between Miss Manners and a pop psychology guru? "Hi, I'm Jonquil Bloom (brightly), and I'm a gift counselor. Gift counseling is ..." Just then, the phone on her desk rang. Rita was nowhere in sight.

"Gift Counseling, Jonquil Bloom speaking. How may I help you?"

"Are you the gift counselor?"

"Yes I am," she replied. *You bet I am!*

* * *

Billy arrived home after her. He'd helped Ramon walk Mrs. Crandon's dogs and then stayed a while to play with Blackie.

Jonquil had his favorite dinner all prepared. He whipped out his test paper and she proudly taped it to the refrigerator door. Then, after he washed his hands, they sat down at the dinner table.

She asked Billy to say grace. After the usual words he added a few of his own. "And God, Mrs. Crandon said anytime Mom says it's okay, I can have one of her

170

puppies. So God, please work on Mom. I'm not having much luck. Amen."

Jonquil shot him a look that acknowledged his resourcefulness for bringing up the taboo subject of dogs within a prayer but she chose not to comment.

"Mom," he said after drinking a gulp of milk, "when's Hanukkah?"

"I think it begins next Wednesday, which is the day I—"

"Next Wednesday? That's Christmas Eve!" he blurted out.

"Yes, Billy, and it's impolite to interrupt when someone is speaking."

"Sorry, Mom." He appeared to be crestfallen.

"Never mind. What about Hanukkah?"

"That's the day Mrs. Crandon is giving her puppies to her grandchildren. Even Blackie!"

"That's enough, Billy. Didn't I tell you not to become attached to those dogs?" she reminded him crossly.

"Yes," he muttered and scowled darkly.

She refused to have a repeat of the contretemps from Saturday night. It was time to change the subject.

"Claude was real happy to hear about your test score."

Billy's mood improved immediately. Jonquil told him about the phone call and the date but not about the television appearance. That could wait. "And Rita's coming over to stay with you while we're out." He felt miffed that he wasn't included on the date but it didn't prevent him from enjoying second helpings of dessert: Moose Tracks ice cream.

She switched on the VCR after he had gone to bed. She liked Poppi Blair with her scarf turban, emerald green caftan, hooped earrings and stellar smile. She handled her guests, the audience and crew with ease.

Yet, each time the screen filled with views of the cameras or television crew, Jonquil got flutters. Her only experience on camera, other than the KTLA interview at Clyde's ten days ago, occurred when she was videotaped running a therapy group as part of her psyche training at UCLA. This would be entirely different.

Was she ready to present her ideas on national television? She had trouble explaining gift counseling to herself, let alone to her boss or co-workers.

With a jolt, Jonquil remembered her faculty advisor, Dr. Paxton's undisguised reaction during that one brief phone call they had had weeks ago. Possibly someone in the department would see her on television and report the news back to him. What if she came off as a total flake? Her theory as well as her hopes for a rewarding career would crash and burn before they ever had a chance.

So, she had to do her best, win over Poppi and the audience, represent Clyde's in a professional manner and also impress any other psychologist who happened to tune in to the show that day.

A loud, prolonged yawn cut short her mounting anxiety, a signal from her brain that it was done with thinking for the day. Quietly, she stopped the video, turned off the Christmas tree lights and trudged down the hall to bed.

CHAPTER EIGHTEEN

Tuesday, December 16th

L eigh Usher was not in the store either Thursday or Friday. Since December was her down-time, the occasional day or two she took off work for personal reasons went unnoticed.

Only her secretary, Sally Tarson, and Mr. Merrill knew her true whereabouts. Her sister's drug addiction had led to a hospital readmission or arrest and necessitated another of Leigh's unplanned absences from work.

Upon her return to work Monday, Leigh wasted no time pruning the grapevine for tidbits on the Constance event. By all accounts, the twenty-minute session between the celebrity and Jonquil Bloom had been deemed a success.

"So after she was counseled, did Constance purchase anything in the store?" inquired Leigh at the weekly executive meeting.

"No siree bob," boasted Al and clapped his hands once with satisfaction. "I had the situation covered. She never even saw the store."

"Aw," was Leigh's biting retort, "all that hoopla for nothing."

Mr. Merrill winced at the tone of her voice. Miss Egnar and others had tried to warn him about this side of Leigh. He'd always associated her moodiness with a family crisis. Yet, it was highly unprofessional of her to publicly lampoon a fellow employee's work.

He deftly moved the staff's attention to the next agenda item. At the meeting's conclusion, he asked Leigh to step into his office.

He began by asking solicitously after Julie, her older sister. Reluctantly, Leigh furnished him with an update. Julie was in detox again and would be discharged, if no other problems developed, on the day before Christmas.

Mr. Merrill was familiar with the details. Julie had been clean for two years and living with their parents when their father died of a heart attack. It sent Julie into a downward spiral. Two months later, it fell to Leigh to put their mother into a nursing home following a crippling stroke. Now whenever Julie needed help or bail, Leigh was called. Mr. Merrill gently reaffirmed his support.

Then he asked Leigh if there were some problem he should be aware of between her and Jonquil Bloom.

"She doesn't belong here. Have you seen the complaints?"

Leigh had a friend (spy) in the Customer Service department who copied her on any correspondence related to gift counseling. True, the few complaints were primarily about the difficulty in getting an appointment, yet a couple of negative comments had also surfaced. Leigh especially treasured one from Dan somebody which summed up Jonquil's skills in one word: shallow.

Mr. Merrill raised his hands in a placating manner and asked her to calm down. The month was half over and so was Jonquil's experiment at Clyde's.

A mollified Leigh returned to her office. She was starting to relax when the ridiculous Poppi Blair Show rumor began racing through the executive offices like a shoplifter on rollerblades.

Twenty minutes later, she found herself back in Mr. Merrill's office, this time with the rest of the executive staff and Jonquil to hear the formal announcement. For the second time in two weeks, everyone's attention was focused on this other woman, this fraud everyone considered to be so enlightened, this nobody. Leigh's resentment grew to nearly choking proportions.

There sat Jonquil, her hair a bog, her clothes the same off-the-rack suit of a week ago. The mere sight of her reminded Leigh that she had a meeting with a social

176

worker that evening at her sister's detox unit. She tossed her head with annoyance.

Mr. Merrill and the rest seemed oblivious to Jonquil's lack of style, so busy were they congratulating each other over the unexpected media coup. Stunned by the topsy-turvy turn of events, Leigh observed the proceedings in silence. She dared not comment so soon after her tete-a-tete with Mr. Merrill. Yet, how this intruder, this faker, this *meddler* could be permitted to appear on a moronic daytime talk show and put her precious Clyde's at risk galled her.

Two things were now clear to her: the "Doc" must be shown up for the phony that she was, either on or before the Poppi Blair Show. As for Mr. Merrill and his apparently revived enthusiasm for running the store, well! One huge television fiasco engineered by Leigh Usher would bring down both Jonquil and her champion, Mr. Merrill, simultaneously. Then the others would know once and for all that Clyde's future rested in her hands, hers alone.

CHAPTER NINETEEN

Wednesday, December 17th

Billy was unaware that his mother was meeting with the Poppi Blair Show's advance crew to prepare for her television appearance next week. While they tested her voice and on-camera look and role played through her opening remarks, the half hour before his lunch period slowly ticked by.

To pass the time, Billy sat at his desk in St. Monica Elementary School, daydreaming about next season's baseball opener. He played left outfielder on his little league team and though he was only a fair batter, he led them in stolen bases. He'd broken his right arm at the end of last season while stealing third base, yet managed to make the tying run before his injury was discovered. After two months in a cast, his arm was completely healed. It ached a little only when it rained. It was raining now.

To cheer himself up and take his mind off the pain, he embellished his fantasy with bright sunshine and friendly clouds that shielded him from the sun's glare. With no outs, the bases loaded, and the biggest kid in the league facing him down, Billy decided to turn his first at bat since the injury into a score. Stepping back, he adjusted his helmet and fought off the urge to glance at his mom seated in the stands to his right. He clenched the bat, wiggled a few times like the Dodgers did, and prayed not to blink. The intimidating pitcher wound up and threw a fast ball. Billy swung hard and smacked air.

Strike one.

Easy now, he imagined Claude telling him. This was turning into one of his better daydreams, he conceded to himself. Before his injury, he would have daydreamed nailing that first pitch and sending it soaring until it landed a block away. He wouldn't have accepted anything less than instant gratification. Now he was finding that a few juicy details, such as having Claude cheering him on, made his fantasy more credible.

"Cla-ass?" intoned his nearsighted teacher, Mrs. Thompson. He ignored her.

"Psst." The student behind him, Leonard Spaulding, slipped him a folded scrap of paper. Leonard was always getting into trouble—the kind that got other kids into trouble, too. He often came to school with no lunch money and stole or bullied kids into giving him theirs. Warily, Billy opened the note, jerked back at the contents, turned the paper over and with enormous relief passed it to the boy who sat in front of him before rocketing back to the safety of his daydream.

In the interval, two balls had stretched out the count. Runners at first and third were edging off base while the guy at second was asleep at his post. A booming voice coming from directly over the scoreboard was inexplicably telling the crowd to put away their computer books and fold their hands at attention for a very important discussion.

Strike two.

He never saw it coming! Now who was snoozing?

The pitcher signaled time out. Billy nodded with comprehension. The pitcher was trying to throw him off his game. Fat chance. The bat felt heavier as he made a few practice swings. Had it started to rain in his daydream? Was that why the umps, the managers, the catcher and pitcher were huddled on the mound?

No. It was Mrs. Thompson's voice again coming from over the scoreboard that had made the pitcher in his daydream call time out.

Billy was ready then, when the folded paper sailed over the right shoulder of the boy in front of him like a fly ball. He fielded it nicely, while Mrs. Thompson's back was turned, spiked it to Leonard and then got back to the game.

"Billy Bloom!"

Everyone on the field froze.

"This is not a laughing matter. Pay attention now."

Billy sat up straighter in his seat, the picture of compliance. Safely hidden behind his innocent demeanor, the game resumed. Yet, in the split second while he was unavoidably distracted, a wild pitch had led to a double play and left only the kid at second on base.

"Now, I don't want to make judgments," qualified the voice from above the outfield. "It's possible she misplaced it. Of course, it was careless of her to leave it out in the open ..."

Billy filtered out the annoying voice and shook out his tension from head to toe, followed by a few neck rolls, before assuming the batter's stance once again. This was it. He fingered his bat, bent his knees and swung, making contact, when that interfering voice called him back to the present.

"Billy Bloom, on your feet!" He scrambled out of his chair.

Mrs. Thompson sighed. "You haven't been listening, have you? We are discussing the very serious fact that someone stole a twenty dollar bill off the principal's desk this morning during recess. What have you to say about that? Stand up straight. No slouching." Mrs. Thompson folded her arms and waited.

Billy made sure he blocked Leonard's face from his teacher's view. He balanced on one foot and then the other while recalling the words he had read in the note. His mother had told him that snitching was bad form unless something dire like blood or drugs were involved. Instead, he concentrated on the last image of his daydream—the ball soaring over the infield, over the outfield, over the stands and out of sight.

"Um, uh, well ..." he said and wrinkled his brow. "Maybe whoever did it needed it more?"

She squinted at the rain, unsure of how to continue. Boys his age were quirky, crying over some nonsense one minute, the next minute surprising you with a complex moral inquiry. Whether he was protecting someone or voicing a genuine compassion she couldn't say, so she reminded the class that stealing was wrong and left it at that.

* * *

Jonquil felt a wave of relief an hour later when the television people finally left. They had pummeled her with so many questions during their visit that her mind demanded a rest. She now sat at her desk between afternoon appointments, carefully wrapping a Christmas present for her grandmother in Ireland while enjoying a quiet respite. Rita was doing an errand when the phone rang so Jonquil picked up the receiver.

"Jonquil Bloom," she said.

"Jonny? It's Claude."

"Oh, hi." Her professional tone instantly became a giddy purr.

"Do you have a minute to chat?" he asked. She heard his chair squeak indicating that he was calling her from the jobsite.

"Sure do." She turned away from her desk in order to give Claude her full attention. She hoped he wasn't calling to cancel their date. That would absolutely crush her.

"I just wanted to hear your voice," he said. "In my business, I have to listen to guys shoot their mouths off all day long and by this time in the afternoon, I need a break."

"You could always dial zero and talk to an operator," she said sweetly.

"That never occurred to me. But they tend to be impersonal, all business. 'What number, please?' I need to hear someone softer."

Relief bubbled up inside of her like a fountain. The man wasn't cancelling, he was flirting!

"Look," he said, "I do have a serious question. Are you allergic to any foods?"

She laughed. "Should I be?"

"No, seriously. I'm planning our menu for Saturday and I want to make sure you have a good time. It wouldn't do if I served you the very thing that makes you break out in purple spots."

"Lima beans," she replied.

"Really?" He sounded surprised. "What happens if you eat lima beans?"

"You'll never know, I promise you."

"That bad?" He paused and exhaled heavily. "Well, then, guess I'll have to scratch the soufflé I'd planned, and the salad, the rolls, the pie and the sherbet, and of course the flavored coffee and start all over."

"Funny!" she said and burst out laughing like she was being tickled. It felt as good as a full body massage to laugh so effortlessly. "What about you, Mr. Chappel, are you allergic to any foods?"

"Nothing that I know of except bad cooking. We Frenchmen, we like our food done well."

"I'll remember that," she said.

Silence followed, a warm, tuned-into-each-other kind of silence. She thought of many things she wanted to tell him that minute; big things like that her car had stalled that morning and little things like that she needed to finish wrapping the Christmas present for Margo Bloom and get to the post office before it closed. They weren't yet sharing freely about their day or their lives but she was already looking forward to the time when they would be.

"Excuse me a minute, can you hold on a sec?"

"Yes, of course." She sat back and heard him speaking to someone nearby who sounded like a woman.

A woman? What was a woman doing there?

He laughed and said good bye to his visitor and then resumed their conversation. "Sorry about that. My sister, Katie, dropped by to invite me over for dinner tonight. I think she suspects I'm seeing someone and wants to drag it out of me.

"Where were we? Oh, right, allergies. So, do you have any others, I mean, besides lima beans?"

"That's a strange question, Claude. You mean, like heights?" This time she couldn't discern what the silence between them meant. "Why do you ask?"

"Eh, just making sure I get things right. It's a picnic and on a picnic there could be bees or wasps in the area or stray … squirrels. Are you allergic to any of those?"

"No." She had the feeling he wasn't being straightforward with her but she couldn't be sure.

"Good, then we're all set. I'll see you Saturday night at seven thirty. Take care."

"Bye, now," she replied and disconnected.

Rita appeared in the doorway.

"Hi, you're back. Claude called me," said Jonquil.

"Ooo, nice," Rita replied. "Can't wait to see you, huh? Mid-week phone call just to say hi? I'd say this is getting hot-hot-hot, sugar."

"Oh, no, he wanted to know if I'm allergic to anything food-wise, and then he asked me about bees."

"Bees? As in the birds and the bees?" Rita asked and giggled. "My, my, he's a fast worker."

"No, silly, not like that. Bees as in allergies. We're going on a picnic, remember?" asked Jonquil with a chuckle.

Rita frowned. "Humph," she said. "Well, are you?"

"I don't know because I've never been stung. But doesn't it strike you as odd? Like, too cautious? I mean, does Al ask you about food allergies before he takes you out?"

"Well, no. But Al and I have known each other for years. You and Claude just met. I think it's real sweet of him to be so caring. Besides, and I mean this for your own good: you analyze too darn much. Why not simply enjoy his attentions? Don't make a big problem out of this. He seems like a good man. Get to know him better. Have fun. Live a little." Jonquil appreciated the friendly concern implicit in Rita's observation.

"Thanks, Rita. My curiosity goes into overdrive and gets in the way now and then."

"My advice is, stop being a psychologist when Claude's on the phone."

"Will do!"

The afternoon passed with appointments and walk-ins and Jonquil worked steadily until it was time to leave. She chose to follow Rita's advice and consider Claude's phone call nothing more than his clever excuse to hear her voice again. She found herself humming a love song and daydreaming about Saturday.

That night Billy and Jonquil went to a neighbor's tree trimming party. Jonquil made no mention of the meeting with the TV people nor did Billy bring up the incident in Mrs. Thompson's class. These things that they kept from each other were unrelated but the withholding behavior was similar, for it was drawing them inextricably toward a secret that wouldn't keep.

CHAPTER TWENTY

Thursday, December 18th

J onquil spread out her stash of 3 x 5 cards accumulated so far that week on her desk. Daily she was confronted with quirky situations and often thankful that no one could read her mind. She was surprised by the many issues about giving and receiving that came up in the sessions. She was no longer testing her theory about hidden agendas, aka, the strings attached to gifts. Instead, she was counseling and offering reassurance. Her psychological training gave her insights along the way.

Her goal to provide a definitive recommendation by the completion of each session wasn't always successful. Occasionally, people came to discuss gifts far afield of Clyde's merchandise. A querulous couple sprang to mind: "You don't love our son or else you'd give him what he wants!" hissed the wife. Her husband shot back: "A car? When he can't even get passing grades? Are you out of your mind?" It had been nearly impossible to keep them on point during the twenty minute session and they left still quarreling. They didn't need gift counseling, they needed a referee!

There were bound to be misses along the way, hopefully few. She shrugged her shoulders, fingered a card, and read the note she had written down verbatim:

"Tell me how to make my husband give me a fur coat for our anniversary. He has the money. He's just a born cheapskate."

She cringed, recalling the venom in that woman's voice. Was it her job to coach people on how to get the things they wanted from other people? It sounded devious and not her style. She advised the client to be honest with her husband, tell him what she wanted, and if that didn't work, to open her own savings account.

Each card brought back a sharp memory, and she became engrossed in replaying the sessions in her mind.

"My problem is my new boyfriend. He doesn't believe in celebrating holidays. He says a surprise when I least expect one is more sincere than a gift on Christmas Day when everyone gives them.

What am I supposed to do? Do I get him something or not?"

Jonquil, based on a similar experience in high school, was tempted to warn the client not to get her hopes up for Valentine's Day! Since the relationship was new, she recommended that the client be true to herself, give gifts when she wanted to, and wait to see how often and what sort of gifts the new boyfriend surprised her with. Perhaps they would be very romantic. The client left with a smile on her face.

What was a gift counselor? She wasn't sure. The job was teaching her session by session. For now, she began an "issues" pile and read on:

"My grandchildren never write me thank you notes. Why should I bother giving them Hanukkah presents this year? I taught their parents better manners than that. What's the world coming to?"

As a parent, she sympathized. Thank you notes were becoming passé; whether due to modern technology or changing norms, she couldn't say. Jonquil sensed that the client's real issue had more to do with feelings than manners. She reassured the woman that, regardless of whether or not they expressed their appreciation, her grandchildren loved her. The woman listened closely, relaxed and then went on to discuss generous gift ideas for each of them. She read on:

"My son's teacher has given him two bad report cards this semester. Do I have to buy her something for Christmas?"

Jonquil suppressed the impulse to ask the client what her son was getting for Christmas, like, maybe a tutor? The client's question sounded sincere and deserved a thoughtful answer. Jonquil suggested the client take the high road and buy the teacher a nice gift. The client nodded as though she already knew the answer. They spent the remainder of the session exchanging mother-to-mother gift ideas for school teachers. She read on:

"I dread opening presents! Why must it always be done in front of a crowd? It's so public! Ew! Even when it's a private occasion, somebody has to be thanked. Oh, I hate getting presents. Am I crazy?"

Jonquil recalled times in her own life feeling awkward about receiving a lame gift. An inspiration came to her. She suggested that while opening a present, the teenage client could concentrate on the giver and the relationship rather than the gift. In this way, it would become possible to smile and simply say thank you. The client agreed to give it a try. She read on:

"I lost my job last April. Been out of work ever since. I can't face the family this year. I got no money. The pressure is killing me—buy, send, give. You can't get away from it. It's depressing and I'm already depressed."

She wanted to hug the thirtyish-year-old man but instead suggested he become the extra pair of hands through the holidays at home and at gatherings. Being useful would be his generous gift this Christmas. He actually appeared more lighthearted when he left her office. She read on:

"A close neighbor of mine's in a bad way. Her husband lost his job over a year ago and now she's been diagnosed with cancer. I want to help. They have young children. My husband and I can do much more than a casserole, but we can hardly hand her a check. Too awkward, you see. Can you help me?"

Jonquil was instantly swept back to the dark days that followed her husband Gerry's untimely death in a house fire. A caring neighbor took her in while she waited for the funeral. One day a thick envelope showed up addressed to her. Inside were ten crisp 100 dollar bills. No note, no clue as to who had gifted her with much needed funds and no embarrassment accepting them.

She shared her story about the anonymous gift with the client. But Jonquil could only wonder to herself, *there* are *gifts with no strings attached. How did I forget?*

She came across one of the easier sessions and read:

"I saw you on television and had to check you out. What's a good twenty dollar Christmas gift for my mail carrier?"

Jonquil had smiled and said: "The money will be most appreciated. Find a nice card to put it in. That way you will have spent time on the gift." The woman promptly headed out the door to Stationary and for once Jonquil knew the store would benefit from gift counseling. She read on:

"I got promoted to exec secretary about a month ago. Everything's fine except the boss has me doing his shopping for him. He's got me picking out his wife's birthday present. Is that right?"

Jonquil knew what she would do in that instance: tell the boss to stuff it! But of course she was much more sensitive about gift-giving than most people. She and the client talked about turning the chore into a game. Could the secretary get to know the wife better each time she called the office? Could she recommend smart gifts that scored points for her boss? The client laughed good naturedly and made a joke about job security. She read on:

"My friends made me come on a dare. You're a social worker or a shrink, right? Anyway, I'm eighteen so you can't turn me in. I ran away from home three years ago. Been living in Hollywood, modeling and stuff. Lately, I've been having dreams about my mom. She goes a little nuts at Christmas with shopping and baking and decorating the house. Only, I think since I been gone, maybe she ain't the same. Sometimes I think I hear her calling my name all the way from Scranton. I got some money saved up. What's a

gift I can send her that will let her know that I
been thinking of her, too?"

With that girl she'd been blunt: "Go back to Scranton
or at least call home. That is the *only* thing your mother
wants this Christmas." Feeling good about that session,
she read on:

"My buddy and I were closer than brothers.
Two years ago he was diagnosed with ALS. I
assume you know what that is. He's not the man
he once was. He's wasting away in a lousy
wheelchair. I hate to visit him empty-handed. It's
so hard to talk to him now. I need something—
anything—to distract me when I go see him."

Frequently, clients would stumble on their own
solution to their problem, as in this case, when the man
realized he could bring a book or newspaper and read to
his friend. It excited Jonquil how people could puzzle out
solutions with someone there to guide them.

Maybe that's what a gift counselor was: a guide. She
read on:

"My friend and I exchange gifts every year.
Yesterday, she gave me what appeared to be a

perfectly lovely neck scarf—wool—in my favorite color—taupe. Today, when I put it on I noticed it had a Pick 'n Save label. Not even a Walmart label let alone one of Clyde's. I was horrified. It would have been better not to give me anything than to insult me. Have you ever heard of a gift ending a friendship?"

She'd resisted the urge to throw the client out of her office. Oddly, while the tit for tat questions demonstrated her theory, dealing with them left Jonquil dissatisfied on some deeper level. She'd have to learn to tolerate them better since they came up often.

Reciprocity formed the basis of gift exchanges in many cultures. Did it apply to old and valued friendships too?

Jonquil sat back and studied the woman, remarking how the wool neck scarf brought out the color in her cheeks. The client looked pleased. Jonquil went on to say how well her friend knew her, that she had spotted such a flattering scarf and hadn't ignored it on account of where she'd found it! The client's eyes flashed with comprehension and she left the suite in a better frame of mind.

She made a note and read on:

"My boyfriend and I do not give each other good gifts. I can't explain it. We're crazy about each other but we seem to be incompatible gift givers. Does that mean we don't belong together?"

People came from different backgrounds with different learned patterns of giving. Jonquil had suggested that the young woman pay attention to her boyfriend's interests and hobbies as she got to know him better and consider a gift certificate for now.

Was Claude Chappel a good gift-giver? She guessed he was, based on the lengths he'd taken to quiet his workmen's tools that one morning. What fun it would be choosing a gift for him if things between them progressed. She let a minute float by in tingly anticipation of their approaching date.

Her glance fell on the last card.

"If I don't get a ring this Christmas I'll kill myself."

Fortunately, the twenty-something young woman had been accompanied by her unperturbed mother who suggested they go shopping. Daughter gave a cagey smile and they soon left.

How many other people were truly desperate for a particular gift and how should she address their expectations in the future? Moodily, she thought of Billy and his steadfast desire for a dog.

She pulled the cards together, slid them into her desk top drawer and sighed. She felt quite alone in a way she hadn't at Children's Home. There, she'd had other people to talk with over challenging treatment situations: the staff, the administrators, the other clinicians. Here, she was completely on her own.

Rita stuck her face in the door. "How's it going, sugar?" Jonquil felt instant gratitude that she had this one agreeable friend in her corner.

"Come in, Rita. I was just reviewing my sessions. I'm curious. How do most people look when they leave here?"

Rita stepped inside and answered without hesitation. "They look to me like they're raring to go shopping."

"Really? The strange thing is, I stopped asking clients what they want a gift to do. That's my theory but mostly I'm going with my instincts. Is that good research? Oh, I don't know anymore." She lowered her forehead onto her balled fists. "I'm missing something. I need to talk to my faculty advisor."

"You're doing fine. Your problem is you think too much. Oh, you have a visitor." Rita left and in walked

Mary Acuna, a graduate school classmate and Native woman who'd shown keen interest in Jonquil's dissertation topic. She wore a denim shirt, jeans and boots. Her dark eyes gleamed above her high cheeks and her glossy black hair seemed to bounce as she moved.

Jonquil pushed out of her chair and hastened over to welcome her.

"I have something for you," said Mary. She presented Jonquil with a large blue feathered dream catcher.

"Oh, Mary, how lovely!" Jonquil held it high and admired the beadwork.

Mary said proudly, "My people invented gift-giving. The dream catcher will bring you good luck, Jonquil."

"I need it! Oh, thank you. It's perfect."

They displayed the dream catcher prominently in the window opposite Jonquil's desk. Then, Jonquil walked Mary to the door and began the afternoon, spirits high.

CHAPTER TWENTY-ONE

Friday, December 19th

J onquil had resorted to crock-pot dinners dressed up with one of her inspired garden salads which sufficed for weeknight dinners. Come Friday, she let Billy choose the menu. That night, though, Billy had been invited to a Christmas party and sleepover hosted by a friend.

Not until she was dropping him off at the party in the highlands above Sunset Boulevard did it sink in that Billy was not going to be home that night.

"Have fun!" she called.

He blew her kisses until someone opened the door. She decided to take the long way home and check out the Christmas decorations along the way.

But though the angels on Santa Monica Boulevard in West Hollywood gleamed and glistened, she found the house decorations in Beverly Hills and West L.A. forced at best. They never matched the snow-covered neighborhoods of her youth.

When she got home, she noticed the large box that must have arrived earlier that day. Gingerly, she placed one hand on it. Gerry's parents as usual had sent their gifts in time for Christmas Day. "I need a shower and a drink," she announced to the furniture. Receiving no objection, she began peeling off her clothes in haphazard fashion and savored the kind of shower only a single mom with a night to herself can enjoy. But long before she slipped on her robe, the memories encamped and enfolded her.

Gerald Will O'Keefe was a grad student when they met. Facing him that first afternoon, she felt both weak and hopeful. Weak because no one else had ever looked into her eyes that way. Hopeful because she never dared believe anyone would. After she agreed to go with him, he took her hand—grabbed it—like it was his already (it was) and off they went. A perfect stranger. Holding her hand. As they took shortcuts across campus, cantering, she had the sensation that her past was disappearing on the grass behind them. Now there was only Gerry and whatever lay ahead.

His shoulder-length, light brown hair and bedroom eyes were a far cry from the clean-cut young men she tended to date. He wasn't much taller than Jonquil yet he was wiry from years of running and rugged from constant interface with the outdoors. He was passionate about Nature and he loved nothing better than to test himself against the elements by camping, rock climbing, competing in marathons, chopping wood, snow skiing. Like the outdoors, he had a wild streak which both scared and attracted her. He could sit for hours in the library writing and researching for his coursework in environmental ethics. Then he'd jump on his motorcycle and lose himself in Washington's heart-stopping beauty which encroached on the campus and beckoned him in every direction.

He once persuaded her to ride with him. The speed petrified her. She couldn't swallow because of the wind and her eyes kept tearing, blinding her. They traveled two breathless miles until she begged him to stop. He did, his disappointment evident, but it did not derail their nascent relationship.

Three dates later, she discovered he was a great kisser. On her part, it was a momentous event. She did not recall a high school date when she ever wanted more than a goodnight kiss. Her college experiences had followed suit. That all ended on the night she and Gerry took in their first movie together, a late snack, and a long arm-in-arm stroll back to her dorm. It was chilly and clear. Other couples stood around them locked in embraces. Jonquil felt self-conscious until he pulled her into his arms. Their kiss unleashed her first stirrings of womanly love. She held onto him tightly and wanted a second and third kiss. Dimly, she was glad she had a roommate with whom she could share the news: she was in love!

Later that night he called from the off-campus house he shared with his dog, Baron, and three other grad students. They talked for hours while her obliging roommate sacked out in the dorm lounge.

How quickly she fell in love! She loved his otherness, his dark eyes, the smell of his skin. The stronger their attraction to each other grew, the more she sensed that a gaping hole in her life created by the loss of her parents was being filled and repaved.

He called her "Bloomie" and she called him "Keefer" when they were alone. Their friends thought they made a darling couple. That first year of getting to know each other flew by. They were separated that summer when Gerry lived on the Makah Indian reservation at Neah Bay to do independent study. However, they stayed in close touch.

The following autumn, Gerry met Margo Bloom over Thanksgiving break and charmed her with his Irish ancestry which dated back to the 1600s. During Christmas break, Jonquil then flew to Philadelphia and met his family.

Until that meeting, nothing about him had indicated that he came from wealth. She found herself in a condo on the Main Line unsure of what to wear to dinner. Her anxiety disappeared as soon as they sat down for roast beef and potatoes. Jonquil's eyes panned the friendly half-dozen faces around the table and got goose bumps. *So this is how it feels when the family circle is complete,* she thought.

The possibility of marriage first arose on their flight back to school after that visit. Up until that point, Jonquil had expected to graduate in June with a degree in education and no definite career goal. Now she realized that her purpose in life was to create a new family circle with Gerry.

True, his flirtation with danger was as much a part of him as the sound of his voice. He called her need for attention and reassurance proof that she was spoiled. Sure, they had their differences but their quarrels were few, their desire to make up mutual. They'd both been raised Catholics. They both wanted children. What else mattered?

The night he proposed, he presented her with an exquisite two-carat diamond. It didn't dawn on her to ask him how he had paid for it, so he had to explain to her that his wild days were over because he had sold his bike to purchase the ring.

That happened more than thirteen years ago, yet it was as clear as yesterday in her heart. She had loved him, loved him body and soul. She had trusted him with her body and soul.

Sitting in the rocker, similar to the one he'd given her soon after they bought their home, allowing only the tree lights to brighten the room, Jonquil sipped a glass of wine and let soft tears roll down her cheeks. The phone rang.

She wiped her eyes and walked out to the kitchen. One of these days she would invest in a mobile phone.

"Hi, Mom," Billy said and giggled. The noise of the party filled the background.

"Oh, Billy, are you having fun, honey?"

"It's a blast. Just called you to say good night. Well, gotta go."

She replaced the receiver and wished for the millionth time that Gerry would step from out of the shadows, take her into his arms and sway her back and forth while they celebrated the treasure of having such a dear son. Then they would waltz a little and then they would make love while the winter night advanced.

On so many occasions when Billy made her proud, she wished Gerry was there to share them with her, and the feeling grew stronger when she was worried about Billy. But the ordinary days were the hardest, when the simple longing to be together as a family still haunted her.

205

Would she ever let go of her anger toward Gerry? Would her old dream of creating a family circle ever get a second chance?

A surprising thrill of excitement coursed through her veins. Tomorrow night would be her first date with Claude Chappel.

"Oh, God," she whispered. "Please, God, help me let go."

She bowed her head and slowly plodded back to her bedroom, deciding to leave the tree lights on for once.

CHAPTER TWENTY-TWO

Saturday, December 20th

The doorbell rang. Billy heard it first and ended his conversation with Ramon with an abrupt, "Well, bye!" Next, he tore over to the front entrance and beat out Rita who was only a step behind him. Swinging open the door, he saw Claude shaking out a large black umbrella.

"You must be Claude," trilled Rita while Billy unlatched the screen door.

"Claude! Claude!" cried Billy, reaching up for a hug.

"Hey there, Billy Bloom," said Claude as he stepped inside. "Who's your girlfriend?"

"Eh, this is Rita. She's not my girlfriend, she's the sitter."

"Glad to meet you, Rita. I'm Claude Chappel." They shook hands while she sized him up on the spot. Solid grip, natural tan, virile, tantalizing build, comfortable around kids, easy on the cologne, yet dripping with confidence. His dark suit and tie—not exactly a given in Venice Beach, California—were enhanced by a scrubbed, groomed look. He'd considerately phoned that afternoon when the downpour began with a change of plans. To Rita's mind, the absence of flowers did not jive with his otherwise suave manner.

"Is Jonquil ready?" Claude inquired.

"Please take a seat and I'll tell her you're here," drawled Rita. She disappeared down the hall. Billy immediately took over the duties of host. "How come I can't go with you and Mom?" he pouted.

"Hey, partner, cut me some slack," said Claude as he grabbed Billy for a man-to-man tickle-tussle. "Remember what we talked about yesterday? Now, how can I work on your mom with you hanging around?"

"Oh, yeah, I almost forgot," Billy conceded between peals of laughter. Stepping back from his tormentor's reach, he gasped and his eyes opened wide. Down the hall, not yet in Claude's view, approached his mom with Rita. Billy had never seen Jonquil look this way. Her usually unruly hair now sat piled high on her head in a soft chignon. Long, wispy curls dangled on either side of her face and down her neck. Her low-cut black dress made a swishy sound each time she moved. She wore eye makeup and shiny red nail polish. Even her sling-back pumps sparkled. To top things off, she smelled more heavenly than the Christmas tree in the main room.

Claude followed Billy's stare. "Hello," said Claude with delight.

"Hi," replied Jonquil with a demure nod.

"Mom, you look gorgeous!" declared Billy.

After a review of the bedtime hour and a squeeze from Rita, Jonquil gave Billy a quick hug and kiss. Then, she pulled a beautiful red and black embroidered shawl around her shoulders, picked up her purse, and ducked out the door with Claude underneath his umbrella.

"That was too easy," she breathed. "I expected Billy to throw a fit. He begged me to let him come along."

Claude chuckled and guided her over to his Jeep. He swung open the passenger door, located the flower he'd left on her seat, and presented it to her. "I never understood the point of sending flowers that sit at home and wilt by the time a date's over."

Pleased, Jonquil took the single long stemmed white rose, tied with a satin bow. "Thank you, kind sir." He helped her inside the vehicle. Moments later they were off.

"This rain sure put a crimp in my plans," he admitted to her. "But they've finally opened the restaurant at that new Hotel Carmel in Marina del Rey. I hear the cuisine is superb. Thought we might give it a try."

"Sounds perfect," agreed Jonquil. She held the flower up to her nose and tried not to guess how long it had been since someone else was in charge of the planning, driving and paying the bill. Afraid she might leave the lovely rose behind, she looped her purse strings securely around the stem and held them both in her lap.

Twenty minutes later Claude pulled into the hotel entrance behind two other cars. An arching carport shielded them from the downpour. As occupants of the vehicles ahead of them emerged in their tuxedoes and floor-length gowns, Jonquil pictured a Christmas ball in full swing inside or a wedding. *How thrilling hotels were,* she thought. On cue, a phalanx of red-vested valets descended upon the Jeep: one to help her out, one to take Claude's keys, and one to escort them inside.

The lobby gleamed with newness. Jonquil could scarcely take in the lavish décor or array of activity because Claude had her arm tucked under his which cancelled out all other sensations. The escort had left them in front of the restaurant's express elevator. Off to the left, a band was playing in one of the lounges. She began nodding her head to the rhythm. *Bossa Nova* always made her feel like dancing. He looked over at her and grinned.

The elevator doors slid open and a throng of people exited. She looked back in the direction of the music.

Claude leaned over and said, "Later." His comment rendered her mute with pleasure on the ride all the way up.

The Bird Cage restaurant was situated on top of the hotel and featured both indoor and enclosed outdoor dining. While Claude checked the reservation, Jonquil surveyed the room. The peach-colored walls were trimmed in gold and lime green. Twenty linen-covered tables dotted the spacious area. All seemed to be occupied by couples. A large beveled skylight held back the drumming rain and provided extra inches for the spectacular tree in the room's center. Adorned with exquisite lovebirds, it slowly revolved on a stand hidden from view with assorted gift boxes. Jonquil could hardly take her eyes away until Claude pointed down at her feet. Shellacked to the wood floor was a collage of newspapers. They chuckled to each other.

Claude requested a table on the deck and they were shown to a table overlooking the marina. In contrast to the restaurant, the deck was dark, lit only by heat lamps, table candles and miniature tree lights. Wreaths hung on the window shutters, half-closed to keep out the dampness. The scent of fresh pine, the flickering candles and the sound of lapping waves created a divine mood.

After Claude ordered a bottle of wine, she said, "Tell me about you."

He related that he was born in French Canada in a small town outside of Montreal. He was the oldest in a family of five. His father moved the family down to California for the weather when he was nine. His dad was a house painter and Claude worked summers for him. That's how he became interested in building things. In the past year, he'd made a dream come true by becoming a general contractor. He paused to refill her glass.

"That's it?" Jonquil asked and blinked. "But you've told me so little. What about your personal life? Were you ever married?"

"I came close once. We met in high school. We went steady for all four years. Eh, but then my father moved us back to Canada. By then my brother and I were both draft age. My folks were both heart set against the war. Actually, Caroline and I stayed in touch for quite a while."

Thin bread sticks, cheeses, and a frosted bowl of fresh-cut vegetables were placed between them.

"What became of her?"

"She went on to nursing school and eventually wound up in Vietnam. Such an ironic twist of fate!" He made a steeple of his fingers and lowered his head.

"Good God. You don't mean—"

"Exactly! The third time a certain helicopter pilot ended up in her triage unit, he proposed and she accepted.

I understand they have a house full of kids somewhere in Oregon."

"Oh, you. You set me up!" she protested with a coquettish smile. He grinned back at her mischievously. Their eyes held.

"And there was no one else?"

He sat back. "No time. Work became my mistress. I moved back down here ten years ago and it's taken everything to get my company started, including the odd paint job. But then they pay such fantastic dividends, for that is how I met you."

She liked that he didn't immediately ask her to tell him her life story. They chatted and joked and found things to tease each other about. He refilled her glass. It was, hands down, her favorite kind of date.

Over grilled swordfish he asked her about her work. She gave a carefully edited description of her dissertation, not wanting to monopolize the conversation. Yet, as he seemed to be truly listening, she went more deeply into the subject.

"It's absolutely mind-boggling. People give, take—withhold—or let go every waking moment of their lives. It's fundamental yet there's hardly any formal research on the subject. I've spent hours in the medical library and bookstores scouring psychoanalytic literature and I rarely find references to gifts, much less their meaning. It's a rather significant omission. Sociologists, anthropologists, historians, yes. Psychologists? No.

"Did you know that Ralph Waldo Emerson wrote a famous essay on gifts? Why, even the etiquette books have more to say about gift-giving than psychologists. The Internet isn't much help either. There's loads of gift advice but hardly any research. Claude, we're talking about a behavior or instinct as basic as eating. It sets the tone of our relationships, from one-on-ones all the way up to international, potentially, intergalactic arenas!" They both laughed.

"Maybe you should try some other books."

"Such as?"

"Aquinas, the New Testament, the Old Testament for that matter." At her startled glance he confessed to having spent a year in a seminary. "Forgive me, I only go off on this stuff with gift counselors."

"When were you in the seminary?" she asked, momentarily confused since he had not mentioned this chapter in his life earlier.

"Long, long ago, Jonquil," he assured her.

"What made you leave?" she persisted.

"I discovered I wanted to be a father not 'Father'," he replied and sketched quotation marks in the air. A vague premonition told her to change the subject. Behind them someone strummed a classical guitar.

"I wonder who chooses the sort of music for places like this."

"Beats me," he quipped.

"Guitars always make me think of troubadours. It's exactly the right sound for this setting, don't you agree?"

"I think," he said, placing his fingers over hers, "that Billy was close but no cigar tonight. You're not merely gorgeous, Jonny, you're shining." The contact with his hand sent shivers of radiating heat into every nook of her body. She wanted to be passionately kissed. *Later*, she smiled secretly to herself.

"You're not from here originally?" he asked as their dinner plates were removed and replaced with dessert and coffee.

"No," she replied and before she knew it she'd told him the essentials of her childhood and then about Margo. "My grandmother was the first person who believed in me. She used to hold me tight and whisper in my ear, 'Bloom, Jonquil, bloom!' Sounds corny but I loved hearing her say that so much that after my husband died, I reverted to my maiden name. I wanted Billy to bloom too, so I gave him my name. He never knew his father."

"How did your husband die?"

She adjusted the shawl around her shoulders and sat up taller while avoiding his eyes. "In a house fire. I never discuss it," she added, figuratively drawing the line.

He changed the subject.

"So ... then you moved down to L.A.?"

"Yes," she answered and shifted into a more relaxed position. "Billy's the native." She went on to describe Clyde's and the many possibilities her work there afforded her. "In fact, Wednesday I'm going to appear on the Poppi Blair Show. Ever hear of it?"

"Sure, that's the one my sister raves about. Television, huh? Pretty heady stuff." He motioned to the waiter to refill their cups. "What's your ultimate goal?"

"It keeps changing, Claude. I know now that I'm not cut out to be a therapist." She paused. "Wow, I haven't confided that to anyone, not even to myself, until now." Her straightforward intimacy heightened her coloring. Excitedly, she continued. "If the store keeps me on, I'll make a career of gift counseling. I've barely scratched the surface but I've never been this happy before in my work. I'll complete my research and maybe turn it into a book. I'll become the expert and give lectures and go the whole nine yards, hell, the whole 100! Then I'll have what I've always wanted: security for me and Billy." Her eyes sparkled and her cheeks flushed.

"Sounds like a very full full-time career." He paused provocatively, and jiggled his dark eyebrows. "Will there be time enough for us to fall in love?"

She took a sip of water and then patted her lips with

her napkin. His voice sounded sincere but he didn't look sincere. *Better pass it off as a joke*, she decided, beginning to feel uncomfortable.

"Fall in love? Come on, Claude. This is our first date. And if we don't leave soon we'll miss the dancing." She placed her napkin firmly on the table to indicate both an end to dinner and to this disconcerting shift in their conversation.

He leaned back in his chair. His body language conveyed to her that not only weren't they leaving yet, but dancing was the furthest thing from his mind. She sensed a sudden stiffness in the air. Their eyes met.

"This is about as real as a guy gets when he finally finds the woman and boy he wants to take care of for the rest of his life."

She swallowed. *Too fast, this is going way too fast. I need air*. Her eyes discreetly searched the far corners of the dim room for an exit sign.

He placed his hands lightly on the table. "Jonquil, please hear me out. I'm forty-three years old. I know what I want. I fell for you the minute I laid eyes on you. I love Billy because he is your son."

Where was this coming from? she wondered suspiciously. Besides, proposals on a first date, if this blundering attempt—"fell for you"—was leading up to one, seemed more apropos of the fairytale romances spun by the Magic Kingdom down in Anaheim.

It struck her that Claude had a habit of being impulsive. Hadn't he jumped the gun by starting work too early on his construction site that first morning? Now, he was doing it again.

"What's your hurry?" she smiled. "You risk ruining a perfectly fabulous evening. Let's take time to get to know each other, all right?" Either she had forgotten how to flirt or else he had brought an agenda on the date that had less to do with romancing her and more to do with a commitment elsewhere. But where, what? In the silence that followed, the tricky connection became clear to her. Sighing with disappointment, she put her cards on the table.

"This is about Billy, right? Billy doesn't have a dad and you are willing, ready and able to step up to the job." She saluted him smartly, unaware that emotional withdrawal, a nearly dissociative state, was creeping over her again for the first time in years. A blunting defense and sure sign that he was coming on too strong, the only evidence of her distress was the wary look on her face.

"It had crossed my mind," he replied like the arrogant teacher who prods his student to think harder. "Jonny, you say you want Billy to bloom. I believe you—"

"Good!" she cut in. "Oh, there's our waiter. Please, let's go."

She made a supreme effort to keep her voice low and placed a hand on her purse.

"But what Billy doesn't need is another stuffed animal." The words, stated flatly, were out of his mouth before he could take them back.

Jonquil slumped back in her chair as though he had slugged her. Briefly they regarded each other across a taut silence. He was a stranger now who could hurt her. He had already hurt her. She wouldn't give him the opportunity to do it again.

"Jonquil, I'm sorry. What I meant to say was—"

"I'll take a cab home," she said softly as she stood up. "Look, you seem like a nice guy and up until now I've had a good time but you haven't the vaguest notion what you're getting into. Lose a spouse sometime, buddy, lose your home, your family, all your dreams and all your happiness in one black night because of a spoiled dog. Then come tell me how to raise my son."

Her eyes filled with tears so that she couldn't see that the shawl was snagged between her chair and the wall. As she tugged and pulled, it ripped. "Margo's wedding gift!" she whimpered, sagging against the wall. He stood up, which made her stiffen.

"Don't," she said with a vehemence that made people in the vicinity look up. Without another word, she grabbed her purse and shawl and ran out of the restaurant.

* * *

Rita could not believe her eyes. She'd just put Billy to bed and was reaching for her knitting needles when she saw Jonquil charging up the walk from the street. Alone. And by the looks of it, she had chosen to be alone. It wasn't quite 10:30.

Rita ran and opened the door. "Rita," Jonquil cried. "Oh, Rita." She collapsed in Rita's arms and sobbed as though her world had come apart.

"There, there," soothed Rita. "I'm here, sugar. I'm right here. Cry it out, baby, let it go." It wasn't long before they heard Billy tearing down the hall barefoot.

"Mom! Mom! What happened? Why are you crying?" Billy wrapped his arms around both women, trembling.

Jonquil extricated herself from Rita's arms and addressed her son in a shaky voice. "Billy, you are not to see Claude again."

"W-why, Mom?" Billy started blubbering too.

"Because, honey, he's not our friend." At Billy's challenging look she added, "I mean he's a busy man. He doesn't have time to get to really know us. And speaking of time, you should be in bed." Billy flinched but stayed put.

Rita had two upset people on her hands and she didn't know which one to comfort first. Plus, she'd either totally misjudged the charming fellow whom she had met earlier that evening or else this distraught woman, her friend and boss, who sounded quite out of her head.

"I'm s-scared, M-Mom."

Please God, prayed Jonquil. *I have shielded him for so long. Help me to do it a little longer.*

"Billy, come here." She felt back in control and the uncomfortable numb feeling she had experienced at the restaurant did not return. "Mommy's very upset but not with you. We're okay, Billy, we're okay. Come on, I'll tuck you in." They lumbered down the hall arm in arm.

Rita bent over and retrieved Jonquil's discarded purse and shawl. The lovely garment was torn at one end. "I'll kill him!" she spat. Then she spied the lone rose that had rolled into a corner. "Or her. Humph!"

CHAPTER TWENTY-THREE

Sunday, December 21st

T he celebrant of the eight o'clock morning liturgy at St. Monica's Church concluded the reading from St. Luke's gospel and indicated that the congregation should be seated.

"This morning's gospel," he began, "tells of a young girl who, besides being told she is going to give birth to the 'Son of the Most High', also learns that her kinswoman of advanced age is with child for the first time. The young girl's joy knows no bounds. She immediately travels to the hill country to visit her relative. When she reaches the house, she breaks into song. 'My soul magnifies the Lord and my spirit rejoices in God my Savior!'"

The priest left the pulpit and walked down the two sanctuary steps to stand in the main aisle.

"Christ said we must become like children if we want

to enter the Kingdom of heaven. I don't know about you but that observation, given to his followers when he had already reached manhood, has always baffled me.

"You and I have both heard numerous interpretations of it. Many are in the vein of: well, he didn't mean this! He didn't mean that! He didn't mean we should all be Peter Pans and never grow up or shirk responsibility or live off Mom and Dad indefinitely. He didn't mean that children are innocent little angels, every one of them. No, he did not."

Seated together in a tight back pew, Jonquil felt Billy squirm beside her and gave his shoulder a gentle nudge.

"So, what did he mean? Some years ago, I was ship's chaplain on a cruise to Alaska. Among the passengers were James A. Michener and his wife, Mari. Michener was in his eighties by then, the recent recipient of a newly installed hip. Still hale and hearty, he spoke on occasion about his worldwide adventures.

"One day I found him looking through binoculars at whales crossing the bow. Michener could not contain his excitement. He pointed to them like a schoolboy, calling out to others in the vicinity: 'Did you see that one? Aren't they fabulous? Look at them go! Oh, this is fantastic!' Those around him, officers and seasoned cruisers, had seen the phenomenon many times before. Michener was viewing it through fresh eyes and his joy was contagious.

Everyone including the captain responded to his joy and took another look, this time with enthusiasm.

"You know, when our God told us to become like little children, he was only asking us to do what he himself had done."

The priest paused while a ripple of coughs from different parts of the church broke the silence and then he continued.

"Recently, one evening I stood in the back of a bus. Every seat was taken and many, like me, crowded the aisle. Glancing around, I noticed a baby girl in her mother's arms. The mother smiled and the baby smiled back. Then the mother propped the baby up on her shoulder so she was facing in my direction.

"Perhaps like me, the little one felt tired yet she was so new to life! She looked around and started making eyes at people, you know, 'batted her eyes' as they used to say. Do infants know they have this power?"

His question garnered a few hearty chuckles.

"She smiled at one commuter and then another. She kept it up until someone returned her smile and then the game was on. She became bolder. She went after the sleepy, the taciturn, and the hard boiled. When someone ignored her, she didn't give up. She batted her eyes at someone else.

"By the time I reached my stop, she had me smiling

and clearly, I haven't forgotten her joy.

"A child receives a smile. A child feels good. A child shares that feeling with others."

He turned toward the manger scene and the eyes of the congregation followed his gaze.

"Once more we come to the manger. Can you and I look at it with fresh eyes? Can we see a Baby Boy unaware that he is poor, unaware that he is being hunted by King Herod, and that one day he will die on a cross? Can we hear his baby gurgles? See him squirm in the swaddling clothes? Smell his fresh baby smell? And rejoice?

"For this is why God was born: to bring joy to the world. As someone has said, we are not made for mere happiness, we are made for joy. Joy spills over. There's no cup half empty, half full. It takes all of heaven to contain God's joy. Joy is the essence of Christmas. Joy to the world!

"How soon these days our children are robbed of their joy! They are born with it. It is their natural state. But there is so much darkness in the world waiting to snatch it away.

"How many of our older people, sick and alone, are bereft of joy? After a long life, only bitterness and anger remain."

He clasped and lowered his hands, reflected briefly,

and then looked up.

"Let me suggest something to you, my dear people. It is simply this: if you cannot receive, then you cannot give. Being able to graciously receive is the first step toward becoming a gracious giver, not the reverse.

"Today, in fact for all the days leading up to Christmas, I want you to practice receiving.

"Sounds strange coming from a priest, right? Maybe you think I expect you always to give with no expectation of receiving in turn. Not today. I can guess some of you came to Mass this morning and the furthest thing from your heart was joy."

A child wailed in the back of church setting off a wave of nodding heads and smiles.

"Fine, little one," he said with a grin. "I don't want you or anyone else to fake it. Nor does God. I want to help you rekindle your joy in time for Christmas.

"See if you can receive something or someone joyfully today. Soon we'll exchange the handshake of peace. Take a moment. Then look into your neighbor's face. Don't mumble some hurried words and rush onto the next person. Listen. Feel their grip or embrace or nod for you shy ones. Receive.

"Soon I will say the words of consecration and then you will be invited up to receive the Blessed Sacrament." He gestured toward the altar. "Clear your minds and hearts of distress. Make room for him. It is a miracle beyond all telling. Receive."

The crowded church had become hushed; all eyes were on the celebrant.

"Stop by the crèche on your way out of church and take it all in, the look on Mary's face, the crib, Joseph, the shepherds, the animals. When you leave church, receive the greetings of friends and neighbors. Feel the sunshine on your face."

He climbed the stairs toward the altar but stopped and turned back to the congregation, a twinkle in his eye.

"To those of you who may want to point out to me after Mass, 'Well, we can't all be James Michener and take a cruise,' here's my reply in advance. There's a breathtaking ocean practically in our backyard. You don't have to book a cruise to enjoy it.

"Slip down there today and receive its size and sights and sounds. Drink in the fresh breezes. Watch the sunset this evening, free. Try to see each color, every shading. Receive the ocean, the sky, the beach, the mountains. These are all gifts. Receive them, cherish them, thank God for them.

"When you are able to receive with joy, then and only then will you be able to give with joy.

"And then you will have a truly merry Christmas and a taste of heaven, too. May God bless you. In the name of the Father …"

CHAPTER TWENTY-FOUR

Sunday Afternoon

For the second time in as many hours, Rita relayed to Claude that Jonquil did not wish to take his phone call.

"How is she, Rita?" he asked.

"Busy," she retorted dismissively and then relented. "Kinda distracted-like. Maybe she's tired. I can't say for sure."

"Thanks anyway, Rita," he replied before he hung up.

Jonquil's door opened and she escorted an elderly man out to the hallway. On her way back to her office, she paused at Rita's desk. "Rita, I'm too pooped to pop," Jonquil said. "I have so much on my mind. And that poor gentleman—he lost his wife last month due to a heart attack and he doesn't know what to do with the Christmas gifts he got for her."

"What did you tell him?" Rita was all ears.

229

"Actually, I listened more than usual. I even cried a little with him. He told me about her, showed me her picture, told me why he purchased this and that. Rita, this work is harder than I expected." Rita nodded sympathetically.

"Claude called again."

"Oh." The perfunctory way Jonquil said it made Rita immediately change course.

"So, have you got all your shopping done? What's Santa giving Billy this year?"

"Oh, Billy outgrew Santa Claus a while back. I used that occasion to begin teaching him the habit of donating his discarded toys each year to the Salvation Army so he'd learn that Santa isn't one person but everyone who shares what they have with others. Now Billy gets his old toys and books packed up without me having to remind him. And this year, Billy's going to get a pile of loot, enough, I hope to make up for ..." Jonquil looked down in silence, then squared her shoulders and bestowed an encouraging smile on unsuspecting Rita.

"Rita, may I ask you something?"

"You bet."

"Would you say you were good at receiving gifts?"

"You mean giving, don't you?"

"Forget that." Jonquil continued to stare intently at Rita. "Try this one. What would you say was the best gift you ever received? Now I'm not talking about life or your kids or love. I'm talking about something you actually got in a box and opened. Something tangible."

"Well now, let me think." Rita gnawed her lower lip in concentration. "Ooo—is this for your research?"

"I don't know. Ever since I heard something at church this morning, I'm having more doubts about my theory." At that point, three little giggly damsels in distress entered the suite and one was clutching a piggybank.

"Your next appointment, Ms. Bloom. The misses Sara, Emma, and Ginger Zembrowski." Jonquil's mood brightened noticeably. "Ladies, shall we?" she said gaily as she led them into her office.

"Tap shoes," declared Rita hours later as they prepared to leave for the day. "The best gift I ever got was a pair of tap shoes my mama gave me after I got my legs back."

Intrigued, Jonquil plopped into a chair opposite Rita's desk and said, "Tell me."

Rita described how as a child she had taken dancing lessons from a member of her church in Lake City, Arkansas, who taught piano and dance. She began at age five, the youngest student in the class. "How I loved Miss Vance and those lessons," she remembered. "I had my heart set on becoming a tap dancer like Shirley Temple. Then, the summer I turned nine, I contracted polio." Jonquil gasped and sat forward. "I wore leg braces for a whole year, not knowing whether or not I would ever walk again let alone dance. My poor folks were more scared than I was."

"Oh, Rita," murmured Jonquil. Immediately, Billy flashed in her mind. Thank God he was safe and well! She could not imagine how she would cope if anything so serious happened to him and instantly barred the ghastly thought from her mind. Meanwhile, Rita continued with her story.

"I dreamed about dancing nearly every night and I think that's what got me through. I wasn't going to give it up. Finally, the ugly braces came off and Mama took me to the store to buy new shoes. Afterward, I remember she made me wait in the car while she ran an errand.

"The next day after supper she gave me one of the shoeboxes all done up with a fancy bow. The box was heavy. 'Open it, Ree,'" she said and I did. Inside was one of my new pairs of shoes, the patent leather ones. I didn't understand. 'Turn them over,' she said. That's when I discovered that she'd had the cobbler put taps on the bottoms of them. Well, I thought I'd passed over and woken up in Paradise.

"My legs were like two sticks. I couldn't try out the shoes for weeks. But I did every single thing necessary to make my legs strong again. Finally, I got to wear my shiny new tap shoes. And, oh, how I danced!" Rita's face lit up with joy. "Yeah, sugar, those tap shoes were the best surprise I ever got."

Jonquil quietly thanked Rita for telling the story. On the spur of the moment, she inquired about Rita's plans for Christmas Day. Rita explained that her two sons and their families were flying over from Hawaii on the twenty-sixth after they spent Christmas Day with their in-laws. Jonquil persisted until she admitted that Al had made reservations at a hotel in Malibu for their Christmas dinner. "Oh no, you don't. You're both having dinner with Billy and me. You two lovebirds do what you want later but come for dinner, please?" Rita promised to check with Al that night.

Driving home, Jonquil mulled over the day's events yet her mind kept skittering back to young Ree and her precious tap shoes. Her bliss. Her mother's courage in giving her those shoes. Her love.

Claude's words from the night before broke into her thoughts: "What he doesn't need is another stuffed animal!" She bristled all over again and was immediately confronted with a scene from her own childhood.

She saw herself on the night of her eighth birthday, sweeping the presents her mother carefully had arranged on the dining room sideboard to the floor. Filled with rage and heartache at her father for breaking his promise to be home that night to watch her blow out her candles, she'd then stomped the meaningless gifts to kingdom come. Her mother watched, speechlessly, while the tree lights flickered in the living room. It was a horrible memory for, as always, she wished her mother had been able to comfort her.

Gingerly, like someone stepping off a ladder onto an unseen surface, she let herself stay with the disappointment of that long ago night all the way home.

CHAPTER TWENTY-FIVE

Monday, December 22nd

By ten o'clock Monday morning the executive staff had assembled for their weekly meeting. Mr. Merrill, however, was nowhere in sight. It was not like him to be late. While the others huddled around the breakfront, sipping coffee and nibbling on Christmas cookies, Leigh Usher kept an eye on the conference room door. Sure enough, Miss Egnar poked her head inside on the lookout for Al Yates. Leigh went over to her.

"What's up?" she asked casually.

Miss Egnar spotted Al on the phone in the back of the room but Leigh didn't step aside to let her pass. Reluctantly, she informed the Head Buyer that Mr. Merrill had been unavoidably detained due to car trouble. He asked that the meeting proceed as scheduled.

"I'll handle it," said Leigh and grabbed the agenda

copies. Miss Egnar withdrew. Rapidly, Leigh skimmed down the list of agenda items. A discussion about the future of gift counseling was the last entry. A plan began to take shape in her mind. Though she had already figured out a way to discredit Jonquil, it never hurt to have some insurance. She invited the others to their seats and then slid into Mr. Merrill's chair at the head of the table.

"Guys, the boss has been delayed by car trouble. Poor man, he shouldn't still be driving."

Big Al jerked his head in her direction and grumbled, "Gimme a break. He's only five years older than I am."

"Oh, what I meant was, the president of Clyde's deserves a chauffeur, that's all." She chuckled and playfully poked his arm. As the others exchanged confused looks, she asked Al to pass out the agenda sheets.

Leigh examined her colleagues now seated around the conference table, weighing the pluses and minuses of each. Al, to her right, was her closest ally in the store aside from Mr. Merrill. They got along well by virtue of the fact that his ambitions did not cross hers. Someday before his retirement he hoped to make vice president, nothing more. Congenial, dependable, that was Big Al Yates. Flirting had always been a pleasurable aspect of their routine. He did it with the reflex of a salesman. Al's esteem for Mr. Merrill was his weakness. That and his obnoxious adherence to rules. Nevertheless, Leigh had learned through her network of spies that Al had adamantly protested the introduction of gift counseling from the start. So, once she became president, she intended to reward his loyalty with a promotion and then find someone more progressive to run operations.

Next to him, Inez Escanaba posed no threat. A bosomy Latino woman who favored vivid colored suits size 2x, she was immune to the store's politics. She had a husband, four boisterous sons, and a home in Hermosa Beach to go to each night. So what if the thousand dollar NuMode vases that a member of Leigh's staff had ordered in April sat untouched in neat rows all December long? It wasn't Inez's headache. Leigh prized her skill at dealing with the press and media. However, Inez should have never taken action on the call from Poppi Blair's people without first consulting the Head Buyer slash CEO and president in waiting. When Leigh took over the store, the high profile PR job would be turned over to someone less weight-challenged and less independent. Inez was expendable.

Cyril Saginaw, seated next to Inez, was a player both on and off the job. Soon after Leigh was hired, Sy began pursuing her from his close proximity in Brentwood. Despite his Brooks Brothers suits and the star-studded practice that augmented his retainer from Clyde's, Sy had one major drawback that Leigh could not tolerate. He drank too much, too often and far too complacently. Three dates spent watching him lose his sobriety was her absolute limit. Replacing him would be a top priority.

Then, there was Cornell Bramson III, at the opposite end of the table, whose nickname behind his back was "Corny." His ears stuck out, he was chinless and his scrawny neck sported an Adam's apple the size of West Covina. She had no dirt on the man save for his single unforgivable transgression: he'd hired Jonquil Bloom. Ten years ago he had hired Leigh, no doubt because of her correct credentials. Airhead, joke, he was mercifully near retirement. He'd be gone before Mr. Merrill.

Rich Ridgeland, to Bramson's right, was an unknown. He'd been with the store less than six months. Everyone seemed to be pleased with his work but Leigh had her reservations. For one thing, he hadn't tried to put the moves on her. Was he gay? Nor had he shown the slightest concern about having a resident shrink on the premises. He cared only about getting his media campaign launched. His advertisements had led Constance to the store. His efforts had helped rekindle Mr. Merrill's drive. His deft management had captured the unwanted attention of a popular daytime talk show host. Rich was history.

Finally, the Burney Brothers, on her left, represented

Mr. Merrill's sentimental side and glaring poor judgment. The story was well known to all of Clyde's employees. In 1985, the *Santa Monica Outlook* featured a front page story about the twins. Under the heading, "2 for 1: CPA Team for Hire," the facts unfolded.

Dependent on each other from birth, accountants by profession, one of them—did it matter which?—was laid off by the prestigious Toddle House Toy chain. On the following day, the other one quit. A reporter discovered them a year later, homeless panhandlers, earning a few bucks playing chess at the beach. At the time, Clyde's was in need of an accountant. Mr. Merrill took matters into his own hands. He contacted the newspaper, interviewed the BBs, recognized their fiscal astuteness camouflaged by their whimsical eccentricities, and put them on staff. Leigh couldn't fault their work. They had kept the bank from foreclosing more than once and their gratitude to Mr. Merrill knew no bounds. Still, with the changes she intended to make in the store, there was no way they would keep pace. She would do the kind thing and fire them both on the same day.

Leigh realized Mr. Merrill could arrive at any time. She decided to act boldly. She dinged her china coffee cup with a silver teaspoon. "Attention, please. I think we'll disperse with the minutes and the department reports this morning." The lighthearted banter around her subsided. "Instead, we'll discuss new ideas for the space currently occupied by the GC department." A confused murmur erupted. "What's the problem?" she bated them. "It shuts down on the twenty-fourth as scheduled."

The surprise was evident on everyone's face. "That's final? Who decided that?" asked Al.

"Why, Mr. Merrill of course. He told me himself last Monday that the experiment is half over and it will end in two weeks." She met their frowns with studied composure.

"Uh—was this before or after the Poppi Blair Show deal went through?" asked Inez with suspicion.

"After," lied Leigh. "Well, you can imagine his dilemma. The last thing he needs to worry about is some loose cannon representing Clyde's coast-to-coast on Christmas Eve."

"He seemed mighty pleased about it to me," said Sy as he tipped back his chair.

"Oh, Sy, wise up. We're spitting distance from Hollywood. Could we actually turn down that offer?"

"How do we explain the closing to our customers on such short notice?" wondered Inez aloud.

"Play it as a seasonal offering, Inez, like Santa Claus."

"It's been years since we had a Santa Claus at Clyde's." said BB1 peevishly. The others suppressed snickers.

"I wish Mr. Merrill were here to concur," snapped the Personnel Director, eyeing Al.

"Well, he's not. And it's a good thing. Listen to you! Do you think he could stomach this bickering?" Leigh asked.

"Revenues are up," said BB2.

"It's the holidays, Bernie," Leigh pointed out harshly. She startled the others by addressing him by his first name. "Have you ever known revenues to go down in December? Jonquil Bloom is a UCLA student. She was here merely to do some research. Mr. Merrill did her a favor by giving her a temporary job. You of all people should know what a soft touch the boss can be."

The BBs simultaneously dropped their bright red faces.

"No need to get nasty," said Al.

I mustn't antagonize Al, Leigh thought. "Right," she agreed. "Barney, Bernie, I apologize. Look, by now you all know that Clyde's future is all I care about. Let me ask Rich a question that's been bugging me since this quote unquote experiment began. How compatible is counseling with retail? I mean, counseling! The very word suggests sick people—therapy—yu-uck! Do we really want Clyde's perceived as some sort of outpatient clinic?"

"Leigh, I can't believe you said that. You're usually so avant-garde. You know as well as I do that retail has come a long way in the last few years. Stores today offer everything from babysitting to mammograms. So why not gift counseling?"

"But she's not needed here, Rich. That's my point. If our customers want help, we've got personal shoppers to assist them. Her job is redundant."

"You're comparing apples to oranges," said Al and he glanced around the table for support. "They aren't the same thing at all."

"No? Tell me, how many customers after pouring out their hearts to Ms. Bloom make purchases in the store? You've seen the numbers, Al. Barely fifty percent. The others go where? Robinsons-May? Saks? Rodeo Drive? Who knows?"

"Yeah?" asked Al. "So how do you explain all our new business, new charge accounts? She's putting us back in the ballgame. You're way off base, Leigh. Why, Rita tells me—"

"Rita," cut in Leigh, bobbing her head, "our best Scents associate, is stuck in a backroom answering the phone. How many sales has that bright decision cost us? Bottom line, people: gift counseling is kaput! Now, as to the space ..."

Inez interrupted. "Does Jonquil know about this?"

Leigh sat back and gestured impatiently that the group was being excruciatingly dense that morning. Privately she thought her plan would work so long as she kept up the momentum. She leaned forward and gave her tone an infusion of gravity.

"No, Inez, she does not. Look, I'll be frank. Mr. Merrill doesn't quite know how to tell her. He's—he's guilt ridden about having raised up her hopes. It's just another sign that the job has become a burden to him. I don't think any of you are aware of how frail he is."

"I played nine holes of golf with the man yesterday," Sy said and scoffed. "If he's frail, tell my scorecard."

Leigh didn't reply. Instead, she contorted her face as though she were on the verge of tears and waited until they all had noticed. She appeared to be struggling to keep her emotions in check and aimed accusing eyes at Sy.

"What? I didn't know. I swear I didn't know," the chastened attorney said defensively.

"Is it his heart again?" asked Al in a husky voice. Leigh froze. She was unaware of a pre-existing condition. Fortunately, Al was facing Cornell Bramson. "When was his first bypass, fifteen years ago?"

"Something like that," Cornell muttered. They all trained their eyes again on Leigh.

"He didn't want you to worry," she said reluctantly.

"Damn," said Al, slamming his right fist into his left palm.

Leigh knew she was on thin ice. It was time to wrap things up. "Now, let's all try to help him out of this mess. Each of you stop by his office today and give him one solid reason for letting Jonquil go.

"Al? Rita. It's that simple." Leigh said with a nod.

"Inez and Rich? Play up the image angle, how she doesn't benefit the store at all." They mumbled reluctant agreement.

"Cornell, pitch the job redundancy point. Head count." He sighed audibly.

"Sy, hit that malpractice thing-a-ma-jig. She hasn't even graduated yet. We've been lucky so far but 'what if'? Dot-dot-dot.

"And Barney, Bernie? Give him the Santa Claus argument. She's okay for the season, perhaps, but year round she has no net worth. Is everyone clear? Oh, look at the time!"

Leigh stood up quickly to indicate that the meeting was over.

Then, she added her parting shot. "Look guys, Jonquil Bloom is going to make a fool of herself on television. Trust me. We'll be up to our armpits in damage control. So let's cut our ties with gift counseling ASAP. Shall we get back to work?"

As soon as Leigh left the conference room, the others sat down and conducted an urgent rehash meeting. Inez pinned down Al. "So what do I do with the Poppi Blair press releases?" He told her to get them out on the double.

Likewise, Rich Ridgeland had a dilemma. His staff had spent all day Friday assembling a rush announcement about Clyde's exclusive gift counselor's forthcoming TV appearance. Forty poster boards and easels waited in the maintenance department for storewide distribution. Rich eyed Corny. "Are we a go?" Corny responded with a vehement thumbs-up gesture that sent Rich bounding out the door.

Sy tagged along with the BBs back to their corner office suite. It took two hours to locate Dr. Paxton, Jonquil's dissertation advisor, who was vacationing with his family in Barbados. Sy explained that the purpose of their call was to explore the possibility of Jonquil Bloom completing her degree work at Clyde's. Once the professor got over the novelty of the idea, he invoked "independent study" as the academic term to describe such an unconventional placement. He recommended that her colleagues draft a proposal with Jonquil's input and present it to the chairman of the Psychology Department as soon as possible. With that, Sy concluded the conversation and the three men wrote a confidential memo to Mr. Merrill. Meanwhile, Al and Corny asked Miss Egnar to beep them as soon as the boss arrived.

* * *

At one o'clock, Al stole up to the fifth floor. He felt a heaviness he hadn't known since the day he learned that his second wife had filed for divorce. Not even lunch in the cafeteria with unsuspecting Rita had elevated his mood. One thing about a new love in later life that he was discovering was that his occasional off mood could be overlooked. Or else Rita Oglesby was the soul of understanding. Thinking of her, he relaxed slightly as he came to a standstill before Miss Egnar's desk. "Is he in?" Al inquired while he grabbed a fistful of red and green candies from the dish beside her computer monitor and popped them into his mouth.

"For you, Al? Always," the secretary purred. *Is she flirting with me—Miss Egnar?* he wondered with alarm. "Go right in." She smiled broadly. Then she winked. There was no mistaking it. *My God, the eggnog or whatever it is they drink these days must be flowing already*, he mused.

"Come in, Al," said Mr. Merrill. "Have a seat. I've been expecting you." He snapped shut the latest "MD" medical bag for ages eight and up and remarked, "This is dynamite."

"Sold like hot cakes, sir. Can't meet the demand. Back orders are in the high two digits."

"No wonder. The good news is that my blood pressure is holding steady, given the day's events."

"Sir?"

"Cripes, Al, it's Marty when it's just you and me." Al slumped into a chair opposite his boss's desk. "Then you know," grumbled Al.

"Cornell just left. Whose idea was it to give me a weak heart, yours?"

Al crossed his legs and cupped his chin with his left palm. "Setting her up was easy, Marty." He watched the frown on his boss's face deepen. They sat in uneasy silence. Al feared that Mr. Merrill might back off from the sticky situation as he had done in recent years. He unscrambled his legs, clasped his hands between his knees and bent forward. "Marty, you've got to do something. She made a reference to that TV show that sure sounded to me like a threat. I think Leigh may be dangerous."

Mr. Merrill tilted back in his chair and sighed. "What's your point, Al? Are you saying I should fire her? I can't do that. Three reasons. The first doesn't go beyond the door. Leigh's plate is pretty full right now. Her sister's had another run-in with the law. End of story. Secondly, it's Christmas. When Emily's father turned Clyde's over to me, he gave me two pieces of advice: don't scrimp on the upkeep of the restrooms and never, ever, short of murder, pink slip anyone between Thanksgiving and New Year's." Al concurred with a nod.

"And thirdly, the buyer's year starts up again on January second. Leigh is well regarded by the industry and highly competent at her job. I can't replace her in a week. Besides, if I fired her today, wouldn't I be giving her further reason to act out? No, I have another plan in mind. I think I will fill Ms. Usher's stocking this year with some good old American black coal. Al, I've made up my mind. I'm definitely not retiring in the spring. And I am going to offer Ms. Bloom a permanent job here at Clyde's." He sat forward. "But if I find out that Leigh interfered with that television show, so help me, she's outta here."

When he left the fifth floor that afternoon, Al felt like clicking his heels high in the air. He remembered Miss Egnar's following eyes just in time.

CHAPTER TWENTY-SIX

Monday Afternoon

Trotting briskly from Santa Monica's jammed post office down Sixth Street, Jonquil berated herself for putting off shipping her out-of-state parcels until the last minute. A pox on the people who completed their shopping by July! That left them five whole months to stand in post office lines. If she lived to be two hundred, her life would never be that organized. She ticked off things that still needed doing, such as taking Billy for a haircut and getting herself fitted that afternoon for her appearance on the Poppi Blair Show two days from now.

It was nuts to be going on live television on December twenty-fourth, she chided herself. She couldn't hope to get everything done in time but then again, what an excuse!

Nearing the end of the block, Jonquil glanced across

the street at Santa Monica's public library on the corner and envied the people who were able to spend a quiet afternoon there. It had been several days since she had last done anything more for her Ph.D. dissertation than type the Clyde's data she had gathered into online spreadsheets. She reminded herself that she was lucky to be employed and doing what she clearly enjoyed, so she continued walking back to work free of envy.

Her gaze now shifted to the sidewalk, a lifelong habit of hers. One of the things she missed most since moving to the beach were more trees. As a Midwest child, she'd been fascinated by the patterns of shadows the branches made year round on all but the most overcast days. Today's breeze made the silhouettes of branches and leaves appear to move around clumsily like shadow boxers, creating ever changing, almost hypnotic images. Nature loved layers, her husband Gerry had often pointed out to her. Look at clouds rolling by, look at rock formations, study the intricacies of budding flowers, or simply dig a hole in the sand. Her previous work with emotionally disturbed children had also uncovered layers of conflict and layers of feelings causing her now to wonder, were gift motivations multi-layered, too?

Deep in thought, she rounded the corner onto Santa Monica Boulevard. That's when Jonquil spotted him, nearly half a block ahead of her. His height and jaunty stride caught her complete attention. Right on schedule, she grunted ruefully, her father's phantom—a John Bloom look-alike—was making his seasonal appearance. Her view was temporarily obscured by a glut of people exiting a city Blue Bus, yet the man's distinctive copper-colored hair could still be seen above the crowd and he was headed toward Clyde's!

Quarreling emotions slammed against her heart. She picked up her pace. Never during previous sightings had she gotten close enough to convince herself that it wasn't him, so she kept hoping. Numerous attempts to locate him, including the Salvation Army's failed search, had led her to believe he was dead, yet, often around her birthday or on holidays, she still thought she saw him. Not as he actually would be now—a man of sixty with graying hair—but exactly as he looked at the time he disappeared, which didn't make sense, but that's how it was.

Well, she wouldn't let him slip away this time.

She began to run. The crowd scattered in different directions while she gained on him. No matter what his reasons were for turning up now, she would grab him and not let him go.

What I am wearing, she worried excitedly, *do I look okay?*

The man paused in front of a restaurant. For once she

had a real chance. That, more than adrenaline, gave her an added boost. At which point he turned in profile and the mark on his right cheek became obvious. A large, purple birthmark covering the area from beneath his eye to the edge of his jaw. Not John Bloom's face. Not her father.

She clutched a parking meter and came to a stumbling halt. People stared as she bent over from a stitch in her side, panting. One mother, pushing a baby stroller, asked her if she needed help. Jonquil shook her head no. The man, whoever, he was, disappeared. Long minutes passed before she could straighten up and continue with any semblance of calm on her nearly completed journey back to work. Even so, her anger boiled over and her eyes clotted with tears. Hopefully, no one at Clyde's had seen her.

That's *it*, she scolded herself. No more false alarms. After Christmas, I'm going to track him down, or his grave, and never again put myself through this torment.

It was a New Year's resolution she aimed to keep.

CHAPTER TWENTY-SEVEN

Tuesday, December 23rd

At 4:15 that afternoon, the Gift Counseling Department was essentially deserted. Much to Jonquil's relief, her last appointment cancelled. Throughout the hectic day, she'd been forced to call on reserves of energy to survive the back-to-back sessions. Had Rita not brought her a piece of cake and glass of milk from the employee potluck, she might have collapsed hours ago.

Rita was over in the Sweet Shop assembling the gifts Jonquil would present to Poppi Blair and her crew. She proposed several jumbo sized stockings full of Clyde's own candy and cookies and Jonquil saw the wisdom of leaving the choice up to Poppi's biggest fan. Rita would bring the gifts over to the apartment in the morning. Jonquil had invited her to be her guest and ride with her to Burbank in the limo. Billy, too. It turned out that Billy could not be excused from a half day of school. Rita promptly offered to sit with him again. Jonquil protested but her protégé insisted. She had a mountain of knitting to finish including Al's Christmas present and it didn't much matter where she got it done.

The suite's reception area was vacant. The gift givers had all gone shopping. Jonquil sat at her desk idle for the first time in weeks. In the stillness, with the winter darkness falling on the streets outside her window, all at once she felt drained. She brushed away a tear and then another. *It's only letdown*, she thought, diagnosing herself, *my job here is over. But come tomorrow, I'll go on that show and knock 'em dead.*

Oh, really? countered her inner doubts. For days, she had managed to block them out. What did they know about her that she didn't yet know, see, or get? She exhaled a loud, frustrated sigh.

The feathered blue dream catcher hanging serenely in the window caught her eye. *Was my dream too big?* Jonquil asked herself.

Her hand strayed to the telephone. One comforting word from Claude would erase the gloom. She had managed to elude him each morning when she left for work. Nevertheless, she had the feeling he was watching her from the jobsite. Or was that wishful thinking?

Stubbornly, she resisted the temptation to call him. It

would only lead to more pain. She must tough it out. The same way she ignored Billy's nagging pleas for a dog. No, no, no! She scowled. Why a third no? Instantly, she was reminded of her elegant theory and her shoulders sagged. Ever since she had chosen "gifts and the strings attached" as the direction of her research, she'd become aware of evidence to the contrary.

It had begun with the man who had needed to fix a problem with his girlfriend. Back then, she had been open to change and happy with the results. So, why wasn't she happy now? Why was Billy sulking? Why was Claude apparently out of her life? And why, on the eve of her television debut, did she feel full of doubt?

Sure, many visitors had left the suite satisfied. Her intuition had gotten her through. She recalled the woman with the taupe scarf and the young, unemployed man. Thankfully, no one else had brought up a situation involving a pet but it could easily happen again. Would she handle that topic any better the next time?

Deep down Jonquil knew her "strings attached" theory wasn't built on a firm, scientific foundation. But what should take its place?

Yet, hadn't there been clues along that she was on the wrong path?

Dan Burnham, she thought with a start. The woman wanting to give anonymously. The Sunday homily on joy.

Rita's tap shoes story. Plainly, she hadn't thought things through and now she was only minutes away from her five o'clock meeting with Mr. Merrill. As she scooped up her laptop and purse, Jonquil had to admit to herself that her poorly constructed notion about gift-giving, Billy's bad moods and Claude's glaring absence—not mere letdown—were the crux of her fatigue.

* * *

The conversation with Mr. Merrill went incredibly well. Almost before she'd taken a seat across from him, he offered her a full-time, permanent job. Just weeks ago, she'd sat in the same chair on the verge of termination. The recollection deepened the smile on her face. He picked up a comment card which had landed in one of the store's suggestion boxes, adjusted his bifocals, and read aloud, "Clyde's is the giving store." He leaned back grinning and said how pleased he was with her experiment.

She brushed the pleats of her tartan skirt. Finally, she blurted out, "But I'm not even sure I'm on the right track. In fact, I wish I could start all over again. There are so many facets to giving. I need to find out what makes gift-givers tick.

"Oh, how can I put it into words? Mr. Merrill, every gift has a story. I need to hear these stories before I can understand how to help people give."

"Fine," he said, throwing open his arms and stretching. "I have no objection to your learning on the job." He leaned forward. "Listen, my father-in-law plucked me out of a high school in the valley, where I was teaching geometry, to run this business. Gutsy, huh? He did it because he had faith in me. Well, young woman, I have faith in you.

"Two things, Jonquil: one, don't worry about that television program tomorrow. Get a good night's sleep. You'll do fine. And two: let's agree to meet back here Friday morning, ten o'clock sharp. In the meantime, think over my offer, please?" Then, he pushed back his chair and stood up. So did Jonquil. They shook hands and after they exchanged Merry Christmas greetings, she hastily withdrew.

Her mind was reeling. His offer was a wish or a dream come true or a prayer answered. All of the above. Which reminded her that there still remained the thorny question of her status with UCLA to address.

Click-clacking her heels down the darkened tiled hall toward the elevator, too late, she caught sight of the back of someone locking an office door. Worse luck, it was Leigh Usher! As her nemesis stepped backward, they collided.

"Sorry," said Jonquil quickly. Leigh frowned, and then traced the shaft of light silhouetting Jonquil back to its source: Mr. Merrill's office.

"So he did it? He actually offered you a permanent job?" Jonquil didn't answer. She continued walking to the elevator but Leigh caught up with her, still venting. "The fool. The old dinosaur. He has no clue."

Jonquil punched the call button and tried to ignore the woman harping at her elbow. Mercifully, the elevator door rolled open. They both got in while Leigh continued to spew venom. "The idiot! The moron!"

Jonquil took a step backward and tried to look away.

"You're bound to screw it up tomorrow. On TV, I mean. You're a flash in the pan. A user!" snarled Leigh while fastening the tie of her black satin cape.

Jonquil became afraid. She willed the descending numbers on the overhead wall panel to light up faster. Four—three—two—suddenly, Leigh hit the STOP button. Both women lurched sideways as the elevator shuddered to an unanticipated halt.

Jonquil had had enough. "Cut it out, Leigh and get ahold of yourself," she ordered. She reached for the alarm button but Leigh leaned her body up against the wall panel and said, "I'm going to embarrass you tomorrow."

Warily, Jonquil took another step away from her. "How?"

"I'm going to phone that show, doc. You'd better brush up on all your theories tonight because I'm going to ask you one tough question."

"Ask me now."

"And spoil the fun? Oh, why not?" Leigh crossed her arms and preened. In heels, she stood four inches taller than Jonquil and enjoyed looking down at her. "Picture it: you—live—coast-to-coast—with no place to hide. I call up and say, 'Hey, gift counseling lady, when does a person have the right to stop giving?'"

Her voice hardened. "When can you walk away? Turn your back? Say 'I'm done! No more money, no more bailouts, no more anything—I'm through!'" Her eyes blazed "Tell me!" she shrieked and raised her arms agitatedly. Her cape flared around her in wide circles.

Jonquil watched the spectacle and steeled herself from showing any reaction though her hands felt clammy and the confines of the space made her want to scream for help. Was this jealousy? What would cause Leigh Usher to feel jealousy toward her? No, it felt deeper, it felt paranoid. Abruptly, Leigh dropped her hands to her side. "Well, what's your answer?"

"Why do you hate me, Leigh?"

"Go back to your patients, doc. You should take care of those people. If more of you worked harder at it, maybe my sister would be clean by now."

"Can we get off this thing and go talk somewhere?"

Leigh turned and released the elevator. With a loud bump, it lowered itself to the first floor lobby. The door slid open onto a noisy first floor scene filled with the after work crowd. Jonquil felt a rush of relief and breathed in the cool air. Though she wanted to move away from Leigh as quickly as possible, she took the time to say, "Leigh, is there anything I can do for you?"

A group of ladies nearby was reading one of the easel displays announcing the gift counselor's TV debut. Leigh didn't miss a beat. "Yeah, break both legs."

Still shaking, Jonquil hurried to the garage. She glanced over her shoulder to make sure Leigh wasn't following her and pieced together what must have provoked the ugly confrontation. It didn't take a professor of psychology to deduce that Leigh must have a sister who was a user and that part of Leigh's rage had to do with longstanding disappointments with therapeutic professionals.

Not all patients responded to treatment as hoped. Readmissions occurred. Changes in doses were made, new medications introduced, new doctors, new protocols. Like anything else in life, there were just some people who for whatever reason did not get well. Tommy Cregier, one of her former patients at Children's Home, came to mind. It was both frustrating to the staff and bewildering to families of patients. Jonquil recalled

Leigh's initial hostility toward her and better understood its context.

Even so, the woman had no right to threaten her. How dangerous was Leigh? She'd have to consider her options, either to handle the situation herself or else seek help from Mr. Merrill. One thing was certain, she decided, as she unlocked her car door. She would not allow the Head Buyer to stand in the way of her taking the job at Clyde's.

All at once she wished Claude was there to hold her and kiss away her worries but she pushed the image away. Yet, as Jonquil settled herself behind the steering wheel after giving the garage one last careful look, she grasped an uncomfortable link between Leigh's wish to withhold and her own behavior with Billy. No way, she told herself and turned the key in the ignition, that's preposterous. Her inner voice gave her the raspberry.

CHAPTER TWENTY-EIGHT

Dawn, Wednesday, December 24th

J ust before waking, Jonquil dreamed she held a book in
her hand. It was a thin volume, the kind people often
make jokes about, entitled, *Gifts and the Strings
Attached.*

She opened it.

The chapter on generosity ran two sentences long.
Another chapter entitled, "Misgivings," plagiarized
advice columnists. "'Tis Better to Take than to Give" was
a long, rambling entry while "Get What You Want, the
Art of Manipulation" was the longest chapter.

She was appalled. Her name was on the cover.

The scene changed to New York City. It was snowing
so hard she could barely recognize Rockefeller Center.
She'd gone there to appear on the Poppi Blair Show but
the guard who reminded her of her father, told her she

was in the wrong state. She remembered she still needed to get Billy a gift. Billy! She must get home before Christmas.

JFK was jammed. All the people held copies of her book. They pointed at her and jeered. The woman laughing the hardest sounded like Leigh Usher. Raucous music and garbled announcements made Jonquil miss her plane. She stood in the center of the terminal and wept.

A serviceman tapped her on the shoulder. His name tag read, "Pvt. Euclid." Without a word, he handed her his stand-by ticket for Los Angeles.

"Why are you doing this?" she asked, floored.

"It's mine to give," he replied.

"Mine ... give."

"Mine ... give."

"Mine ... give."

CHAPTER TWENTY-NINE

Afternoon, Wednesday, December 24th

Billy was sequestered in his mother's bedroom closet. Across the room, her thirteen-inch television screen flickered. He had dragged in the stepladder and was poised on the top step, reaching for the highest shelf. Regardless of how many times she scolded him not to search for his Christmas presents, he always did. You had to be a kid to understand.

It was one o'clock in the afternoon. Rita was in the kitchen doing the lunch dishes. She had the volume on the television in the main room turned up high. It wasn't necessary because everything about Poppi Blair was loud, from her big hair, noisy jewelry, garish clothing and booming voice to her even louder laugh. The set was generously adorned with Christmas decorations and the Los Angeles audience appeared to be loving every minute of the show. Billy glanced briefly toward the small TV set when he heard his mom talking to Poppi Blair. She spoke in that funny voice he didn't like. "Poppi, I'm so delighted to be a guest on your show today," she enthused. He tuned her out.

Billy and Jonquil had hit a snag on the home front over Claude. Anyone with a brain could see that he was a great guy. Billy missed him. It didn't help that all the kids at school were talking about family vacations and family get-togethers. Why couldn't they be friends with Claude anymore? Life sure was complicated. Adults were complicated. His mom was the limit.

He stood on tip-toe.

"Jonquil? I've never known anyone called Jonquil before. Darlin', how did you come by that moniker?" asked Poppi.

"Actually, I was named for the gift my father surprised my mother with in the hospital on the day I was born. He brought her a bouquet of her favorite flowers—jonquils. It was wintertime in Minnesota. We never learned how he managed it."

"Far out! Us blooms should stick together, am I right?"

Rita's roar of approval, even from several rooms away, distracted him. A box fell down and nicked his head but didn't hurt him. It was just a dusty cardboard shoebox. Papers cascaded out of it and he jumped down to retrieve them.

"We'll be right back with your questions for the gift counselor," said Poppi.

They weren't papers after all, they were old snapshots. The first one he picked up captured his full attention. It showed his dad standing outside of a tent. The next one showed his dad and mom hugging. Cool. The third photo made Billy's jaw drop. In it, his mother had her arms wrapped around a dog, a setter! Billy's heart started thumping. Carefully, he scrutinized each of the remaining twelve photos. His mom and the dog appeared in seven of them.

What was his mother doing with a dog? *She was allergic.* Yet these photos showed her laughing, holding the animal and petting it. Billy's head ached from concentration. There was only one possible explanation. She had lied to him. Her face filled the television screen. She had on a fancy red outfit he didn't recognize and she looked like she had been to the beauty parlor. A toll-free number flashed across the bottom of the screen. He dropped the snapshots, slammed the closet door shut behind him, stomped across the bedroom and grabbed her telephone receiver.

He was kept on hold for quite a while and used the time to rehearse what he would say to her. Suddenly, his ear was blasted with a burst of sound—music, laughter, clapping.

He reached for the mute button on the TV remote. That helped some.

"Hi, Billy. This is Poppi. Where are you calling from and what's your gift problem today?"

"I'm calling from Venice."

"Darlin', I sure hope you mean Venice Beach, California, or else I hope your mom knows you're on the phone."

The camera panned to Jonquil's alert face.

"She does now."

The audience followed Poppi's cue and tittered. Jonquil sat forward, straining for something the audience couldn't catch. She'd braced herself for Leigh Usher's whacky call, so the sound of her son's voice astonished her.

"Okay, what's your question Billy?"

He'd intended to stay calm but when the time came to speak, he took a deep breath and shouted, "What should you do when you want something very much but your mom won't let you have one 'cause she says it'll make her sick, but then you find out she used to have one?" The camera closed in on Jonquil's face and Billy cried out, "You lied to me my whole life, Mom!"

"Hang on there, honey bunch, what are we talking about?"

"A DOG, A DOG, A D-O-G DOG!" Billy flung the

receiver down hard before he tore out of the room and into his.

Meanwhile, Rita came rushing down the hall calling his name. She filled his doorway. "Billy, was that you on the phone just now?"

Billy didn't answer her. He snatched up his wallet and slipped on his jacket. He scanned the room one last time. The woodcarving from Children's Home sat on his nightstand where he'd placed it on the night his mother had given it to him. He stuffed it into the pocket of his jacket.

"Where are you going?"

"Outa my way, Rita." Before she could respond, he pushed past her and banged the screen door on his way out of the apartment. She hurried down the hall and outside, calling his name to no avail. She scurried around the pool and when she finally reached the front sidewalk, she saw a boy on a bike pedaling furiously up the street. It was Billy.

Unsure of what to do next, she returned to the apartment. All her nerve endings were hanging out. This was absolutely the last time she would sit for Jonquil, boss or no boss. Nor was it possible to ignore what was happening on the television.

"She left the studio?" Poppi shouted to someone offstage. Nodding, she turned back to the camera and rolled her eyes. "Well, y'all, sorry about that. We'll be right back … at least I will!" Rita killed the television.

* * *

At the end of Billy's rant, Jonquil leapt to her feet. "Sorry, I must go now," she told Poppi and ran off the set. A few of the staff tried to block her path but she barreled her way through to the exit marked "Talent Parking." Her limo driver stood slouched against the vehicle, combing his hair. "Is there a phone in there?" she demanded, pointing to the car.

"Like, yeah."

"Take me home—step on it. Don't be shy about short cuts. Burn rubber, buddy."

She threw herself into the back seat, called home and got a busy signal. She punched the redial button until Rita answered. Rita was beside herself with concern. Jonquil told her to sit tight in case Billy came back home. She yelled at the driver to hurry; this was a true emergency. But Christmas Eve afternoon traffic was so heavy, that it took nearly two hours for them to reach the beach. It gave Jonquil ample time to replay Billy's words in her mind over and over again: "You lied to me my whole life."

* * *

Mr. Merrill, a very pleased expression on his face, had just concluded a phone call when Leigh burst into his office unannounced at 1:20 p.m.

"She's walked off the show!" Leigh hurled the words at him, visibly angry and elated. She scanned the area around his desk for signs of toys or games and noticed the inert television on the credenza. "You weren't even watching," she said accusingly.

He gave her an appraising look. "Cornell is taping it for me, Leigh. Please sit down and *calm* down."

"I'm too angry to sit. Gift counselor, my derriere. She's a fraud, that's what she is, a disgrace. I knew it all along and I tried to tell you, but no. You went and offered her a full-time job behind my back. How could you, Marty?"

"I'm still president of Clyde's, Leigh, and I don't have to tell you everything. I don't know what happened today, so, till I do, I will reserve judgment," he added testily.

Leigh glommed onto the edge of his desk and leaned forward menacingly. "I'm telling you what happened," she said in a nasty tone. "A whiney kid called in about wanting a dog and she literally jumped up and ran away with barely a good bye. The kid said 'Mom' but I don't know who he meant, Jonquil or Poppi or whoever. Can you imagine? With the whole world watching? What a mess. And I thought *I* had a tough question to ask her—" She straightened up, tight-lipped, and studied her nails.

"*You* had a question for her? *You* were going to call that show?"

So, Al's suspicions had been right. Mr. Merrill vigorously scratched his jaw. Hadn't he mentored and guided this woman for nearly ten years and offered her emotional support when she needed it? Hadn't he regarded her as both colleague and friend? Hadn't he been her willing advocate? He'd always believed she had the store's best interests in mind, that her loyalty was unimpeachable. Now he questioned whether she had ever cared about Clyde's. Her lack of character quite simply stunned the man. It felt like being brutally jarred awake from a gratifying dream.

"Marty, now … Marty," she faltered, taking a few tentative steps backward. "Look, I never made the call."

Mr. Merrill's phone buzzed loudly, adding to the tension already in the air. Yet, he welcomed the interruption. After listening for a moment, he broke in.

"Yes, Iris, let me put you on speaker. Leigh's here. Please repeat what you just told me."

The conversation with Iris took only a few minutes to complete. Afterward, Mr. Merrill addressed Leigh who had finally slumped down in a chair.

"Two things you should know, Leigh. One, I'm not retiring in the spring or anytime in the foreseeable future."

She shot to her feet and glowered at him. "Then, I resign."

"That," he said, "was number two."

* * *

Rita jumped when the doorbell rang. A dark-haired man in a broad-striped knit sweater, slacks and loafers stood on the other side of the screen door. Not until he removed his sunglasses did she recognize him.

"Oh, Claude, thank God you came!" she exclaimed as she let him inside.

"Where's the boy now?" asked Claude while he scanned the main room.

Rita shook her head. "He ran out of here like a bat out of you know where. Jonquil told me to wait here in case he came back."

"So, it was Billy. I had the television on at home but only caught the tail end of his call. Guess you're surprised I don't give up on Jonquil but there is something about that impossible woman. I'm hooked. Hell, I drove so fast on the way up here I got a ticket," he confessed.

Rita touched his arm. "Glad you're here. I don't know what set him off."

"Where was he? What was he doing?" She led him down the hall toward the bedrooms.

"He was in his mother's room watching the show 'cause he used her phone." Except for cradling the receiver after Billy left, Rita hadn't touched a thing.

They both entered the room. Claude glanced around

272

quickly and noticed that nothing seemed out of place. He peered into the wastebasket and poked under the bed. Just to be thorough, he swung open the closet door and saw the stepladder. "Aha!" he chuckled. "The boy was in her closet—uh-oh. What have we here?" He bent down and picked up the snapshots. "Who's the guy?"

"Gerry, her husband. I recognize him from the photo in the redwood frame in the other room."

"I get it," said Claude slowly after he had looked through the entire pile. "Look here, Rita." He stood up and handed her the pictures. "Ever seen Billy's room? Ever thought about all the junk in there?"

"Claude, I'm so nervous I don't know what to think."

"Hey, Rita," he said and grinned before throwing one arm around her shoulder. "Steady, woman."

The phone rang. She started down the hall on the run. "All these people have been calling here—the store, her friends, neighbors, the media." Abruptly, the phone ceased to ring. Rita's charge to the kitchen ended about where the oval shaped rug in the main room began.

"Bet that was Jonquil again," she tossed over her shoulder to Claude as she peered out of the front window and down the street. "She's been calling every fifteen minutes or so. Poor thing, she's stuck in traffic. Why, she doesn't even know that Poppi called here!"

"Who?" called Claude from halfway down the hall.

"Poppi Blair, herself. She phoned here not ten minutes ago—oh—my—God, Claude, I actually spoke to her!" Rita's delayed reaction took the form of high pitched cackles.

"Yeah?" he asked and took a quick glance at Billy's room.

"Glory be! So I told her that Jonquil was Billy's mother. Oh, well, that shook the worms right out of the apples. Know what she said then? She said she would have done the same thing—I mean, left the show and gone after him. I must remember to tell Jonquil to call her 'cause she wants her back on the show to explain everything. That's my Poppi!" gushed Rita proudly. The phone rang again.

"You stay with the phone," he said, "while I drive around the neighborhood. Some of the kids might have seen him."

Before he moved, however, the front door banged open.

"Billy?"

It was Jonquil. Frantically, her eyes darted in all directions until she saw Claude coming toward her. "You," she murmured and let her coat and purse drop to the floor. His arms encircled her like a haven.

"Jonny," he whispered, kissing the hair at her temple. "We'll find him."

Rita hung up the phone, a wrong number, and joined them. Trying to appear calm, Jonquil asked what had happened.

"I think he was looking at these," Claude volunteered and handed her a couple of the snapshots.

She nodded. "I guessed as much. Claude, I did this. I made Billy run away."

"It will be all right. Trust me."

"Oh, sugar," groaned Rita. "I let you down."

"No, Rita. I'm responsible. Only me."

"We need a plan," interrupted Claude. "What time is it?" They checked their watches and discovered it was going on three-thirty. The phone rang again. Jonquil ran past them to the kitchen.

"Billy? ... Oh, Georgina, how good of you to call ... Yes, yes, it was Billy who phoned the show. Have you seen him? It's terribly important ... I see, okay. Please call me if you do ... thanks, bye." She disconnected and looked anxiously at Claude.

"Jonny, I'm going to case the neighborhood. He took his bike. You got a cell phone?"

"No."

"Here's mine. Beep me if you hear anything. Here's my pager number."

He handed her his business card. "We'll keep in touch. You call his friends and whoever else on the cell phone.

Rita, you take the incoming calls. Walk me out to the Jeep, Jonquil."

Once outside, he drew her close.

"Listen," he said, "have a little faith in Billy."

"But Claude," she pointed out in a faltering voice, "I've been through this before. When someone leaves me, they don't ever come back." She bit her lip to avoid losing her composure but her eyes glistened with tears.

"I came back. And I'm not leaving you." He took her in his arms and kissed her again and again until she threw her arms around his neck. She leaned into him and didn't want to let go. When she realized this, she drew back and spoke fiercely to his fathomless eyes.

"Find him."

* * *

Once aboard his bike, Billy carried out a plan more specific and successful than the adults'. He made a bee-line for Mrs. Crandon's house. After he rang her bell, he kept an eye out for Rita. "Open, open!" he ordered the door until it budged a crack. "Hi ya, Mrs. Crandon, is Blackie still here?"

"Why, Billy, come right in. How nice to see you. They're all out back," she gestured vaguely. "I was just leaving to get my hair done."

"Mrs. Crandon, guess what! My mom said I can have a dog now."

"Mazel tov, Billy! See? I told you she would change her mind."

"I know you want to give Blackie to your grandchildren."

"You still want him?" she asked surprised. "He's all yours."

"Honest? You mean it?"

"Yes, yes. He's been barking up a storm and bothering the precious poodles. My daughter-in-law could never handle him. Now let me see, I have an extra leash. Oh, you'll need his toys and rug. He won't sleep without them." She made a face. "May as well take his water bowl, too."

"My bike's outside. It's got a rack."

"Let me think now." She paused.

"Mrs. C.? I'm kinda in a hurry."

She smiled indulgently at the eager look on his face. "Sure you are. Well, then, go get him while I scare up a carrier. I think I have a small one here somewhere."

Soon, Billy was back on his bike with a panting passenger. He pumped frantically over to Ramon's house and came to a screeching halt.

"Ramon!" he shouted from the street. "Yo, Ramon!"

"Hey, Billy," shouted back Ramon from a second floor window. "What's up?"

"Get your bike."

"'K, dude."

Minutes later, Billy and Ramon rode off toward the ocean. Ramon had considerable trouble keeping pace with his younger friend and the barking puppy. But he was glad the problem between Billy and his mother about having pets had at last been resolved.

* * *

Jonquil watched the late afternoon shadows gather with mounting trepidation. Soon it would be dark. She'd called everyone she could think of. Few people were home and those who were hadn't seen or heard from Billy. There was no answer at Mrs. Crandon's house.

Unable to sit still, she slipped out of the red silk dress the store had lent her and pulled on the first clean pair of sweats she could lay her hands on. It was a relief to be back in her own clothes.

She wandered down to Billy's room. The stuffed animals seemed to glare at her from every corner like gargoyles. *I can't bear this another second*, she told herself.

On top of his bureau, her eyes rested on the statue of Saint Francis of Assisi which Father Tim had given him on the day of his First Communion. She crossed over and placed her fingers on its base. "Dear God, Gerry, Saint Francis, please bring him home safely to me." She gave herself over to prayer.

"Sugar!" yelled Rita. "Ramon's mother is on the phone." Jonquil flew to the extension in her bedroom. "Yes, Juanita? … I see. When was this? … About 2:30 … Thank you. Call me when Ramon gets home, please?"

She reported the news to Rita. "At least he's not alone, Rita. Ramon's little sister saw them leave together. She was playing up the block and only came home just now. I'm going to beep Claude."

* * *

Billy had himself a day to remember. Though he'd broken many rules in the past hour, he did not compound them by going down to the Venice Beach boardwalk unchaperoned. Instead, he and Ramon took Blackie to Palisades Park and then down to the beach. He put Blackie on the leash and strutted—or more truthfully, was dragged—down the length of Santa Monica Pier as though he'd always owned a dog. He bought Ramon and himself snacks along the way and treated Blackie to a hotdog.

Later, the boys relaxed on a bench facing Malibu and watched the awesome sunset while Blackie slept in Billy's lap.

"I can't take him home," said Billy with stoic regret.

"I know, dude," said Ramon. He was dismayed when he learned how Billy had actually come to have Blackie.

"Can you?"

"Nah, we can't have pets in our building. Sorry."

"He needs to be around kids. Old people make him jittery. He likes kids." The sun blinded Billy's eyes for a moment. The gulls wheeled and screamed overhead as the beach slowly became deserted.

"I gotta go, Billy—it's getting late."

Billy's shoulders slumped. "Yeah, I know. I just want to sit here a while longer with him."

"Sure. See ya, dude."

"So long."

"Hey, Billy?" Billy turned in Ramon's direction.

"Yeah?"

"Your mom. Maybe you should call her."

"Bye, Ramon."

Billy swung back on the bench, fighting tears. It was getting hard to make out shapes on the shore. He considered where he could take Blackie. Mrs. Crandon's was no good anymore. Home was out of the question. He could run away with Blackie but where to? Besides, he was exhausted, they both were, and he had spent all his money. Billy sat there for another hour testing out various ideas until a solution finally came to him.

CHAPTER THIRTY

Evening, December 24th

Though he hated to abandon the search even briefly, Claude headed back to Jonquil's apartment. It was dark, his stomach was rumbling, and her voice had begun to show strain. Perhaps it would be best to notify the police if Jonquil agreed, though he doubted they would do anything this soon. He switched on the 6:30 p.m. news to hear the weather report. Cool and clear was the Christmas Eve forecast. How "cool" was cool to a ten-year-old in a jacket? He drove faster.

Jonquil was on the phone when he arrived. She pointed to sandwiches, coffee and fruit neatly laid out on the dining room table and he filled a plate while she sat down and brought him up to date. He was telling her where he had looked when the kitchen telephone rang. Jonquil got up to answer it and became very excited.

"Yes, Miss Hamilton ... No, of course not, Miss
Hamilton! ... Yes, yes—just stay with him until I get
there." She cradled the receiver. "Billy's at Children's
Home. He has a dog with him." She punched out Mrs.
Crandon's phone number for the fifth time. Still no
answer.

"Let's go, Jonny," prompted Claude as he grabbed his
keys.

"Rita, will you stay here in case—" Rita nodded and
shooed them out the door.

"Hey, Jonny," said Claude, once they were in the Jeep.
"Why can't Billy have a dog and why did he accuse you
of lying to him?"

"Not now, Claude, please? Let's go." Without another
word, she buckled her seatbelt and tensely turned away
from him as he pulled the Jeep away from the curb.

Traffic had dwindled considerably. They reached
Children's Home just before seven o'clock. Miss
Hamilton herself greeted them at the front door with a
dour expression. The foyer's dark, vacant status gave
Jonquil a chill.

"Oh, I thought you'd never get here," said the Head of
Social Services while closing the door firmly behind
them.

"Where's Billy?" demanded Jonquil as the familiar,
clinical odor assaulted her nostrils. She scanned the area

but didn't see her son.

"My dear," said Miss Hamilton, patting Jonquil's arm while giving her a meaningful look. "I had no idea you had such a problem child of your own."

"Where is he, Miss Hamilton?" Jonquil repeated through clenched teeth.

"When I think how he showed up at the door with that cage in his arms, so grubby and pushy. Pitiful, really. One of the volunteers let him in. He claimed he had a gift for the children." She tsked-tsked.

"Billy! Now!" Claude and Jonquil shouted in unison.

"Oh, the boy is with the other children I imagine."

Jonquil lost her temper. "I told you not to let him out of your sight until I arrived!"

Miss Hamilton kept her voice even though the muscles around her mouth twitched spasmodically. "Ms. Bloom, we are short-staffed as you so well know. I did my best under the circumstances."

But Jonquil wasn't listening. She took the foyer steps two at a time, Claude right behind her. From far off, she heard the murmur of voices and her heart started pounding fast.

"This way," she told Claude.

She ran down the hallway—the walls now featured drooping holiday decorations—into the community room. A fake Christmas tree occupied the corner by the beat-up piano. Otherwise, the cheerless, mismatched furniture looked exactly the same as when she had last seen it. The children, half a dozen or so, were either listlessly watching cartoons on television or playing with staff. Jonquil didn't recognize the adult faces. Holiday help.

"Miss Bloom, is that you?" cried Tommy Cregier. He walked right over to her. All the other children looked up, too.

"Yes, Tommy, it's me."

"See?" he pivoted and addressed the other children. "I told you she'd come. Miss Bloom, thank you for the nice puppy dog." The other children echoed his appreciation.

"It's not from me. It's from Billy. Where is he?" she asked softly, her eyes darting from face to face.

"Hah! He told us it was from you. He's gone."

Jonquil faltered, all her hopes for a speedy resolution undone. "Gone? Did he say where he was going?" Tommy shook his head no.

"Did he tell anyone where he was going?" Her voice rose higher.

"I know where," bragged a raven-haired little girl with blotchy skin and an irritatingly strident voice.

Jonquil didn't recognize her and surmised she was a new admission. It was always startling to see regressive behavior in a six year old which her baby talk and demeanor suggested, but Jonquil had to let it go. She sensed this child knew something helpful about Billy's whereabouts.

"Tell us," ordered Claude and lunged forward. Jonquil put a restraining hand on his arm.

She got down on one knee so she could be eye level with the child. "Hello, sweetie, what's your name?" she asked.

"Muriel."

"Muriel? That's a very pretty name. I'm Ms. Bloom."

"Are you Billy's mommy?"

"Yes, darling, I am. Now, did he tell you where he was going?"

"Uh-huh. He's goin' ta see his daddy." The words hung suspended in the air until Jonquil's heart rolled over and she began to tremble. Her eyes fastened on Claude, imploring him to take over. He knelt down beside her and followed her example by lowering and gentling his voice.

"What makes you think so, Muriel? Hi, I'm Claude, a friend of Billy's."

"Um, 'caud when a toy fell out his jacket, I said, 'Who's dat for?' an' he said, 'I goin' ta take dis to Fadder … um … um …'" She kept repeating the same grating syllable like a telephone's busy signal. Claude tried building on the clue she'd given them.

"He did?" Claude asked encouragingly. "My goodness, aren't you a smart girl. Father who?"

The query jumpstarted Jonquil's breathing apparatus and she stood and snapped her fingers with excitement. "Sure—Father Tim—old family friend—St. Monica Church—let's go!" She reached for his hand and they were ready to dash out but Miss Hamilton stood in their path.

"Not so fast, you two. You can't leave the mutt here."

"Aw," chorused the children with varying degrees of regret.

"It's absolutely forbidden. You'll find him in the backyard in that contraption the boy left here. Why, the thing isn't even house trained." She sniffed in disgust. "Take the dog or I'll call the police."

"He's house broken all right, just scared out of his wits," said Jonquil. "Claude, will you please get the dog and meet me out front? Hurry!"

"Oh, I'm quite sure he's feeling no pain. You see, Ms. Bloom, I'm more resourceful than you think. When the little beast wouldn't calm down, I mixed half of a valium into a plate of raw hamburger meat. He never knew what hit him."

Jonquil's face darkened with anger. "You drugged an innocent little puppy?"

Claude stepped between the two women. He ordered Miss Hamilton to take him to the dog, tossed his car keys to Jonquil and told her to open the rear of the Jeep.

Moments later, Claude came crunching across the gravel yard holding the carrier. "He's out cold," he reported. "What should we do, take him with us or drop him off somewhere? My sister would take him. It's your call, Jonny." Jonquil's nerves were stretched taut like rubber bands.

On one hand, she and Claude hadn't a moment to spare. On the other, she felt paralyzed by the dog's sudden proximity. Claude waited. Though she hated having to choose, she sensed Claude's unspoken support. A strange idea streaked through her brain. *No,* she protested silently, *I'm not ready to receive him. But I don't have time to quibble about it either.*

"Put him in the back and let's go," she said gruffly. He placed the carrier inside the Jeep, shut the hatchback, and climbed into the driver's seat. "Where to?"

"Seventh and California. Turn right at the corner. Tonight's the children's Christmas liturgy. Billy and I were supposed to go together," she remembered with dismay.

Claude squeezed her left knee. "It's going to be all right."

She murmured, "I'm so glad you're here."

He met her unwavering gaze and nodded. "Me, too."

* * *

St. Monica Church had reached the lull between its two distinct Christmas Eve rituals. The evening children's Mass had concluded and most of that keyed up congregation had departed. In about three hours, the church would be packed again with a more reserved crowd for the traditional Midnight Mass.

The building was a study in contrasts. Its clean, limestone exterior and tall spire, refitted after the 1994 Northridge earthquake, connoted sturdiness bordering on severity. Inside, the bright vestibule and adjoining glass doors opened onto an intimate, cheerful interior. The white walls, both pulpits, and the altar were not stark so much as unpretentious. High above the side aisles and overlooking the pews, the Stations of the Cross and the confessionals, a row of stained glass windows provided colorful though slight distraction. Both side aisles were lined with pillars, softened that night by holly sprigs and berries. Banners depicting the Nativity gospel drew one's eyes up the center aisle to the sanctuary and main altar. However, during the Christmas season most attention was drawn to the manger scene in the space left of the main altar.

There, facing it, on two folding chairs sat Billy and Father Tim.

Billy loved and trusted Father Tim. He was the only adult that the ten-year-old could turn to after giving

Blackie away. His heart ached, and fortunately, the old priest didn't pester him with silly questions. Another lie—that his mom would be picking him up at church—had gone unchallenged. Anyway, it no longer much mattered.

He showed Father Tim the carving of the Irish Setter. "Father, can I put him up there?" asked Billy, indicating the crèche.

"Well, now, let me think," said the old priest. "Those shepherds must have had a sheepdog, right?" He nudged Billy to go ahead. Billy placed the tiny carving by the tall shepherd with the lamb slung around his neck. Then, he reclaimed his seat and snuggled closer to the priest.

"Why'd He do it, Father?" asked Billy with a loud yawn.

"Do what, son?"

"Why'd He get Himself born in a stable?"

The priest pursed his lips. "Hmm, that's a mighty good question. Some say He did it to show us that the poor have dignity and that we should always treat them well. Others think He was letting everyone know early on that He was going to die on a cross, just as poor as the day He was born."

"Nah, that's not the reason."

"What do you say, Billy?" Father Tim lowered his head and listened.

"He did it so He could be near the animals: the cows, the donkey, the sheep and all. He loved the animals. Like me and my dad. And, Father Tim?" His voice broke off in a wail, taking the old man by surprise. They heard a commotion in the back of church.

"Billy Bloom, are you here?" cried out his mother. She and Claude came storming up the main aisle. Billy sprang up.

"I'm not talking to you!" he shouted before he darted out of the side door. Claude cut through a row of pews after him.

The old priest struggled to his feet. "Jonquil!" he called, "what's wrong?"

Claude re-entered from the side door. "Quick, Jonquil, he's on his bike."

Answering Father Tim with only a vague gesture, she flew down the aisle and out of the church. The priest called to her in vain. They were already in the Jeep, heading down California Avenue.

Ahead of them, they could see the decal on Billy's bike. Claude unhitched his seatbelt, reached across her and opened the glove compartment to retrieve a bulky object.

She looked at it dubiously. "What is that thing?"

"A siren from my volunteer fireman days," he said and plugged the cord into the cigarette lighter.

She placed her hand on his wrist, thinking how wonderful it was just to touch him in the slightest way. "No, it'll scare him and he could fall." Claude, with a nod, let the gizmo fall back into his lap.

A red light at Fourth Street made them slow down but not Billy. "Good God—he's riding into oncoming traffic!" Jonquil screamed.

"Don't look, Jonny. Pray." She closed her eyes. California Avenue, with its wide center strip, street lamps, and mix of architecture, was one of her favorite streets in Santa Monica. Two of Billy's classmates lived there. Yet, as they neared the coming intersection at Ocean Boulevard, she gasped. Across Ocean lay Palisades Park and the California Incline which linked the surface street to Pacific Coast Highway below. What would her son do? Would he maneuver the sharp left turn onto Ocean, avoid the triangle of diverters and continue south along the park? Or—good God—would he find himself trapped in the right lane? In that case, he'd have to cross Ocean, veer sharply down the dark incline in traffic and join nonstop PCH. His new bike helmet, together with his other presents, sat in the trunk of her car, no help to him now. Her eyes popped open.

Claude yelled, "He's turning left, he missed the diverters, he's jumped the curb. He's in the park." Claude made a wild left turn and then crossed over one lane of traffic. The Jeep hit the cement curb and bounced across the pavement. Fortunately, at that hour no one was out walking or jogging in that area of Palisades Park.

Jonquil leaped out of the Jeep first while Claude turned up the headlights. They picked up the bike's decal about twenty feet away. Jonquil knew that the eucalyptus trees and grass ended about where the bike stood. Beyond lay a concrete pathway and benches paralleled by a waist-high rock hedge. Beyond the hedge, cliffs dropped down to treacherous PCH.

"Billy Bloom, I know you're there!" she yelled.

"LIAR, LIAR, PANTS ON FIRE!"

"Billy, please," she pleaded, setting off across the grass.

"TAIL AS LONG AS A TELEPHONE WIRE! LIAR, LIAR, LIAR!" He screeched so loud that his voice cracked. Her ears strained to hear the direction his voice was coming from as fear gripped hold of her.

"Wait, Jonny," cautioned Claude in a low voice as he came up behind her, "don't crowd him."

"Claude, I can't even see him." In the winter darkness, there was no telling how close Billy was to the cliffs.

"Billy, it's me, Claude. Come closer where we can see you."

"No!"

"We'll stay here and you can take a step toward us."

"No, and you can't make me!"

Jonquil sensed that Billy now stood directly in front of them and gestured to Claude to keep talking. He nodded.

"Well, then I won't try. But your mom has something important to tell you. I think you better listen to her."

"You're on her side," Billy shot back.

"Now, that's not true. I don't know her side yet. Come on, pal, it's only fair to hear her out. Then, we can both decide which side we're on. Deal?"

They waited.

"I'm listening," Billy grunted but he didn't move. Jonquil gauged he was leaning against the front wheel of the bike. Fight or flight, Billy was ready. She sank down on the grass. It felt damp and bumpy but her legs were shaking so hard, she could no longer stand.

"Billy, I want to tell you about The Red Baron," she said quietly, hoping he might come forward. They heard a twig snap. Jonquil could now see the shape of Billy's high tops.

"Who's he?" he taunted.

"He was a dog, your father's—our dog."

"Ha! I thought you hated dogs."

"N-not always. You see, those pictures you found today were from a camping trip your dad and I made to Yosemite. We'd just found out we were going to have a baby—you, sweetheart." She paused and fought back tears. She had been keeping this family history and the feelings surrounding it secret for so long that exhaustion was setting in rapidly, but she willed herself to go on. "We were overjoyed. To celebrate, we took one more camping trip. Baron, too."

"So?"

"So ..." her voice grew more constricted but not on Billy's account. She was reliving it.

"About a week after we got home, one night our house caught on fire. No one knew how—it just did. Your dad got us out. We got out, Billy. We were safe. Then, your dad remembered Baron and he went back in ... and ... and I never saw either one of them again." She sat back on her haunches, rocking and keening.

Claude reached down to comfort her but she waved him off and, summoning her strength, she continued. "Billy, listen to me. Your father chose that dog over me. Over us. Can you understand? We could have been a family. *We were a family.* He destroyed all that. Now, do you see why I could never give you a dog? You're so like your father, Billy. And I could never, ever bear to lose you. Oh, my sweet Billy, I love you so much." She fell back again, sobbing.

Claude shook his head as he bent down and gave her a folded handkerchief. "Jonquil, haven't you got it all mixed up? Your husband didn't choose a dog over you."

"Were you there?" she asked, loudly blowing her nose. "You don't know."

"No, woman, but I'm a man and I can guess what another man was thinking. Gerry was young. Maybe cocky. He made sure you were safe. You just said so. Only then did he try for the dog. He thought he could do it all. That was his only mistake. He didn't intend to leave you. My God, he loved you. Oh, Jonny! All these years you have kept your love at bay." He groaned.

Jonquil sat up slowly. "He was a marathon runner," she mumbled. "He loved to run." She took great gulps of air and wiped her eyes on her sleeve, Billy-style.

Minutes passed. The din of the traffic pierced the night. A siren wailed in the distance, cars honked, a car alarm started and ended abruptly.

"Mom?"

"Yes, Billy?" She rubbed her eyes again with the back of her hands and waited.

"I wouldn't have left you, I don't think. But, Mom?" His voice quivered.

"Yes, sweetheart?"

He came into full view and her heart relaxed like a sigh in her chest. "I have the gift. I know it. Like you do, only you help people. I want to help animals. Please, Mom, please?"

"Billy!"

He flung himself into her outstretched arms. She nearly lost her balance, but not quite. A breeze lifted the branches of the eucalyptus trees as she tenderly rocked Billy's sobs away. Claude watched and waited.

She became aware of a faint yapping sound. Yapping and scratching. Then, a distinct, demanding bark. The dog. She held Billy more tightly and over his head glanced at Claude. *Wait*, she thought.

Jonquil wanted time to absorb it all. Claude's take on the tragedy. Claude implying that she must forgive Gerry's tragic, impetuous miscalculation, the years of barren refusal, the agony of lonely decisions, the once sealed part of her heart that had sprung wide open, and now the solid feel of Billy safe in her arms. That above all else she wanted to savor.

But life rarely allows such indulgences.

A disoriented, hungry puppy wakes up in a strange, cold vehicle. He needs attention.

Time to let go. Time, if there was still time, to begin again.

"Billy?" she whispered in his ear. "What is it you always say? We're a team, we need a mascot? Can ours be Blackie?"

Billy backed away from her, alert. "Blackie?" he repeated unbelievingly. "Blackie's here? Where?"

"Go and see."

What father, if his son asks for bread, will give him a stone? she thought. Weird, a scripture passage, but how fitting. *And what mother, if her son asks for a dog, gives him pieces of plastic and cloth?* She shivered from head to toe.

* * *

"Jonquil, Jonquil! You found the lad. Thanks be to God." It was Father Tim. Had he huffed and puffed his way down the seven long blocks from church?

"Father Tim, you shouldn't have!" Jonquil protested, getting to her feet.

"I didn't. I got a ride from a parishioner." He waved at a car that honked and pulled away from the curb.

"Father Tim, meet Blackie. He's my new dog," said Billy. The puppy wagged his tail with excitement and licked Father Tim's face.

"Oh, yes, charming. So who's this?" he demanded, pointing with a shaky finger at Claude.

"Father, this is Claude Chappel," said Jonquil, drawing her man close. "And I think I love him."

The two men eyed each other. "Oh, you do, do ye?" he asked crustily. "Well, now."

They dropped Father Tim off at the rectory first. Jonquil reminded him that she would be picking him up the following afternoon for Christmas dinner. Claude walked him to the door. "A word, young man."

"Yes, Father?"

Father Tim's eyes became slits. "She's so …" and his voice trailed off with unspoken emotion. "And the boy, too. So, you stick by, man." He jabbed Claude's chest with his finger. "Stick by, hear? Or so help me, the ghosts of ten thousand Irish martyrs will come down and smite your eager gonads like a bolt from Hell!" He paused. "I'm glad you passed muster, son."

"Sleep well, Padre," replied Claude with a straight face.

"Aye, that I'll do."

* * *

Claude swung around the Jeep and headed toward Venice. In the back seat, Billy dozed with Blackie. In the front passenger seat, Jonquil leaned against Claude's shoulder and gave his arm a grateful pat. "You were wonderful back there."

"So were you," he smiled back at her. They drove in silence for a block until Jonquil's agile mind started up.

"Oh, well, that's that. I'm probably out of a job again. Mr. Merrill will think I lost my mind when he hears how I ran off the show." It all seemed so long ago, Billy's call, Poppi Blair's bulging eyes. Leigh Usher would have a field day with Jonquil's behavior. She sighed. "I can't see going back to doing therapy. Still, if I want to finish my research, I don't have much choice."

"Well ..." He checked his rearview mirror. "Maybe for a while."

"I'm not going to complain. The good thing is I know now what I want to do. And if I could get through tonight, I can get through anything." Her eyes glanced at the rearview mirror and the comforting sight of Billy holding Blackie. Glimpsing her mussed up hair and make-up free face, she sighed again.

"You'll find a way," Claude assured her. He wasn't really paying attention because something else was on his mind. "Man, was that place deserted tonight or what? I seem to recall a lot more kids there the day I painted offices." Jonquil realized he was referring to Children's Home.

"Oh well, Christmas passes. You know, only the orphans are there now."

Claude smoothly pulled over to the side of the street and switched off the ignition. "Say that again."

Billy stirred.

"Sure, the kids with parents go home on holidays. Too much staff are out for the shifts to be covered adequately. But the orphans do have to stay there. Standard operating procedure."

"That stinks."

"Life's unfair. You're not surprised, are you?" Before tonight, she might have sounded sarcastic but not now.

Claude peered straight ahead and then closed his eyes. "Jonny, I'm an orphan."

She stared at him speechless. Was it her or was this guy one constant new revelation?

"My parents thought they couldn't have children and then after adopting me, they went on to have my two sisters and two brothers. Happens a lot, I'm told. Anyway, I was adopted when I was four. Before that, I was in an orphanage. Damn!" He struck the steering wheel hard. "Christmas in a hell hole."

"Claude," Jonquil said, cutting her eyes to the back seat.

"Sorry, big guy," he said to Billy via the mirror.

"No sweat, man." Billy grinned.

"Got an idea," said Claude, resuming his course through the quiet streets. "What say we set 'em loose for the day? You got a tree, Jonny, and you were already planning on a nice early dinner, right?"

"Only for Father Tim and Rita and Al and … and you?" she added, meeting his glance. He smiled and nodded. "You aren't seriously thinking of kidnapping those kids. Claude, you can't!"

"Not at all. That would be breaking the law. Whereas, if I evacuate them from, say, an unhealthy situation brought on by a recent paint job, I'm a hero."

Billy giggled appreciatively and then added his two

cents. "Remember Mom? Celebrate the good times and really celebrate the bad times."

"Hey, I like the sound of that. Give me five, good buddy." Billy obliged.

Claude continued planning aloud with enthusiasm. "And with a few phone calls here and there—some of my guys are all alone, too."

"But Claude, it's unthinkable."

"Really? I thought of it, right?"

She sat up straight and spoke sternly to both of them. "No, no you guys, you can't do this."

"Eh, where's your sense of adventure?" Claude murmured and gave her knee a roughish squeeze. Despite her qualms about his plan, she nudged his arm and laughed.

He parked across the street from where the Blooms lived. When Jonquil unlocked and opened the door to her apartment, she heard the television blaring and quickly found the remote. Poor Rita, she should have phoned her ages ago and told her to go home. Claude and Billy tiptoed inside but Blackie leaped out of Billy's arms and headed straight for Rita's exposed face on the couch.

"Ech—ech! Help! Get him off me!" cried Rita.

Billy sprang to her rescue.

Rita wiped her face with her apron, sat up and wearily took stock of the situation: one woman, one man, one boy, and one dog. Perfect. "Can I go home now?" she begged.

"Yes, but can you come back tomorrow around noon?" asked Claude.

Rita frowned. "Why so early?"

"Claude will explain when he walks you out to your car," said Jonquil. "Now, Rita, I should warn you, what he's planning is sheer lunacy."

Rita grumbled and groaned to her feet. "If he's your honey, I'm not one bit surprised. Humph."

CHAPTER THIRTY-ONE

Thursday, December 25th

CHRISTMAS DAY

At one o'clock on the afternoon of Christmas Day, under fair skies, three men huddled within sight of Children's Home. Besides Claude, there was a drywaller named Jay and a carpenter named Bobby. They reviewed their plan one more time. It was simple: bamboozle their way inside, hijack the kids, and scram.

"I'll handle the old crow," said Claude. "All set? Let's go!"

The street was deserted. The men climbed into their respective vehicles and drove caravan style to the home's driveway entrance.

At that point, Claude gave the signal to halt while he surveyed the vicinity one last time for any pesky squad car. Seeing none, he plugged in his siren. When it was wailing full blast, he and the others sped up the driveway to the front door. Before disembarking, Claude put on a pair of thick goggles while the other two men clamped on gas masks.

A child's face appeared in an upper window. Next, the front door opened wide. As soon as Claude saw Miss Hamilton perched on the threshold in a long dark velveteen gown and white apron, he unplugged the siren. Then he and the others donned their hard hats, grabbed their gear, and strode up to the door.

"What's the meaning of this?" exploded Miss Hamilton. "Who are you?"

"City inspector, ma'am," replied Claude. He whipped out his contractor's license and held it up for a split second. "Who's the head honcho?"

"I assume you mean Dr. Shore," she sniffed. "He's away."

"I see," Claude nodded. "We need to inspect the premises."

"Now? Today? It's Christmas!" she protested and attempted to bar them from entering.

"Safety don't look at no-o-o calendar, ma'am," he drawled and gestured for his men to enter. "Hurry up, men, there's no time to lose!"

"You can't barge in here like this!"

But Bobby and Jay, each lugging a portable gas

detector, dodged past her and up the foyer stairs.

"Sorry, ma'am, but we got a complaint about—er—
NFLs—you know, noxious fume levels? Paint any walls
in the past month?" he inquired in an official tone as he
sauntered past her and up the stairs.

Unwillingly, she followed him inside. They both heard
a high pitched beeping sound coming from Jay's detector
down the hall.

Jay ripped off his mask and yelled, "Getting something
over here, boss."

"What's your reading," barked Claude as he pretended
to make a note on a clipboard.

"Ooo-ee, ballistic!"

"Impossible!" shouted Miss Hamilton. "Only the
offices were painted, not the hallways."

From the opposite direction, the second detector went
off. "Over here, boss," came Bobby's urgent tone.
"Yeow, this stuff is lethal!"

"Okey-doke, men. We gotta evacuate. Round up the
kiddies, check the upper floors, too. Bring them and the
staff down here. Don't scare 'em now."

At that point, Claude removed his hat and goggles and
flashed Miss Hamilton one of his most charming French-
Canadian smiles.

"You!" She staggered back, dumbfounded.

He watched the surprised look on her face harden into contempt.

"Did that Bloom boy ever turn up? My, what a pathetic child."

"Oh, you mean, Billy?" Claude kept his tone folksy and light. "Why, it's real sweet of you to ask, ma'am. We found him soon after we left here last night. He and the dog are practically joined at the hip, if you'll pardon the expression."

"Humph. So what do you want? Why did you barge in here like the place was on fire? Who are your two friends? And good heavens, what are they doing with the children?" She turned toward the main staircase, straining for a glimpse of the men or children while Claude continued talking as if they were having a polite conversation.

"Bobby and Jay work for me. We're here to take the children to a Christmas party at the Blooms's. You're invited too and anyone else you've got stuck working here today."

Though they were at eye level, she managed to cast him a superior look and slowed down her words as though she were speaking to a child. "For your information, Mr ..."

"It's Claude, Miss Hamilton, Claude Chappel." He stepped forward and extended his hand. Miss Hamilton ignored the gesture. Overhead they heard the men going from room to room and the children's excited voices.

"Well, Mr. Chappel, there are procedures which I must follow. These children can't come and go as they please. And I certainly wouldn't allow you to take them, not even to Ms.—especially not to Ms. Bloom's home. Now, call off your men and leave here this instant. As for these children, they are wards of the state. They aren't going anywhere."

"Oh?" He slowly stroked his jaw, letting the harsher interpretation of her last remarks dangle between them. The muscles around her mouth began to twitch while he shifted his weight to his other leg. The time had come to state his case.

"Fact is, these kids are kids. Christmas is for them, too. As for your rules and regs, ma'am, it can't be much different from when I lived in one of these—uh—places. We both know that all it's going to take is for you to call this an outing or a day trip and come along with us. Ms. Bloom has a turkey in the oven."

"Cook's got their Christmas dinner all prepared."

He sniffed the stale air. "I bet. Give the cook the afternoon off. Stow the peanut butter sandwiches for later. Here, use my phone and call her, I mean, Ms. Bloom. Call the doctor, call the governor, do whatever it takes." He held the phone out to her but she waved it off.

"I suppose she put you up to this?" Miss Hamilton sneered.

"Eh, not at all. This was entirely my plan. I'm sorry if the siren scared you. It's just that seeing these kids here last night, I remembered what it was like to spend Christmas Day in the orphanage. I cooked up the fake inspection because I didn't think you'd welcome me back today with open arms." He could see by her expression that he hadn't yet won her over. Frustrated, he said, "Come on, be a sport."

Meanwhile, Bobby and Jay reappeared, each holding a toddler in their arms. Muriel and Tommy Cregier came down the hall with a nurse. Two other frightened Asian youngsters and a male volunteer rounded out the group.

"We got 'em all," announced Bobby proudly as he shifted the little girl from his arms to his hip.

Miss Hamilton snapped her fingers and pointed at Claude. "If I recall correctly, it was you who painted our offices this month, sport."

She crossed her arms and rocked gleefully back and forth on the balls of her feet. She reminded Claude of a giant totem pole bobbing in the wind. His eyes flicked uneasily from Jay to Bobby.

"Yeah, spaut!" brayed Muriel. To Tommy Cregier, it sounded as though she had said spot. "Yeah, spot!" he teased Claude. One child chimed in and then another until all the children were giggling and the hall rang with the words, "Yeah, spot!" The staff, even Claude's men, began to snicker. Miss Hamilton's mouth twitched again. All eyes focused on her and they waited. At last, she untied her apron strings. "Extra diapers! Clean faces and clean shirts. Medications in case we aren't back by change of shift. I'll call the doctor." Her orders were drowned out by a chorus of cheers.

* * *

Meanwhile, Jonquil got into her ruby red Volkswagen and drove to the rectory to pick up Father Tim. Once back home, after taking his coat and packages and getting him comfortably settled in the rocking chair, she looked around the apartment and marveled at how effortlessly the party had come together. All it had required was a flurry of early morning phone calls.

Rita, who arrived before noon, came laden with her home-made coleslaw, cranberry sauce, red and gold candles and a handmade linen tablecloth with candy-cane designs. Al came an hour later bearing assorted paper plates, cups, napkins, cutlery and fruit salad "a la Al." Bobby, one of Claude's men brought over a honey-baked ham and enough corn and mashed potatoes to fill two dozen plates. Another of Claude's workers, Jay, had dropped off a case of soda, a case of beer, an ice cooler, and two bottles of wine before heading for Children's

Home. Claude contributed two pumpkin pies, four gallons of ice cream, milk, a second ice cooler and flowers for the centerpiece. Even Father Tim managed to scare up a couple of bottles of champagne—gifts from his fortieth anniversary in the priesthood which had never been opened. He would offer the blessing as well.

Billy pitched in, too. He'd awakened very early and taken Blackie outside to do his business. Jonquil heated up some leftover chicken and rice and fed it to the puppy while Billy filled his water bowl. Then, they opened their presents and had breakfast. As soon as she and Billy returned from early Mass, she put the turkey in the oven while he moved their presents into her bedroom closet to make more space for their guests in the main room. He also placed fresh towels in both bathrooms and helped Jonquil baste the turkey. Then, he slipped on his new Dodger jacket, put Blackie on his leash and took him down the block to meet his friends. It gave Jonquil and Rita time to set up the dining room buffet-style.

Still, she couldn't quite believe her eyes when the men returned with six children, two staff members, and tight-lipped Ida Hamilton in tow. Jonquil was glad to see that Big Al Yates had brought a camera with him to record the amazing event.

* * *

That is how the Bloom apartment came to be full and overflowing on Christmas Day with grownups, children, good food, laughter, music, and in the center of it, the most incredible sight of all—a cocker spaniel named Blackie.

After dinner, the puppy napped on the floor between Billy and Tommy Cregier's feet. Across the room, still seated comfortably in the rocker, Father Tim was reading a story to Petey and Maggie, the two sleepy toddlers. Muriel was busily coloring pictures on the coffee table with Nurse Carol. Jay and Bobby, the construction workers, had just finished giving piggyback rides to all takers and were sprawled in front of the television, scanning football scores. Al, when he wasn't attending to the CD player he'd brought, was taking pictures for posterity. And Rita was making the rounds with a fresh pot of coffee. She paused in front of Miss Hamilton, seated on the couch with the two Asian children, Kim and Hanh, on either side of her.

"I want to thank you for firing Jonquil," said Rita sincerely as she bent to freshen up the older woman's coffee mug.

Miss Hamilton's eyes flickered. "The children miss her," she grumbled. "She's a talented clinician despite her aloofness. Maybe it was for the best. I see big changes in her. She seems much happier now."

"Right," replied Rita, "it was a blessing in disguise. But you're wearing Gardenia. Now, that is a mistake for a woman of your—" Rita eyed her up and down, "qualities. Drop by the store someday and I'll fix you up with one of my premier fragrances on the house." Miss Hamilton, unsure whether she had just been complimented or criticized, crossed her ankles and slurped her coffee.

In the kitchen, Jonquil attempted to answer the intrusive wall phone on the first ring. Gary, a bearded, ponytailed volunteer from Children's Home, helped Claude with cleanup. Rita came into the kitchen and deposited the empty coffee pot. "Jonquil, I adore that color on you," she said.

"Thanks, Rita. It's a gift from my grandmother in Ireland." Jonquil was attired in a clingy tangerine-colored knit top and fringed skirt, accessorized by a large reindeer pin with a glowing red nose.

"And dig those crazy earrings," said Jonquil, giving the tiny sleigh bells hanging from Rita's ear a shake.

"Gary, I love that belt you're wearing," deadpanned Claude.

"Thanks, Claude, and your socks are to die for!"

"Hardy, har, har," broke in Rita. "Say, isn't it time to open presents?" she demanded loudly above the racket.

Jonquil put a warning finger to her lips. "We don't have any gifts for the kids," she whispered.

"Well, sugar, I've got one for you. Let me go get it."

The wall phone rang again and Jonquil spoke a few words into the receiver. "I better take this call in my bedroom," said Jonquil, mouthing "Mr. Merrill" to Claude before handing him the receiver.

No one looked up as Jonquil tiptoed through the main room and down the hall. She dreaded the conversation about to take place and hoped Mr. Merrill's withdrawal of the job offer would not upset her so much that she would not be able to enjoy the party. She rubbed the palms of her hands on her skirt before picking up her phone and heard Claude disconnect in the kitchen.

"Mr. Merrill? Hello," she said, blinking back prickles of anxious tears. "I want to apologize and explain," she added in a rush. "I'm so very sorry about what happened yesterday."

"Merry Christmas, Jonquil." His terse retort sounded genuinely cheerful.

"Thank you and the same to you. About yesterday ..." She paused. What should she say?

"Yes?"

"You see, my son was watching the show at home and discovered something I hadn't yet explained to him about his father's death and when he ... when he ..."

"Jonquil, I missed the show. I heard about what happened later. It was good of you to telephone Iris with everything else on your mind. How is your son doing?"

"Billy's fine, Mr. Merrill. Thank you for asking. It was a long night but he's fine now."

"Good, glad to hear it. Leigh Usher and I had a short talk yesterday after which Leigh resigned."

"Oh!" Jonquil clutched the receiver more tightly.

"Resigned, I should add, with my firm recommendation. That's between you and me for now." Jonquil didn't know whether to be glad or unnerved by the news. If Leigh was gone, did that mean her own job was secure? Or did he intend to lower the boom on her as well?

"I … I see …" The noise in the other room kicked up a notch. Jonquil stretched the extension cord as far as possible across her bedroom, still holding the phone to her ear, and kicked the door shut.

"Maybe you had an inkling about Leigh's intentions to sabotage the show but let's discuss that later. Now," he said, "you haven't asked me yet why I wasn't watching the show, so I'll tell you. I was on a phone call from Paris."

"Paris?" This time Jonquil flopped down on her bed, totally mystified until it hit her who might have made that call. Constance! *Oh, no*, she almost groaned aloud, *out of the frying pan and into the fryer.*

* * *

"Good news, Jonny?" asked Claude, eyeing her flushed face when she returned to the kitchen. Gary turned off the sink faucet and they all waited.

"That was Mr. Merrill on the phone. After he asked about Billy, he reminded me about our meeting tomorrow morning at the store. Not only that," she added, turning to Claude, "he's invited me ... and you ... for cocktails at his home on New Year's Eve." They gazed at each other intently, the room receding, as their smiles broadened.

"Glory be! In that case, sugar, you may want to wear this," chirped Rita and handed Jonquil a bundle of white tissue paper tied with a shiny gold bow. Jonquil tore open the paper bundle. Inside she found the shawl from her grandmother, neatly mended and ironed. Tears of gratitude welled up in Jonquil's eyes. To receive a precious gift not once, but twice! "Rita, you are the best!" The two women flung out their arms to each other and hugged.

"What about your job, Jonny?" asked Claude.

"Mr. Merrill missed the television show, Claude, because he was on the phone with Constance. You see, it was already Christmas Eve in Paris. Do you know who I'm talking about?"

Listening as he dried dishes, Gary struck his chest with the open palm of his hand. "Constance? *The* Constance?" he blurted. Both men laughed.

"So? Jonquil, give already!" cried Rita.

"So, Constance had such a happy Christmas with her mother because of my advice, that she-wants-me-to-be-her-Gift-Counselor-at-her-new-Beverly-Hills-boutique!"

Rita inhaled sharply and clenched her fists.

"But how can I do that when I'm already Clyde's brand new, full-time, exclusive gift counselor?"

Rita let out a relieved, ear-splitting whoop. Jonquil grabbed her hands and squeezed hard. "Ouch!" they both cried. Jonquil snatched away her hands and examined Rita's fingers.

"Aha! What's this?" she asked while she held out Rita's left hand for Claude to see.

"It's—it's—well, it just happened at a stoplight on the way over here," stammered Rita, both pleased and flustered.

Jonquil dropped Rita's hand and fled the kitchen. She stepped gingerly over the bodies sprawled on the floor in the main room. "Where is Al Yates?" she demanded. "Al Yates, front and center!"

Al had just switched off the CD player and tuned in a radio station that featured all-day holiday music. "Here I am," he called calmly from the opposite end of the room. He wore bright red suspenders and a blinking red bow tie.

"Congratulations, you brilliant man!" She gave Al a hug and kiss and then, taking his hand and flinging it high in the air as if he were the champ, she addressed the room.

"Hey, everybody, Al and Rita are engaged! Talk about your M-A-R-R-Y Christmas."

The groans that greeted her lame pun were immediately followed by a round of applause and whistles for the middle aged couple, during which Rita bashfully showed off her ring.

The phone rang again. "Let it go to the machine," ordered Jonquil to the room in general. "I don't want to miss another moment of this fabulous party."

Claude and Gary emerged from the kitchen. "Can I get anyone anything before I cave in?" offered Claude, drying his hands on a dishcloth.

"Sure, you can open that bubbly now," quipped Father Tim as he smiled over at glowing Rita. The adults chuckled but indicated that they were full.

Muriel looked up from her coloring task at the two stockings draped over the desk above Billy's head.

"Did Sanna Caud come ta yo haut?" she quizzed Billy in her most grating voice.

The adults glanced uneasily at each other and shrugged their shoulders. Their preparations for a spur of the moment Christmas party had overlooked one vital detail. Hmm, they now shrugged uncomfortably to one another, the question was bound to come up. The room became quiet, all the good cheer draining out of it as fast as the soapsuds disappearing down the kitchen sink.

"Yes, he did," answered Billy on impulse, scrambling to his feet. "And he brought everybody presents." Blackie woke up and started yapping. "Tommy, hold him for me, all right? Don't let go of him."

"Sure, Billy," said Tommy and gathered the excited puppy in his arms.

Jonquil peered quizzically at the back of her son as he disappeared down the hall toward their bedrooms. She'd hoped that his behavior on the previous day had been an aberration. What was he up to now? Claude crossed the room to her side. "Trouble?" he mouthed.

"I don't know—unless—but we haven't got any presents for little girls that I'm aware of," she whispered back. All eyes focused on the hallway.

Soon, Billy reappeared, his arms bulging with stuffed animals. He gave Muriel first pick. Initially, she chose the ponies, then changed her mind and lunged for the fanged animals, so he dumped them all in her lap and ran back for more. He distributed them to both the children and the adults and topped off each gift with one of his warm hugs, Miss Hamilton included, upon whom he bestowed his favorite teddy bear. That gesture finally put some color in her cheeks.

There was laughter and a few guffaws as various

species found themselves in the hands of new owners. Finally, Billy stood in front of Tommy, poised to give him a slick T-Rex model.

"Aw, man," griped Tommy, "them's baby toys."

Billy switched gears without showing the slightest hesitation. "I almost forgot! Santa brought you something else!"

He tore off again and this time was gone for several minutes.

"I better go see what he's doing," said Jonquil to Claude in a low voice. She hurried down the hall to her son's room and found him rolling up a poster that he had just removed from the wall.

He looked up, relieved to see her. "Mom, will you help me tie a bow around this?"

She walked swiftly over to his bed and sat down. "Billy, have you thought this over carefully? Do you know the trouble I went through to get you a signed poster? Not to mention the cost. Billy, this was my special birthday present to you.

"Now, I suppose I can see that, with Blackie here, you may not want to keep your stuffed animals. And your idea to give them away was wonderful, it got us out of a jam. Besides, Claude's right—you've outgrown them.

"But sweetie, this is different. We can give Tommy something else—maybe your new computer game. That will be easy to replace."

He frowned. "But Tommy will love this poster. Please tie a bow around it, Mom. He's waiting."

Feeling somewhat bewildered, she darted off to her room to retrieve the spool of scarlet ribbon sitting on her vanity, thinking, *Why was Billy doing this?* He could be so obstinate. At least they were having this conversation privately and not in front of their guests.

She also felt hurt. Hadn't the poster meant anything to him? Her fingers closed around the ribbon while she confronted her reflection in the mirror. Her eyes were still pink and soft from last night's watershed. She closed her eyes and tried to compose herself.

In that instant, the words from her dream drifted back to her: "It's mine to give." Billy's point, exactly. She'd given him the poster. A gift, freely given. Now, he wanted to pass it on to someone else. Freely!

Before, when he had given her pens and paper on her birthday so she could do her work at Children's Home, he did so because he truly believed she loved her job. Hadn't he listened to her talk about it avidly throughout the summer and fall?

But Billy didn't know that since taking the job at Clyde's, she had come to realize what her true calling was. So, by forcing her own interpretation out of his choice of gift, and turning it into her theory of gifts with strings attached, she had set the bar on gift-giving too low.

Her eyes opened wide with comprehension. *Gifts—true gifts—have no strings attached!*

Jonquil sensed something deep within her yield to the simple truth about gifts. She grabbed the ribbon and hurried back to her son.

Billy reappeared in the main room, this time holding the rolled up poster in his hands behind his back. He headed straight for Tommy.

"Here, Tommy, Merry Christmas from me and Santa Claus." Billy handed him the poster and scooped up Blackie, freeing both of Tommy's hands so he could undo the bow and unfurl the gift.

"Sammy Sosa!" cried Tommy. "Hey everybody, I got Sosa, I got Sosa, Miss Hamilton!" He turned in every direction so everyone could see.

Bobby came over and held the poster higher. "Look, Tommy, it's signed, too." The room responded with loud applause for both the Cub outfielder and the generous gift.

"Man-o-man, Billy. I'll hang this over my bed!" Tommy flashed him his incandescent smile and then one of Claude's men helped him roll up the poster.

Jonquil gazed lovingly at her son.

Billy had Margo's gift—of loving, of sharing, of

sacrifice, of joy. She leaned sideways and happily found Claude still there, leaning toward her.

"Can we do this next year?" he asked and then kissed the curls on top of her head.

For a mere second, she wanted them to disappear so she could be alone with her new love. A cacophony of sounds made her change her mind: a toddler needing a diaper change; a tug of war over a Beanie Baby, a burst of Rita's infectious laughter, the telephone ringing again, the dog barking, one of the children on the couch erupting in nonsensical jabber, a rush to clean up another glass of spilt milk, life! Over or under or through it all—she couldn't say for sure—the power of Tony Bennett's voice on the radio implored:

"O, be a giver everyday
In your own inspired way.
You're the only one
Who can give your love."

ACKNOWLEDGEMENTS

My grateful thanks to Babe; to the generous personnel from president to perfume clerks at former Henchey's of Santa Monica; to Dave Strauss; to the Chicago Barnes and Noble Book Store-on-Diversey writers group; to Tamara Shaffer, for her enthusiasm, insight, and wit; to the Head Buyer and perfume sales clerks at Marshall Field and Co.'s former State Street store; to the Great Books Foundation in Chicago; to the Career Transitions Center of Chicago coaches and staff; to all of my readers along the way; special thanks for encouragement to Adriana Loomis, Marsha Staley, Rick Goldman, Kate Leatham, Jooley Johnson, Beverlee T. Nelson, Rachel Mayuga, the late Gwen Thompson, Chris Sutton, Laura Stokes-Gray; to Chloe Bolan for her insights; and to Ellyn Rose and the Cronin clan who were supportive in bounteous ways;

To Rev. Martin N. Winters; to the memory of V. Michael Vaccaro, MD, and the faculty of the former Hahnemann Medical College and Hospital Graduate School of Psychology; to my grandparents' beloved cocker spaniel Knickerbocker who reappeared in this story as Blackie; to John Hoffman for the tagline; and to Jim Brogan for many kindnesses;

To Cara Lockwood, my generous and supportive editor, and to Beth Hill, who pointed the way;

And to my three parents: James R. Cronin, Sr., Jean Hayes Cronin and Pat Somers Cronin.

Ultimate thanks to the Giver of all gifts. Thank You.

Have Jonquil and Claude found true love?

How will Billy face the darkness ahead?

Will Jonquil find her father?

Find out in

***Best of All Gifts*,**

coming soon.

To contact the author, please visit:
www.giftcounselorbook.com.

To support this book, please: tell a friend, choose it for your book club, order a copy at your public library or write a comment on **amazon.com or goodreads.com.**

Thank you!

Made in the USA
San Bernardino, CA
11 October 2015